BETWEEN JOHN AND A HARD PLACE

ANITA YOMBO

Publisher: Babou Publishing

ISBN: 978-0-578-31083-1

Cover Design: Verity Anne Casey

Editor: Kirsten Rees | Book Editor & Author Coach

Formatter: Claire Jennison

To Congolese boys and girls around the world.

CHAPTER 1

The day the soldiers came and took over my little town of Lusa was only the start. Everything was destroyed little by little. They took away the kind of simple life that we were used to.

Waking up to the sound of the rooster outside my window, getting ready for an exciting sunny day, and looking forward to spending time with my friends and family. That was the type of life I was accustomed to in the Congo.

My name is Grace Munia, I was born in Lusa, in the eastern part of the Democratic Republic of Congo. I am the firstborn of five children. My little sister, Mwinda, always on the go and with so much going on in her mind that sometimes, my parents forgot she existed. My younger brother, Kwenu, was the quiet and smart one. My parents treated him as if he was the firstborn. They knew they could rely on him because of his sense of responsibility - and his perfect composure.

Next came the twins, Iman the girl and Kano the boy. They were both treated like royalty because in my culture, twins are celebrated like a God-given gift to a family. My parents cherished them with all their heart and soul and believed that the family's good fortune came from them.

The five of us lived in a four-bedroom house that our father designed and helped build. My father was a strong man, my personal hero, who worked hard to give us everything we needed. He not only supported us, his children, but he also financially helped a big part of our extended family. My mother was a perfect match for him. She was just as strong as my father but wiser. She carried herself with such charisma that even strangers were afraid to disobey her orders. She was the perfect matriarch. People respected her but never feared her. She was always open to lending a helping hand to the needy and never turned down friends in despair.

My life as a girl from a small town was typical. I woke up every morning at the same time, to the sound of a rooster. No one else in my family did, but for some reason, the sound signified the beginning of a new day for me. Making sure my younger siblings were awake and ready to go to school was my responsibility.

From the age of seven, I was taught by my mother to make breakfast and iron clothes. My parents knew that I was a scatter-brained person at times, so they counted on my brother to share the responsibilities with me whenever I embarked on an imaginary journey. We all went to the same school, at the same time, and returned straight home after school. Except my sister, Mwinda, who always had something else to do after school. I dreamed of life in a big city, with carefree people and luxurious cars. And every day I made the same wish to get out of Lusa, to go explore the rest of the world. When I look back, I realize how much time I wasted hoping to get out of there. Now, I look back and wish I had taken the time to appreciate it more.

Lusa was a beautiful town and the people were its pulse. We only had one season, because most of the year the sun came up glorious and shiny. When it rained, the grass looked greener and the town looked like a fresh young bride on her wedding day. The month of April was my favorite because of the butterflies that took over our gardens and made it look so colorful.

My siblings and I love playing with them. My brother Kwenu liked killing them to make art with their wings. He dried their wings and attached them to a piece of canvas.

One day my mother caught him, and to make him stop killing the butterflies that she loved so much, she told him, "For every butterfly that you kill, a different spirit will come to hunt you at night. For butterflies are our ancestors' souls coming back to bring happiness into our lives".

We believed her, and from that day on we all had so much respect for them and made sure that we let them fly free to shower us with their good spirits. The best part of my day was after school, we all gathered around the kitchen table to eat the food that my mother had cooked with so much care and so much love. We ate in the kitchen because the living room table was only for big occasions, such as birthdays, visits from important people, or family reunions. We sat very close to one another to enjoy our meals, especially my mother's specialty, chicken with crushed peanuts. My mother was the best cook in town, and because of that most mothers sent their daughters to her before sending them off to 'matrimonial bliss'.

The women in Lusa believed the way to a man's heart was through his stomach. So, women revered my mother for being able to keep my father for such a long time in spite of the many concubines and mistresses. Most men ended up leaving their first wives, but my dad usually came running back to my mother six months into an affair.

People attributed it to her skills in the kitchen. Some people said it was her skills in bed, but I won't get into that. Because girls didn't talk about sex in Lusa, let alone their parents' or any adult's sexuality. Sex was, and always will be, the biggest taboo in Lusa. Girls weren't allowed to have sex before marriage, but boys were encouraged to train themselves sexually to later become good husbands. But what most people did not realize is that boys were going to explore their sexual urges with the girls that everyone wanted to keep virginal. So, the town was full of so-called virgins, and so-called potent men.

My mother insisted that my sister and I stayed away from men until marriage, and we both made sure to just do that. She used amazing scare tactics to warn us from boys.

"They will have sex with you to get you pregnant and then leave you", she would say, or "they will infect you with all sorts of diseases and you will be worthless".

That was enough to keep me completely away from boys. Besides, I lived my fantasies through my promiscuous friends who helped the boys experiment with their virility. It's funny that my brother, Kwenu, was not expected to stay a virgin; in fact, every time my parents saw him on the street with a girl, they'd get so excited and invite the girl over. His attention to girls was encouraged from when he was barely five years old. They wanted him to show his interest in girls and his ability to control them, and he certainly did not disappoint.

My Uncle Johnson - whose real name was Kasu but changed it to look cool - had seventeen kids from different women. He was the poorest man in town and yet he considered himself rich because of his progeny. To him, a man's wealth was in his children. Although they were the cutest kids, he turned them into real beggars. He didn't have enough money to feed them, so he sent them around town to beg for money from different members of the family. By the end of each day, he had more food and money than the average working man. Everybody in town knew his ways but couldn't resist his beautiful children.

People in my town were too compassionate to tell him in his face that they resented him for being so lazy. Everyone talked about him behind his back, including my parents and the rest of the family. Each time his children came over to my house, my parents swore that it would be their last. But the next day, they still gave them food and money. His wife walked around with her head down, she planted some vegetables in her backyard, but it was never enough to feed her children and the concubine's children.

My mother bought her a sewing machine, it sat merely as a decoration never to be used. The women in the family asked her to stop having kids, but she just couldn't say no to her husband. She had to compete with the other women in my uncle's life who also liked getting pregnant in the hope to dethrone my aunt. A few times, he had four women pregnant at the same time and when the children were born, he gave all four of them the same first name.

His favourite daughter who was probably the most beautiful girl in town and he knew that people couldn't resist her. She was gentle and her eyes could light up the meanest man's heart. From the moment she was born, people talked about her beauty. Her skin was dark without scars, and she had a full head of hair. She was very quiet and well-mannered.

Until one Saturday morning, he sent her to go beg and she never came back. She was only eleven years old. He waited a few hours and when the sun set that day he panicked, running around town asking after her. He showed up at our house completely disheveled. It took him a few minutes before he had the courage to tell my father that his favorite daughter had gone missing. My father, who had already heard the misfortune from the neighbor, didn't hesitate to give him a piece of his mind.

"You have been shamelessly exploiting your own children, now you lost one of them? You are a poor excuse for a man."

My uncle was so preoccupied thinking about his daughter that he didn't respond to my father's remark. He got up from the chair and walked out of our house silently with his head down.

He looked for her in and out of town, and no one had seen her, nor heard from her.

For weeks, he kept looking. While his wife and children stayed behind, starving and weeping. We didn't see him for a few weeks. So whenever Mother could, she sent food to his family.

On one rainy day, he came back, still without her, defeated. He isolated himself to mourn her disappearance. We all thought the incident would change him, make him get a job or at least stop sending his kids all over town, but that same year, he got two women pregnant and came up with new ways to beg for money. From then on, his concubines and wife were sent along with the children to beg for money.

Rumor had it that his daughter was kidnapped, others suggested she had been attacked by an animal. Some even said that her own father sold her to tourists or sex traffickers. The mystery of her disappearance remained unsolved for as long as I lived in Lusa. The children that he had with my aunt, his first wife, came to have lunch with us often. Our house was crowded when they came around. My mother welcomed them, but I protested.

"Why do we have to share our good meals with them?"

My mother answered my question with a proverb. "To whom much is given, much is required."

I wasn't convinced but decided to protest in silence instead. If there is one thing I had learned, it was to never contradict my mother. Because both my parents could make life a living hell until you agreed with them, or at least abided by their rules.

Because my father was well off compared to most people in his family, he took it upon himself to be the provider, both because he was a compassionate man, and a man with a big ego. The more he gave, the more people feared and respected him. Either way, he was very generous. Some of my uncle's concubines had the audacity to come with their children and get their own piece of the pie.

Every day after lunch, we distracted ourselves with soccer. Most children in town knew how to play soccer well, and we all met at the town square to play the boys against girls' match. Even though the girls always outnumbered the boys; the boys managed to win each match we played. As my father would say; "Nature has a funny way of proving that men are superior to women."

A comment that always started an argument between my father and my sister Mwinda, who refused to be considered inferior to anybody else.

"I am equal or superior, but never inferior, never," she would say.

My father would just laugh at her. 'With time you'll learn that you are inferior, trust me'.

I didn't agree with my father that women were inferior to men, but I still wasn't convinced that we were equal nor the same. I always believed that we were created by God with the same amount of love and rights, but that we were also different. Men and women have different capabilities whether emotional or physical. As I saw it, women were emotionally able to handle more. Women were the ones to carry babies in their womb for nine months and the ones to sacrifice the most to raise them, while men never needed to change their lives for fatherhood.

Women in my town didn't do anything to contradict my father's view on men's superiority. From the day they were born, girls were taught to be good future wives. Their mothers trained them to be submissive and always ready to please their men.

There were many words of wisdom shared every day from mothers to daughters, repeated over and over like mantras. 'Wash your downtheres (aka vaginas) very well, no husband wants to marry a stinky girl', 'Make sure not to burn the dish, a good wife cannot afford that', 'don't talk to the boys alone in the dark, no man will marry a girl who has been around', 'make sure you smile properly at all times, it's all about presentation', 'learn to cook as many dishes as you can, food is the best way to a man's heart'.

I wondered what fathers told their sons to prepare them for marriage; apparently not so much, considering the number of bad marriages caused by men's infidelity and lack of consideration. My view of marriage was very distorted, and it took a very long time to realize that some people were happily married, but people in my town just had their own way of doing things. To me, society concentrated so much on what women should become once they got married, that they forgot to teach men to be good husbands, and the women paid for it.

Most mothers had the same wish; for their daughters to marry a man, not necessarily a good man, just any man. However, my mother pressed on the issue of marriage just as much as on education. She often said, "There is nothing wrong with being an educated wife and mother". She didn't have the chance to complete her education, so she dreamed through us. And my siblings and I wanted to keep that dream alive.

We all did our best to stay on top of our education. We wanted our education to be the least of our mother's worries because we knew that she had enough on her plate. She had to deal with my father's family and his concubines almost daily. They all wanted a piece of what we had. When Mother had a new pair of shoes, everyone else wanted a pair of shoes. When we bought new furniture, the concubines waited for their turn as well.

My mother knew she was living her life under a microscope, so she was careful about everything she said or did. She kept quiet about her business, and only gave a strong and collected facade. My father allowed people in his family to run his life sometimes, and his concubines took a lot from him as well. He lived a normal life with us, but always had to give just as much of himself to his family and women.

The situation was getting out of control to the point that my mother decided to never buy anything new, at least not for herself. We knew the sacrifices that she had to make every day, so whenever we could cut her a break, we jumped on the occasion. Good grades in school were our little way of saying, 'we understand, Mother'.

People in Lusa were very close and knew each other's business. Parents arranged marriages between their children, men helped their peers get jobs, women gave each other advice on how to be good wives and good mothers when it was time. Life wasn't perfect, but it was good enough for us. The children were mostly happy and healthy, and the town was growing steadily.

Although Lusa was a small town, it was part of a big country. The Congo was a Belgian Colony until June 30th, 1960. And after gaining its independence, the country went through its fair share of problems and wars. The only constant factor was the second president Mobutu, who took power after the coup d'état to dethrone the very first president, Kasavubu. He took power in 1965 and became the perfect example of an African dictator. He wore a leopard skin hat and always carried a cane with him wherever he went.

During his reign as the president, he looted the country of all its wealth while the inhabitants were left to fend for themselves. The president, his family, and his entourage lived a lavish life and amassed a wealth that no one can possibly estimate. In the early nineties, the people of the Congo were tired of living in deep poverty while the president and his entourage got richer with each passing day.

In 1997, a troop led by Joseph Desire Kabila went on a crusade to invade the capital of Congo, Kinshasa, and overthrow

President Mobutu. The Congo was already fighting ethnic tensions in the East and had been since 1994. After the Genocide in Rwanda, various armed groups of rebels fled to the Congo and started the war against civilians and other armed militias. The government was not equipped to control nor stop them.

It's apparently men's nature to sometimes take advantage of the power given to them. Most soldiers led by Laurent Kabila were on a mission to enter the capital and take over the country, but for some of them the situation was an opportunity to run wild and abuse the arms given to them.

Meanwhile, other rebels and militias took advantage of the chaos to start terrorizing the population as well. We began to hear rumors that they were coming, but none of us thought we would be affected. Most of the population in Lusa was known to be for the dictator Mobutu, not because he was a great president, but because we didn't know any better than what we had. We just couldn't conceive why anyone would want to disturb our peace with another doctrine or philosophy.

It had become the norm that the president was ridiculously rich while most of the population was dirt poor. The country had the potential to have a better economy, but we were just afraid of change and hoped that the rebels would stay away from our town. But at the same time, we were hoping for a better life.

CHAPTER 2

Our lives were forever changed when the old government collapsed, and the new force took over. The country was a disaster, and the rebels took over most regions, especially the ones in the eastern part of the country. Their leader, Kabila, was about peace and order, but with the liberation of old power, chaos followed. The situation led rebels from surrounding countries and refugees from Rwanda to enter and want their share. Lusa was unfortunately one of the regions that fell under the rebellious hands.

During that time, our parents kept us at home and school was canceled. Most people remained inside their homes. We were afraid and weren't sure whether our little town would be affected.

"God forbid the rebels get to the town while you are at school," my mother said.

We spent our days watching TV and listening to the radio. We followed their progress and waited. For weeks we were forced to spend time together at home, and it turned out to be somewhat of a blessing in disguise. Despite the tension and the fear of being attacked by rebels, our days were filled with board games and our parents sharing stories about their childhood. By the end of the first week, we were running out of food at home and the markets were closed. My resourceful mother baked bread at home and we helped. We bonded and comforted each other in those very frightening times.

One day as we were making bread in the kitchen, I asked my mother, "What if the rebels invade our town? What would happen to us?"

My siblings all went quiet at once. We looked at our mother, waiting for her to give us an answer. She had the power to make any situation better and always knew the right thing to say.

She took a moment before answering, then said, "You must get rid of all the negative thoughts in your little head, Grace. We are going to be fine. God will protect us." She turned away, her hands back on the dough.

I sensed fear in my mother's voice. My siblings and I stayed very quiet; we all knew that our lives were about to change and my mother couldn't do anything about it.

The rebels invaded the city on a Sunday morning. We heard gunfire early at around 4am. We all gathered in our parents' room and started to pray. I had never been more afraid in my life. Outside, we could hear people screaming and such a commotion that the town felt like a war zone. We held each other quietly and hopelessly. My mother sang under her breath to God and wanted to appear strong to us.

My father only said, "I will not let anything happen to any of my children".

Ironically, I thought then about all my half-siblings who didn't live with us. *Did they want our father to protect them at that moment? Were they as frightened as we were? What about their mothers? Didn't they want their partner to be there with them?* I felt a wave of sadness take over me and saw the worry on my father's face. I was afraid and so unsure about everything.

Later that evening, we heard a bang. They were trying to break through our gate, and within a few minutes, they were inside. My father went out to talk to them, but he was handcuffed and taken back inside the house. They were knocking things over and breaking furniture. They smelled of tobacco, sweat, and alcohol. I dared to look one in the eyes, and all I saw was anger and evil.

We sat on the floor in the living room, while they had fun terrorizing us. The twins cried loudly until my mother put her hands over their mouths to quiet them. After about half an hour of complete terror, they took us outside where most of the people were. That's when I witnessed the most horrifying scene of my life.

They raped the women and killed our men, at least the ones who tried to defend their wives. Death had knocked at our doors, and we didn't know what to do. Life was a nightmare, for a while we didn't know what the future had for us. We were all forced to leave our homes and made to sleep at the town square where rebels were guarding us. We slept on the pavement and waited for our turn to either get killed or get raped. The guards were usually drunk and passed out.

One night, while the guards passed out, my uncle and my dad were able to get all of us to escape and go hide in a church. To our surprise, we found a few of our neighbors there that we thought had been killed. The women were sitting huddled together with fear in their eyes, while the men paced the room anxious and worried. To feel so powerless and unable to stop the fate that awaited their wives and daughters. Some boys from our town turned to the rebellion after watching their families murdered; they joined the militia not because they wanted to, but by lack of better choice or any choice at all.

People had to find a way to survive and if it was by joining hands with the enemy, they were willing to do just that. Their purpose was to save their loved ones, the few who might still be alive.

Those young rebels were just as dangerous as any predator in the wild. Nothing stopped them from doing the unthinkable. To them, the feeling of making other people powerless with their weapons was satisfying. They went around and enjoyed watching people fear them or hide from them. It was a newfound power, and they were determined to use it to the fullest. At first, people tried to resist them at the risk of losing their lives, but the wives begged their husbands to just obey the rebels, and children watched their fathers get beaten up. It all seemed like a nightmare, and we all were in total shock. I looked at those men and wondered what their motivation was, they looked very satisfied with what they were doing.

I watched my father fight tears more than once, and that hurt me more than knowing what could happen to me. I felt the urge to stand up and run to the rebels to fight them. My mother and I kept exchanging worrying glances. I looked at the rest of my family and felt hurt for them. If only I could take their fears and sorrow away. Why was this happening?

We spent weeks hiding behind the church, hoping that the rebels would leave our town after destroying everything. We prayed with each passing day for the moment that we could all go back to our normal lives. Even though we knew that normal life was never going to be part of our vocabulary again.

The church had mangoes and avocado trees so that's what we fed ourselves with. Most of us had no appetite, at first, the little hope we had made us believe we were going to go home and eat real food soon. But by the end of that second week, mangoes and avocados were just as good as roasted chicken and fried plantains. My mother's strength amazed me; she was even stronger than my father. She tried so hard to hide her fear.

"Think positive, always think positive," she repeated to us, or maybe to herself. Her optimism irritated my father to the point that one day, he snapped. In the sixteen years I had known them, my parents usually went to their bedroom to fight. But the tension was so palpable, they fought in front of us, in front of the rest of the family and the neighbors.

"You have to stop with your nonsense. How would your optimism help us right now?" my father shouted at my mother.

The exchange continued for what seemed like an eternity. I resented my father for that, because I agreed with my mother and her hopes. I wanted to believe that nothing was going to happen to us, not because we were perfect people, but because we tried to be as good as possible. My father helped people in the neighborhood when they needed him, my mother cooked for her rivals' kids and my siblings, and we were good kids. For all those reasons, I believed that God would grant us his mercy and miraculously get us out of hell, literally. Hope is what kept us alive.

We sat in the cold for several days, and only had rotten mangoes to feed ourselves with. But it was amazing how hope kept us strong; I realize that hope is indeed a very powerful thing. My father couldn't feel hope, he was angry.

At the beginning of the third week, one of the men from the group decided to go back out to see what was really going on. We all gave him a list of the things we needed.

"Please, get me a toothbrush," my sister said.

And everyone came up with something.

"A blanket, please."

"Get me water if you can."

"Can you go in my house and bring me underwear?"

"Can you just see if my father is somewhere out there?"

We all asked for something, except for his wife.

She begged him to stay. "Think of our sons, what if something happens to you out there?" she implored.

"Don't jinx it, I will be fine, the town has been quiet, I am sure they are all drunk and asleep," he replied.

The man took his jacket and left at the break of dawn. We all prayed for his safe return but pitied his wife and sons for what could happen to him. Deep down, I was glad it wasn't my father risking his life out there. The sun rose and set that day, and our friend did not come back. We all went to sleep, except his wife. I woke up a few times in the middle of the night to check on her, and every time she was down on her knees whispering a prayer.

The next day came and we were all still waiting. The sun came up and set five times and still nothing. Until the sixth day, our friend came back not with what we expected but with a group of rebels. They had used him to guide them to where we were hiding. He came back with our enemies and without his arms and left eye. He took his last breath in front of us.

The rebels took us all out of our refuge and led us to the town center at gunpoint. They started with us, the young girls. Making us dance with them and hand feed them in front of our families. They undressed us and made us dance with each other. I wasn't embarrassed or angry; those words do not begin to describe what I was feeling that day. I was beside myself, feeling hatred from within. For the first time in my life, I knew what it meant to feel real hatred, and it made me sick. I fantasized about setting them all on fire, but they were stronger than us and armed.

For two days, they used us as their sex toys. They took turns, one after another. Our parents were sitting there, unable to do anything. We all cried at first, but after so much violence, tears were out of the question. When someone violates your body like that, crying would only motivate them. So, we held on to our tears for our own sakes and the sake of our families. On the third day, the men couldn't take it anymore and decided to fight the armed rebels with their bare hands. It was a disaster; we all started to run in every direction possible.

"Just run, don't worry about me and the twins, just run," my mother yelled to me and my sister and brother.

We didn't have time to hesitate nor debate, the rebels were shooting at everyone. My mother tried to run behind us to keep an eye on us, but we lost her. There were trees all around us and it was dark; amid the chaos, I also lost my siblings. I looked back and couldn't see a single member of my family. As if I was reacting to a punch in my stomach, I screamed. I called for all of them by name, but everybody else around me was screaming too.

This old lady stopped in front of me. "I lost my people too, but do them a favor, just keep running," she said.

Before I could even say anything, I heard gunshots approaching in my direction, so I ran as fast as I could. I couldn't feel my feet anymore, my stomach was aching, and I wanted to throw up, but I couldn't stop. I had to run and meet my family on the other side. I ran through the trees and grass. I just kept going. I had to run because my mother was counting on me to be okay. I ran for hours, maybe even days, until I collapsed. I couldn't run anymore, my feet had given up on me, my strength had left me, and my hope irritated me. I laid on the floor and everything went dark.

I woke up inside a tent, on a bed with a man sitting by my side. For a moment I thought he was an angel, and then he said something. I didn't understand him but he kept talking to me. As far as I was concerned, the man had saved my life.

When I tried to say something, my throat was so dry it hurt. He stood up to get me a glass of water; I took a sip and asked him in my dialect, "Where is my family?".

He nodded and answered in my dialect too. "I found you not far from here, two days ago. You were alone."

I tried to stand but was too weak. "We have to go find them, they must be waiting for me somewhere," I said in tears.

He asked me to go back to bed and promised to talk about it when I felt better. But wild horses couldn't keep me in the bed, I gathered the little strength that I had and stood up. That's when I realized that I was naked. He looked at me and paused, I was petrified but he had a smirk on his face. After a bizarre moment, he handed me a shirt.

I walked out of the tent, there was nobody around, just me and him. Without shoes, I ran frantically toward the trees, but after a short while I realized I wasn't getting anywhere. So I decided to go back to the strange man who had saved my life. When I got back, he was sitting in front of the tent, apparently waiting for me.

"I knew that you wouldn't get far, so I waited," he said as soon as he saw me.

I couldn't think straight, was that a good thing or a bad thing that he was waiting for me? I just sat on the floor beside him, and my strength abandoned me again. I fell asleep.

This time when I woke up in the tent, I was more lucid. I wanted some answers and needed to get to know the man who was possibly my last chance. I took a good look around me and the tent was practically empty. He had a small duffel bag on the floor next to the bed. Close to the window, I saw a small table with a radio and a few books on top. The tent smelled of alcohol and clay. The fan was on and making a very loud sound. The man was neat because everything was kept in order, even the empty bottles of beer in the corner, were neatly placed.

He was having a warm beer outside the tent, and I went outside to sit with him. We both couldn't look at each other. I didn't know what to think of him or myself. He just didn't want me to read through his eyes. We sat there quietly, and then I eventually fell asleep. When I woke up, he was staring at me.

"We need to talk now. My name is John, I am an anthropologist, and I am conducting social research here in the Congo," he said.

I wanted to scream out of my lungs that I wasn't interested in knowing him, really. All I wanted was for him to help me find my family. But he kept talking about what sounded like rubbish to me.

"I know that you want to find your family and friends, but I heard the report on the radio, and they are all dead," he said coldly.

Time stood still, everything around me stopped abruptly, and I felt numb. He kept talking but all I could hear was 'They're all dead,' which he had said so casually. I don't know how long I stayed like that, but I couldn't speak, nor stand up for several hours.

John went for a walk after our talk. He knew I was too afraid to go anywhere - I had nowhere to go. My life as I knew it had ended, the people I cared for the most had vanished from my world, and I was inconsolable. The next day, I got up and left the tent again. I started walking with the hope that I would end up where the rest of my family was. Still very weak; John had told me the day before that I had some kind of infection. I did not care, I had to find my people, and nothing could stop me.

I walked for what seemed like days. So many thoughts went through my head, and I couldn't think straight. I was scared and hopeful at the same time. In my heart, I was having a conversation with my mother. Repeating over and over, 'I will find you. I know you are out there'. I cried and screamed as I was walking. Unsure where I was, at some point, I lost all my strength and collapsed again.

John found me and took me back to his tent. He had total

power over me from that point on. I didn't give it to him, he just took it. I was like a lifeless doll he could just play with. When I woke up in the tent that day I was empty and sad. I felt like I had to stop thinking to start breathing. My mind frightened me. It became a place that scared me. I didn't want to think about what was happening to me. Only wanted to survive. He gave me some medicine in the morning and fed me until I started to regain my strength. He seemed nice. Yet, my instincts sensed something wrong about him, but the fact that he was so nurturing made me trust him a little bit. He spoke my dialect and French fluently, so we were able to communicate. He made me tea and fed me some canned food. I still wondered why he was taking care of me, but I learned to appreciate it. Still, I told him again that I wanted to go find my family, so he took me back to my town.

He had a beat-up Peugeot behind the tent, I was genuinely surprised when the engine started. We drove for what seemed like an eternity, John knew his way around. I didn't want to think too much or hope for anything. I just wanted to get there and see with my own eyes.

My heart was heavy when we entered the town. It was quiet and felt like a ghost town. I saw unrecognizable dead bodies everywhere. The car windows were down so we caught a whiff of the pungent smell coming from outside. The smell of dead flesh and burnt woods. There was no sign of life whatsoever and most houses were burnt down and destroyed.

"You see, there is nothing left here," John said to me, as I was looking out the car window.

I felt a knot in my stomach. He drove around for half an hour, we went in front of what used to be my home but it wasn't there anymore. My family house was reduced to ashes. I looked only once; my body couldn't handle it anymore. The shock was unbearable. I wasn't prepared for that reality. We turned around and drove back to the tent. I was quiet all the way there. I refused to think and react.

The next morning, John and I went to the city nearby to work on my passport. I was just following his lead, not sure why. But the pain I was feeling inside put me in a trance. I needed something to hold on to, something else to occupy my mind. So, I followed John and didn't pay much attention to anything else.

Within a few days, we packed all his belongings and got on a plane to Kinshasa, the capital of Congo. From there we flew to Brussels, where we took a flight to Los Angeles. He told me about the chaos in my country and promised that after my complete recovery, we would come back and try to find my people, if they were still alive. At that point, my life had taken so many bad turns that I felt like I could trust him and his help, so I did. John made it sound so exciting, or at least he tried.

"You are going to have a brand-new life, I promise." He kept telling me this. "I am going to marry you when you turn eighteen and give you a family, no one is ever going to hurt you again," he said. "We are going to find your family if they're still alive, and we are going to take them with us."

After what life had thrown at me up until that point, I wanted to find something to live for again. But no matter how much John embellished our future together, my heart felt heavy. Nothing settled right, nothing got me excited, and nothing could take the pain away from me. So, I pretended to listen to him when he went on about what America was going to be like.

It's ironic how life had turned out for me, because when I was younger, my siblings and I used to dream of America. One of my father's friends had visited America and stayed there for six months. His name was Tutulu, an arrogant but intelligent man. My father didn't like him much but respected him enough to pretend to be his friend. He was my father's competition with the women in our town. Women in Lusa loved Tutulu because of his power and influence. He had been around the world and had fabulous stories about his trips. Once he told us that he had dined with the Prince of Monaco. We all knew it was a lie, but we loved the fantasy he brought to our lives. Every time he spoke of America, I listened so carefully. I wanted to know about the different states, and the people of different races and cultures. The idea of tall buildings, a thousand television channels, fast food, freedom of speech, people with fast cars, and even different seasons fascinated me.

I dreamed of going there, and I told him, "One day I'll live in America, and I will become one of them".

They laughed at me. "You will always be Congolese, no matter where you live," my mother said. "A dog doesn't turn into a crocodile when you throw it in the water, does it now?"

I didn't know what she meant, and went on dreaming. Now that John was taking me to America, that dream seemed so far away and bitter. I didn't want to go to America. I wanted to go home to my family, and I wanted everything to go back to normal. I wanted to be able to lie down on my mother's lap; I wanted to watch my parents talk about the small stuff; I wanted to see my siblings play around the house; I wanted to smell the aroma of freshly cut grass, the smell of the sand after a rainy day and the sound of the rooster at the break of dawn.

The feeling of wanting something that I couldn't have any longer troubled me. I felt powerless and helpless. I wanted to jump off the plane, take off my clothes, scream, hit something, or just kill myself. My mind was scattered, I asked myself questions about God, fate and life. But all the questions in my head remained unanswered. John, who was sitting right next to me, felt so distant. I couldn't reach him, and he couldn't reach me.

We were strangers. The people on the plane were strangers and I had never felt so lost in my life. *What was going to happen to me? What if I never find my family? Why am I taking this chance with him? Maybe I didn't look hard enough for my siblings?*

I had a thousand questions, and I was going crazy. I was screaming inside, but John looked calm and happy. He looked like a man who had just conquered a battle. I felt very distant from him and everything else around me. The plane felt so confined, even though we were sitting in first class. The people irritated me, and I felt trapped in my own fate. I could not shake off the darkness within me.

After two very long flights, we landed at Los Angeles Airport. I had never seen anything like it in my life. I didn't know an airport could be so huge. The people, the airplanes, the weather, the sounds, and the smell were all foreign to me. So foreign that it all felt hostile to me. I was blown away but scared at the same time. I was in a new environment with a strange man, and nothing seemed normal.

John held my hand the entire time, from the moment we got out of the plane, as we were getting his luggage, until we got a taxi. He was quiet for a long time. He looked like he was working on a plan in his head. He didn't want to let go of me and didn't want people looking at or talking to me.

To me, everything was moving at the speed of light. I was living in Lusa, the rebels took over, I lost my family, ended up in John's tent, and then I was in America. I couldn't digest all the changes, and when it hit me that my life had completely turned upside down, I felt nauseous and dizzy. John asked the taxi driver to stop the cab so that I could throw up outside. I threw up a green substance that I had never seen before, and it smelled so strong.

"It must be the stress of the flight and everything else, you will be fine," John said as he patted my back.

It always seemed so strange to me that John spoke my dialect. By then, I realized he spoke at least ten different languages, because at the airport he communicated with some Asian people in their language that I couldn't place, then to some foreigners who looked maybe Hispanic in their language. And the taxi driver, who looked Somalian, had a conversation with John in his dialect too. I guess I admired that about him, it was strange but amazing.

We got onto the highway, cars were moving so fast and people looked crazy behind their wheels. The driver kept swearing at those who were cutting in his line, and the people swore back at him. I thought to myself, I'd rather go back to Africa where life was sometimes chaotic, but I was used to it. I like the overcrowded markets in Lusa, and the uncontrollable cars on the streets. Congolese people had a lot to be sad about, but always figured out a way to be merry. We didn't trust our politicians, worshiped our entertainers, and revered our church leaders. Whatever the priests or the pastors said was the absolute truth. We believe in the spirits of our ancestors, but also in God. We were one of the richest countries in resources, and yet one of the poorest economically. People drove the same cars for years and figured out a way to maintain them. The poor both admired and hated the wealthy. The Congo is a standing contradiction, but I was deeply in love with everything it represented.

And then we got to our destination, a beautiful building with orange bricks and a glass door. "This is our temporary home. Don't get too used to it because in a couple of days we'll move from North Hollywood to Bakersfield. You'll love it there better."

That's what John told me. "Okay," I said back.

North Hollywood or Bakersfield sounded all the same to me, I had never heard of either. We got all his bags inside the apartment that looked like no one had ever lived in it. Everything seemed so lifeless; the single sofa, the television, and the bookshelves.

I stood there motionless and frightened to the core. I had

never been in a room alone with a man other than my father and brothers, and this was a strange moment for me. John gestured for me to take a seat on his sofa. Without another word, he got on the phone for a long time while drinking his beer. And that is how the adventure I didn't sign up for began.

CHAPTER 3

As promised, John moved us from North Hollywood to this town called Bakersfield in less than two weeks. We drove for a few hours and I slept the entire time. My life had become a tale of surprises, and I was on the outside looking in. *Who was I? What was going to happen to me? Why didn't I question John?* It felt like a living nightmare.

When we got to John's house in Bakersfield, John forbade me to go out, answer the phone, or watch television in his absence. My life became this uncanny routine. I had to wake up an hour before John; he set the alarm for me. I took a cold shower, got dressed, ironed John's clothes, and went to the kitchen to make breakfast. All at the tender age of sixteen.

John came to the kitchen with a pill on his upturned palm that he forced me to take. I don't know what it was, but he started giving it to me since the night we had sex for the first time.

The memory of that night still keeps me up at night, even though we had several nights of forced intimacy after that. The night we arrived at John's house in Bakersfield, I didn't know what to do with myself.

"This is your new home. Make yourself comfortable," he said, with a smirk.

The place was somewhat organized but needed some fresh air. He guided me to his bedroom and commanded me to unpack his bags for him.

"We'll get you a few clothes this week. Okay?" I just nodded. "You will sleep on this bed with me," he continued.

I felt like someone had just punched me. He expected me to share a bed with him. After I unpacked his bag, I took a cold shower. I sat in the bathroom for a very long time, trying to collect myself. I felt wrong. It all felt like something was amiss. I couldn't read John and his intentions. But as I sat in the bathroom that day, I knew that once I got out of it, something bad was going to happen to me.

John came and knocked on the door. I stayed quiet. I was scared. He knocked again and I finally opened the door. He took me by my hand and led me to the living room. I followed him, and my heart felt like it was going to come out of my chest. He put a tape in the VCR, and images of people naked and having sex came on. I looked away, but he forcefully held my head and turned it toward the screen. To me, sex was sacred. The rebels back home had turned it into a disgusting act. And watching some folks doing it on TV really made my stomach turn. I wanted to run out of the house but couldn't.

"You can't go out of this house," John told me. "You are illegal in this country, and trust me you don't want to know what they do with people like you."

I had heard of porn, but it was all a big taboo for me. Some boys watched it secretly in Lusa, and one of my uncles encouraged them. "You could learn so much from it," he would say. But John was using it to manipulate me. So, I sat on the couch and watched the tape with him. Within fifteen minutes, he took my hand and led me to the bedroom. I thought my heart was going to stop beating at that point. I was scared and didn't know a way out of what was awaiting me in the bedroom. He took his clothes off and ordered me to take off the towel that I had wrapped around my body. My eyes were staring at the floor, I couldn't look at John. I resisted and he slapped me hard, so hard that I thought my jaw exploded. I started to cry as he pulled me toward him.

"You are going to do to me what those girls were doing to their men in the video, you hear? Now get down on your knees," he said in a cold and cruel tone.

I knew that I had to obey because my life depended on it. So I got on my knees and did what I saw in the video. I sucked on his penis and wanted to throw up. Then I laid down on the bed, he went on top of me and penetrated me. He smelled of alcohol and I couldn't breathe. I held my scream inside; the rage felt like a volcano was ready to erupt inside of me. John didn't care. That moment brought back the memory of what the rebels did to me back home. They penetrated me, played with my breasts and fingered me. He kept riding me like a madman on a horse, and I zoned out. My body wasn't mine anymore. I was being violated once more.

I decided from that point on that John was never going to see my tears. I made a promise to myself to never show emotions around him; no fear, no hatred, no love, no panic, or anything else. When he finished that night, he rolled away from me and fell asleep. He snored all night, and I stayed awake. I was a whore who had sex with rebels and now with a stranger. I felt dirty and ashamed of my body. I chased away the image of my mother in my head.

Every day, we did the same thing. John left for work after locking the entertainment center and locking me inside the house. At night I served him dinner, we watched pornography, and then had sex. My soul had left me completely; I didn't know who I was anymore: a slave, a maid, a whore, or just a toy. John and I barely communicated; he gave orders and I followed them. The only English words that I had learned so far, I learned from the porn we were watching: 'fuck me!', 'yes, do me!', 'right there!', 'Yes! Yes! Yes!', 'spank me' and many more. I was a puppet and John was the master. He wanted me to repeat what I heard in the porn and I did.

One day when John left for work, I dared to open the kitchen window and saw a neighbor. This older blonde lady saw me and kept looking at me strangely, as if she was wondering what I was doing there. I closed the windows and the blinds because I knew that if John found out, I was not only going to get beaten, but also the sex was going to be extremely violent. Those were my two punishments whenever I did something that John didn't like.

I remember one day, I threw up the pill that John gave me every morning. I thought he had left the house, but he caught me. He slapped me hard, then he said, "Wait until I come back tonight, you'll get punished".

That day felt like the longest day of my life, I wanted John to come back and get it over with. I wondered what he was going to do to me, so I cleaned up the house at least ten times. I paced back and forth in the living room awaiting my sentence.

When John came home that night, he brought a new tape. He didn't even look at the dinner table and ordered me to watch the tape with him. John opened a bottle of beer and focused on the TV. People were having violent sex: some were choking each other; some were using whips and the others were just physically torturing their partners. So, John did most of those things to me that night, and for the first time I broke the promise I had made to myself, to never cry in front of him. I didn't deliberately cry, tears escaped my eyes, because I think even my inside was shocked at what was happening.

My body was doing things that I couldn't control, a scream

came out of my lips, tears dropped, and my legs were trembling out of control. I wanted to die, but everything except death happened that night.

"This is what you get for being a bad girl," John said, over and over.

I stared at the ceiling and hoped for that moment to just pass. I wanted to throw up because the smell of alcohol was overwhelming. And that was just the beginning of my life with John.

As the days passed, whenever I felt like breathing fresh air, I'd open the kitchen window from time to time, but just briefly so that the lady across didn't see me. I longed for those days back home when everything was so pure and simple. I wondered about my family, even though John told me that they were all dead, something inside of me was telling me otherwise. Maybe I was just in denial, but hope kept me alive. I kept thinking about my mother.

"You are going to make a good wife, I tell you," she used to say.

She was so proud of my sister and I every time we completed our chores. I hated doing them, but it was our responsibility to do them, besides I loved the look on my mother's face when she congratulated me. She was a good wife to my father, always there for him even when he didn't deserve her. My mother never showed her disappointment in front of us. She loved him and cared for him unconditionally.

And I always prayed to be half as good a wife as my mother. I remember one time, my father came home late after work; he loved his food completely warm and fresh out of the oven. But that day, he came in an hour later than he usually did, and the food had gotten cold. He sat down to eat and after the first bite, he stopped. He looked at my mother with rage and threw the plates of food on the floor. The food that my mother had cooked with all the love and care in the world was on the floor.

"It's cold, you know I don't like it cold," my father yelled at my mother.

We all stared at him, petrified to see that side of him that we only saw a few times a year, but we knew existed. My mother got up gently, picked up everything and went into the kitchen. My father left that night, and only came back the next day after work. He spent the night with one of his concubines. Something that he seldom did.

When he came back the next day, my mother welcomed him with open arms as if nothing happened the day before. I was mad at my father for his lack of consideration but couldn't say anything. My mother was a strong and intelligent woman, but she valued her family more than anything, and didn't want her children to carry the stigma of 'children of divorced parents'. That's why she fought to save her marriage like a lioness. I couldn't stand it, but I understood her.

"I love your father, don't ever forget that. He is the only man I have ever loved," she told me the one day I asked her to leave my father.

She loved him - with the good and the bad. On one hand, I admired her strength but on the other, I wished she had had the courage to leave him. Through thick and thin, they were there for each other.

John had killed the life that I dreamed of; he took away my dream as a young girl and somehow, I felt responsible for it. I should have tried harder to escape from him, or I should have tried to stay with my family while we were running. It was all my fault; I was a failure and I was paying for it.

One day, I got caught in my own reverie with the windows

open, and the neighbor came close enough to talk to me. As soon as she said hi, I slammed the window shut. I felt a shortness of breath, as if I just ran a mile. *What was I doing? What if John finds out?* And he did. That night, John came home and he slammed the door behind him and shouted:

"Grace, come here!"

I was hiding in the bathroom because I had a feeling that something bad was going to happen to me that day. I heard him going into the kitchen, then the bedroom. He paused for a while, then came storming into the bathroom as I ran out. He followed me into the living room and caught me by my hair. He pulled me, I knew that there was no point in fighting him; he was bigger, stronger, and furious.

"You know what you did, that's why you are hiding?" He screamed. "What did I tell you about opening doors and windows?" he continued.

I couldn't utter a word, before I even got a chance, he slapped me as hard as he could. He unzipped his pants and aggressively pushed inside of me. It only lasted a few minutes, time stood still. I wanted to throw up, but the disgust that I felt stayed inside and made me feel sick and filthy.

I belonged to John and my emotions didn't matter. According to John, the lady asked about me on his way home, and he didn't give her an answer. He told me to never try to talk to her or anyone, and that if anyone ever dared to knock at the door, I wasn't allowed to open it under any circumstances.

That morning after, he gave me all these new rules and restrictions. I listened while taking the pill that he gave me. I looked at him and wondered if he was capable of loving and caring for another human being.

His eyes had no expressions or emotions. The only times that I saw something in his eyes were when I was performing a sexual act on him like the girls on the videos. I saw something in his eyes that I cannot describe, it was unique. He looked like a defeated beast.

He left for the day, and sure enough the neighbor came knocking at the door. I was tempted to answer, but I knew the consequences. She insisted for at least ten minutes, but I stood by the door, fighting the urge to open it. She gave up and I sighed. The day went on; I cleaned up a few times, cooked, and waited for John to come back from work.

I stood by the windows a couple of times, wanting to open them and scream for help, but the fear that I had of John stopped me. I feared John like I feared the rebels back home. To me John represented danger, evil, hatred, and all that I grew up trying to stay away from. My mother warned me about strangers my whole life, and there I was living and sleeping with one.

———

When I was twelve, my school had guest speakers that came from different countries. I was just curious to know what it was like to live in Belgium, France, Germany, the USA or just from another continent. These people fascinated me. I loved the way they carried themselves with such carelessness, the way they spoke, and the way couples showed affection in public.

In my little town, couples didn't kiss and cuddle in public often. But the couple among the guest speakers felt free to do that in public, and everybody in town felt embarrassed and uncomfortable around them.

My mother warned me. "They are not even married but look at the way he is touching her. Poor girl is ruining her reputation."

"I think they are in love. Love makes you do crazy things like that," I replied to my mother. She got up from her chair and came to sit close to me. "I don't care where they are from, but no one touches you like that until he marries you," she said with all the authority in the world.

My mother was beyond traditional when it came to marriage, and I just didn't know what to think of her opinion. So, I never contradicted her on anything she told me, I learned to take it in.

She warned me against the guest speakers, to her they were like the virus that was going to infect the children of Lusa. But the more she warned me, the more I wanted to get to know them. I started staying after school to talk to them. When my mother asked about my after-school activities, I told her that I had to improve on my math skills and stayed with the smart kids to practice. She was so proud of me, and I took advantage of it.

A few other kids and I stayed for at least three hours after school to hang out with the speakers at the school's guest house. I asked them questions and they were more than happy to answer. I learned terms such as passion and lust. I tried alcohol and witnessed them smoking herbs. I enjoyed being around them to get a taste of foreign cultures. I didn't think their culture was better, but I enjoyed being around something different.

But one day, I drank more than one glass of wine when I was left alone in the kitchen, and soon I began to feel dizzy and nauseous. I managed to walk home slowly. I stopped a few times to catch my breath and compose myself. The world was turning around me. As I approached the house, I saw my mother waiting for me at the door.

"Where have you been?" she asked calmly.

I couldn't focus on her or anything for that matter. I went straight past her, and she must have smelt the alcohol because she grabbed me by the arm and swung me at the door. She yelled like a mad woman, and I started to laugh. The more I laughed, the more she got upset. But after a few minutes, she realized that there was no use in yelling, so she took me to my room, and tucked me in.

The next morning, I woke up with an aggressive headache and couldn't get up to go to school. My mother told my father that I ate something bad at school, and that she would take me to the doctor. My father and my siblings left for work and school, and I stayed home with my mother. She stormed into my room and gave me the beating of my life.

"Do you know what your father would do to you if he found out? So you have been hanging out with the foreigners who teach you promiscuity?" she kept shouting.

I screamed, but it was no use because it was just me and her in the house, and the neighbors didn't care. After beating me up, she ordered me to stop crying and we sat down at the special dinner table to have a talk. She had a way of making us feel good after a punishment. She made sure that we knew that everything she did was out of love, and I never doubted that. I apologized for my behavior and never went back to the guest house. I was ashamed of myself for disappointing her, but she told me that it was normal for people my age to experiment with different things. From that day on, I stayed out of trouble and avoided my foreign friends.

John came home earlier than usual. I guess he was afraid that I had gone to the lady next door. He got inside the house and the first thing he did was call my name. I was in the kitchen cooking. When I heard his voice I got goosebumps, not the good kind. At first, I didn't answer. He went into all the rooms panicked, but finally found me, waiting for him at the kitchen table.

He looked at me and made eye contact. He stood by the kitchen door for a moment to catch his breath. As soon as he left, I smiled to myself; the man was a fool.

CHAPTER 4

A day had turned into a week, a week into a month and I lost track of the time, my life was monotonous. I lived for John. At that point, he was convinced that I wouldn't go anywhere.

The lady next door attempted to knock several times at the door, and each time I ignored her. John and I didn't have sex every day the way we did at the beginning; we had it three or four times a week. Some days, he came home late and too tired to have sex or nag about stupid things. He would order me to serve him beer in the bedroom and to leave him alone for the rest of the night. To me, those nights were my nights off. When he came home on time and was not tired, I had to deal with him and his grumpiness.

He always found ways to push me. Why is the table so dusty? Why is there so much salt in the steak? Did you try to open the entertainment center? It looks like someone tried to read my books. He complained without any reason. He just took pleasure in torturing me and making my life a living hell. He stopped speaking to me in my dialect and switched to English only.

I never smiled nor cried, and it bothered him. John wanted me to show emotions, or cry for him at least, but my heart was frozen. I wished that one day he would leave and never come back. But I disappointed myself every day when I heard the keys turn and saw him walking through the doors.

John was present in the house and in my nightmares. He was the only human being I interacted with and I started to forget what other human beings looked like, except my neighbor. I tried to close my eyes and concentrate on my past, my blissful past that I was probably never going to get back.

I wondered what my neighbor was doing, and who she lived with. I imagined what her house was like inside, and had a relationship with her in my mind. She had become my imaginary friend in my lonely times. I spoke to her and told her my hopes and fears. That pretend friendship kept me going.

When I was young I prayed to God as if he was a magician, because God, according to me, had tricks up his sleeves. All I had to do was pray and whatever I wanted came true. What I didn't understand was that children have microscopic needs that parents can help fulfill. The older we get, the bigger and more complicated the dreams get. I remember when I wanted to get into the regional junior soccer team, my sister made fun of me and my father tried to dissuade me.

But my mother looked into my eyes and knew how bad I wanted it. "Listen, it's hard to get onto the team," she said, "but if you have faith, God would get you in and even help you win the championship".

That night, I went and got on my knees to pray. I went to bed with a heart filled with hopes and dreams. The next day, I went for the tryout and got onto the team. It was that simple, God had answered my prayers and amid the excitement, I forgot to thank him for it. I realized that I asked God for help in desperate times, forgot about him in happy times and blamed him for all the bad times. And of course, I blamed him for everything that had happened to me and didn't want to speak to him anymore.

I developed an astonishing imagination; my mind went places that I had never been before. I went to Europe, Asia, and some places that only existed in my mind. I needed to occupy myself and get my mind off of reality. I even imagined John chained down in a dark room with rats and snakes. I made up this older woman who would come and rescue me from John. Basically, I was very detached from the real world and it felt darn good.

But I couldn't always ignore reality, because some days, John slapped me back to it, literally. He hated it when I daydreamed in the morning while serving his breakfast. One morning, I was so absent that I forgot to toast his bread. He grabbed me by my hair, took me in the bedroom and beat me so hard that I threw up blood.

I knew that it wasn't over, because whenever John was angry with me, he spent his entire day thinking of a punishment. My day was spent waiting for my reprimand. I didn't have the strength to cook or clean, but I did anyway. I couldn't dream or think of anything good in my life. I couldn't escape in my mind and shut down John. He got under my skin like a snake's venom. I was so angry that I physically couldn't stand straight on my feet, the anger paralyzed me that day.

My heart felt heavy like it wasn't mine anymore. I wanted to scream. I wanted out of the pain and the misery. I felt tempted to run outside and ask for help, but I was too scared. The combination of my anger, frustration, helplessness, and hatred made me nauseous

I asked myself, "What is it that I had done that was so bad, that my life had to be so unbearable?" I had questions going through my head, and the fact that I wasn't going to get answers made me even more upset.

When John came home that night, I was sitting on the floor in the living room waiting for him. He brought another tape that we watched together. For the first time, I begged him to leave me alone because I was still hurting from the morning. But he went ahead and did all the nasty things to me anyway. The pain that I felt that night went beyond unbearable; I was numb.

I spent the following day trying to heal myself with salted water. I rubbed myself with warm oil and put the water in my bruises. I dipped my legs in warm water for a couple of hours when John left for work. I looked at myself in the mirror and laughed, I was a mess. What was becoming of me? Where do I go from here? What happens next? The questions were endless.

I wanted to talk to someone, so I went and dared to take the key from John's drawers and opened the entertainment center. I turned on the television and watched the news. It felt good to watch something other than pornography on television. I was so excited that I kept switching the channels. John had captions on so I enjoyed watching and reading at the same time.

On one channel a man was cooking, I found that odd because I had never seen a man cooking before. My dad didn't know his way around the kitchen. Then another channel seemed to be dedicated to nature documentaries. And on another, a lady was talking while a group of people sat attentively listening. I thought to myself that she must be an important person. I didn't know that television had a variety of programs like that; I made a discovery and loved it.

For a very long time, the Congo was called Zaire, and Mobutu was the dictator at the time. He made sure that we only had one television channel. The population watched the same programs. A few years before the end of his regime, people who could afford it paid for cable and were able to get some international channels, but in Lusa, we were way behind the big cities. I was so caught up in my discovery that I forgot about the time and John's return.

Luckily, the lady next door came knocking at my door and got me out of my fantasy land. Her knocks startled me, and I thought that it was John coming in. A chill went down my spine at the idea that John had caught me watching television, cold sweat started running down my armpits. But when I realized that it was the neighbor, I turned off the television, locked the center and neatly returned the key where I found it. I finished my chores and only had an hour to cook dinner before John came back.

I was afraid he was going to come home before dinner was ready, so I rushed like a madwoman. He came home late that night; I had plenty of time not only to finish cooking but also to watch a little more television. The thought of getting caught sent an adrenaline rush through me.

When I heard his car pulling in, my heart was beating so fast that I started to sweat. It took me less than a minute to turn off the television, lock the center and return the key. But when John got in the house, he asked me to hide in the bathroom, and I obeyed him. He went back in the car, and a minute later he came into the room with a woman. I couldn't see her, but I heard her voice. They had sex for a couple of hours, and for the first time, I heard a woman give John orders. After sex, she asked him to bring her a glass of water, and he did. Whoever that woman was, I already liked her. It was quiet for a moment, then they got up and he took her out. She left and John came back to the bathroom to take a piss. That's when he remembered that I was there the entire time.

He looked at me and smiled. "Did you enjoy the sound of my girlfriend and I making love?"

I just got up and went into the living room, I didn't want his filthiness rubbing off on me, the mere sight of him disgusted me. That night, I didn't sleep, the fact that John was worse than I could have possibly imagined dawned on me. He was a monster, an evil man, or something worse, but there was no way that he had a normal human heart and soul, no way. With all the sex we had, or rather that he did to me, I didn't think it possible for him to want another partner. But John's sexual thirst was insatiable. That next morning, he woke me up from the sofa and we had more sex before he went to work. He walked out the door that day without giving me the pill. I was surprised but before I even finished my thought, he came back and gave it to me.

I watched more television after he was gone, and surprisingly enough I understood around half of what they were saying in English. The brain is an amazing thing; I had already learned the basics in school, but now listening to John and watching TV and the pornography meant I had picked up even more. So I started to repeat words and tried to put sentences together, but the only problem was that I had to concentrate to understand what they were saying. After watching for three hours I felt a violent headache come on, so I turned the set off and fell asleep.

John came home late that night, I pretended not to hear him. He brought another girl, I didn't see her face, but she sounded different, maybe a lot younger. I stayed on the sofa with my eyes closed. Normally, John would have yelled my name to wake me up. But that night, he wanted to spend the night alone with the girl. She noticed me and asked him who I was, he told her that I was his maid.

"Let's not wake her up, she works so hard to keep my house clean. A sweet girl, very sweet," he said.

I couldn't believe what I was hearing; John called me a sweet girl. I was disgusted and wanted to hurt him. But I kept my eyes shut and remained in that position until the morning.

When John and his lady friend woke up, I was in the kitchen making breakfast. I thought that he would have had the courtesy to at least spare me the torture of meeting his lady friend, but it was just an absurd wish. She came into the kitchen with John's shirt on looking young, pretty, and merry. Smiling, she introduced herself to me.

John looked uncomfortable but couldn't say anything. He

realized, a little too late, that his friend was taking an interest in me. I was in heaven; the only thing was that I had to pretend that I didn't speak English well. I didn't want John to know that I understood a little bit of English. So, she kept talking to me and I kept smiling and nodding at everything she said. I loved the fact that another human being was in the kitchen other than John and I. I wanted her to stay and keep talking to me, but John saw the delight on my face and couldn't bear it. He asked the girl to get dressed and leave, she declined his request, at least that's what she thought it was. He tried one more time, but she said that she wanted to stay. I saw the fury in John's eyes the third time she said no. He couldn't contain himself, his anger dominated him. He literally grabbed her arm, dragged her into the bedroom, made her put on her clothes and threw her out.

I witnessed John unleash his wrath on someone other than me. It was disturbing to watch the terror in that girl's expression. She went from being so jovial to looking scared, like a child attacked by a big mountain lion. John was roaring and acting like someone had just invaded his territory. He was in action, and I was there to witness it. When the girl was gone, he came back in the kitchen, sat on his chair, and finished eating his breakfast.

Once again, John had just revealed another layer of his diabolical personality. I didn't know what to do or what to think. I felt a lump in my throat, my eyes got teary, but I wouldn't allow myself to cry. My life had sunk to the bottom, and I was defenseless. I stared at the dishes that I was washing, until John snapped me back to reality to give me my pill. I took it from him and swallowed it with a heavy heart.

CHAPTER 5

It had been almost eight months since John and I moved in. I saw the months pass only through his television. I had gained weight and cut my hair short per John's request. I concluded that I was going to die in John's house, and no one was ever going to find out.

My life was completely meaningless and nothing in the world mattered to me. I started to die inside and waited for the day that John was going to kill me with his violence once and for all. He brought girls back on Fridays and locked me in the pantry to avoid any incident. During the day, I still watched television and spoke English even better in my head. I understood almost everything. I lost all hope of ever having a normal life again. I forgot that I had the right to live, because John killed the little girl in me.

The girl who loved the simple things had died. I felt dirty, ashamed, and worthless. I saw an ugly girl when I looked at myself in the mirror and couldn't face what I had turned into. It hurt so much that sometimes I laughed at myself. Life had dealt me a bad card. John had a collection of pornographic tapes, and his very personal sex toy, me. Every day, I woke up to the same routine. John didn't have to set the alarm anymore, I got used to waking up early. I took a cold shower and cooked breakfast. John would eat it, give me the pill, and head to work. I stayed home to clean, cook, and watch television until he came back. I knew exactly when to turn the television off, when the five o'clock world news started. John would walk in thirty minutes later, eat dinner and take me to bed when he wasn't too tired. Some days, he came in later and went straight to bed without the porn and the sex, and I celebrated in my heart. I began to like it when he brought other girls home. For me, those were my extra nights off and I enjoyed them.

The lady neighbor stopped knocking at the door after several attempts. For about two months, she didn't stop by, and I was surprised. I was starting to like the knock, to me it felt like someone out there cared for me. I developed a connection with her without even knowing who she was. I had seen her from afar only. I knew that opening the door would only put me and her at risk.

John was a dangerous man, and I didn't want him to hurt the neighbor. I resisted the urge to ever answer the door. It took strength and willpower that I didn't think myself capable of. One of the days, I'd had to lock myself in the bathroom away from the sound of her knocks.

"Please go away! You don't want to know what's on this side of the door. Just go." I whispered to myself, hoping that she would hear and never come back. And that was the last time she came. I don't think she heard me, but she didn't come back. I missed her and found myself crying over her. We became close strangers; she was closer to me than the man I shared a bed with. I didn't know her, but I knew that she cared enough to come back every day and knock on the door. She cared and it had been a long time since anyone had cared about me. So, for the first time in a long time, I cried when she didn't come back.

I cried but got over it because I wasn't expecting anything good from life anymore. I learned how to deal with the bad and ignore the possibility of anything good. So when the neighbor stopped coming to the door, I cried and moved on.

One night John came home with another girl, and he locked me in the kitchen pantry. I fell asleep thinking of my mother. I dreamed that she came to Bakersfield, and everything was different for me. I looked so happy when she was holding my hand. We were walking together and life felt good again. She looked beautiful in her pink satin gown, and I was wearing the same gown in white. My dream was cut short when, in the morning, John came to wake me up.

"You overslept again. Wake up and make me breakfast," he said.

I woke up with a smile on my face that John couldn't take away. I made him breakfast, took the pill, and went to take a shower. During the shower, I tried to revive my dream and thought of my entire family. I missed them so much. I remembered how we used to take turns to shower. We had two bathrooms, one in my parents' room and the other in the hallway that we all had to share. I usually woke up first to shower during the week. Whoever woke up first had the right to shower first unless he or she wanted to trade it for part of his or her allowance. I remembered one time; my sister gave me her entire allowance so that she could shower before me. She had to go meet her cool friends, and to her that was priceless.

"Take all the money, I just can't be late. They'll think I am uncool," she said.

I shamelessly took her money and told her she could shower before me. But my brother came running and hit the shower before her. She was fuming out of her ears, and I wouldn't give her back her money. We had a monumental fight that morning, and to calm us down, my mother grounded us and took both our allowances to give to the less fortunate. We spent that Saturday in our room. At first, we didn't talk to each other, but after a couple of hours we started talking and sharing stories. She didn't go see her friend and I didn't go play soccer that day. Instead, we stayed home to talk and play with the twins. My mother was proud of herself every time she turned a fight into a party. And from time to time, she proved that she was very good at it.

"I can't tolerate my own children fighting like enemies," she said. According to my mother, 'where there is love, there is room for disagreement but not hostility'. A lesson that was embedded in me then, and still today.

At John's house, television was my only outlet to the world. I learned how to fix my hair, to pretend to put on makeup, to sing, to walk like a star, to speak English, but most importantly, I learned to draw. They had a show that taught viewers how to become amateur artists and I watched it regularly. At some point, I went to John's office and took paper and pencils. I knew that he wouldn't notice because he rarely worked at his desk. I found a new activity to occupy myself during the day. I started to draw pictures of flowers and African landscapes. I drew what I remembered of my country: the animals, the land, the people, the blue sky, the outside clothing lines, and more.

Drawing became my best friend; I found a way to express myself freely and without interruptions. I hid the pictures in the pantry; John never set foot in there. To him, everything in the kitchen was my business, not his. I hated drawing when I was younger; my attention span wouldn't allow me to sit and focus. I always had a lot going on in my mind and wanted to know and understand everything. My curiosity got me in trouble for the most part, but I was always the first to know about scandals waiting to happen in our town. When I was fourteen, my dad's sister was cheating on her husband, which is completely forbidden in our culture. My father heard the rumor and confronted her about it. Of course, she denied it. But by looking at her, I knew that something was up. I knew she was lying.

My aunt was mean to us, she never really cared about anyone but herself. Her husband had a hard time living with her as she was selfish, talkative, a gossip and troublemaker.

One day, I decided to start ditching school to follow her for a week and record her activities. Sure enough on the third day, in the morning when most of the husbands were at work, the children at school and the women too busy cooking, my aunt went to visit her lover. A much younger guy, the shoe repairman's son, who was only eighteen. I saw them going into an abandoned house together and I followed them. I climbed the wall to peep through the window, and with my own eyes I saw the young man undress my aunt.

I wanted to make her pay for all the gossip she spread about my mother and some other women in the community. I went home and told my mother about what I had seen, and she yelled at me.

"First of all, you ditched school. And then you go spying on your aunt?" my mother said. "Are you trying to separate this family? Is that what you want? You better keep quiet, this conversation never happened," she continued.

But to me, the information that I had against my aunt was too hot to keep to myself. I couldn't contain myself, and that same night I told my sister. The next morning at breakfast, she told my father. My mother was furious, so furious that she asked me to stay home and go wait for her in my room. When everyone left for school and my dad had gone to work, my mother came into my room and gave me another beating.

"What are you doing spying on older people? I told you to keep quiet, but you told people anyway." She yelled as she was beating me up.

When she finished, my mother told me to get dressed and go

to school. I went to school late with my eyes red and a sore body. I was hurting all over, and when people asked me why I was late, I told them that my mother beat me for talking too much. Most of the kids at school could relate, so we spent that day sharing the stories of our mothers and their ways.

After school, I found the entire family at my house; my grandparents, my uncle's parents, and the town's wise men and women. My father had followed my aunt to the abandoned house and caught her red-handed with her young lover. My father dragged my aunt and her lover all over town and made sure to humiliate them in front of everybody. When I walked in, my aunt was sitting on the floor with just a cloth around her torso, and her lover with his shorts only. She looked sad and humiliated, I felt bad.

My mother blamed me, I could tell by the look on her face. I wanted to disappear. What was done was done, my aunt had been caught, and she was going to pay for it. After hours and hours of deliberation, the family decided to punish her by isolating her in a room for forty days, and for her lover to leave town forever. When they all left, the house was so quiet, and my mother was in a killer mood. She came to my room, and we had a talk. She told me that there was nothing wrong with denouncing evil, but that there was a better way to do it. I had nightmares that night; the guilt wouldn't let me sleep. But we all lived through it.

After cleaning and cooking, I watched television for a couple of hours, but got bored. I drew flowers and butterflies until I fell asleep on the couch surrounded by a couple of my other drawings and the new ones.

I felt a tap on my shoulder and when I opened my eyes, John

was holding my drawings. Thankfully, I had already turned off the TV. It felt like a kick in my stomach, John had a defiant look on his face. A look that I had never seen before, he was beyond furious.

"What is this?" he asked.

I could not utter a word nor move. I was paralyzed and knew what was going to happen to me.

"This is what you do when I am not around. Instead of cleaning the house, you spend your time drawing these awful pictures?" he yelled.

I was sweating bullets at that point; my whole life flashed right in front of me. He grabbed me and threw me on the floor. He kicked me with his foot with unnatural strength. I tried to run from him, but he caught me and kept beating me. John was not only twice my size, but his anger made him incredibly strong. After beating me up, he tore the house apart looking for the rest of the drawings.

He handed me a pair of scissors and made me cut them into small pieces. A part of me died a little more with each picture, and John's eyes were blazing with fury. I only looked at him once, and my heart was filled with an emotion that I can't describe. I hated him. To add insult to injury, we went back in the bedroom and had sex. A beast was on top of me, and I suffocated in my own anger and disgust.

The next day, he came into the kitchen, sat at the breakfast table, and ate the food that I had made him. I wasn't angry anymore; I felt numb inside and out. And of course, he gave me the pill. I spent the day rubbing alcohol on my bruises and massaging myself. I wondered where God was but couldn't say a prayer. I cleaned his house and cooked for him, and that day for the first time in a long time, I didn't watch television.

When John didn't come home at 5:30, I knew he would be coming home with one of his lady friends. I hid myself in the pantry. I did not want to deal with him, or even hear his voice. I put cotton balls in my ears and fell asleep. I woke up the next morning to the sound of a girl in the kitchen. She was loud, so I took out the cotton balls and listened.

"You are going to pay me three hundred. You made me do crazy things that I never do for anyone else," she screamed.

"But you consented to it. You are a whore that's what you are supposed to do, now get out!" John fired back.

But she wouldn't have it. She started to break things in the kitchen and open the pantry, there I was. She screamed. "Who is this? Who are you?"

I just sat there, silently. John grabbed her by her arm, gave her the money and kicked her out. He didn't have breakfast that day, nor did he give me the pill. He took a shower and left for the day. I was happy knowing that he was having a bad day, that made me have a great day. But in the middle of the day, I stopped myself. I had been thinking so negatively about John. I was letting John turn me into a monster. It wasn't like me to carry so much hatred in my heart. Sitting down, I tried to get the anger out of my system but couldn't. I promised myself to at least try not to hate John. The hatred I felt was weighing heavy in my heart. A burden I wasn't used to carrying.

When he came home that night, his shirt was wet from his sweat. He looked feverish and his face was red. He went straight to the bedroom and asked me to bring him water. When I got in the room, he took some aspirin and gave me my pill. He tossed and turned all night and kept waking me up to go fetch him water. I ended up sleeping in the living room. The next morning, John did not get better. He still had a very high fever and an aggressive headache. Pitying him a little, I tended to his needs. I helped him go to the bathroom, helped him take more aspirin, and cooked onion soup for him. Two days passed and he didn't improve. He finally decided to go to the doctor but couldn't stand on his own. He called an ambulance to take him to the hospital. He was very sick but still managed to tell me, "Don't do anything stupid."

The lady next door saw me through her window. I went back inside and within fifteen minutes, she came knocking at the door. I took a deep breath and opened the door.

She stopped and looked at me first. I was shaking a little but smiled. "My name is Margaret. May I come in?" she said.

I shook my head.

"Well, that's fine. What's your name?" she asked.

I hadn't been asked that question for such a long time that I had to think before I could answer. A minute later, I answered, "Grace Munia."

"That's a pretty name," she responded. "Is your husband in?" she asked.

I knew that she had the answer to that question, and that she wanted me to give her more information. But I couldn't and did not want to. I enjoyed her presence at the doorstep and loved talking to someone other than John; but I had to protect myself.

"I am sorry," I said as I was shutting the door.

She held the door and gave me a sheet of paper. "That's my phone number, don't hesitate to call me if you ever need anything."

I thanked her and shut the door. She stood by the doors for a few minutes. She knocked again, but I did not open the door. My heart was beating so fast that I felt dizzy. I was not ready to take that step and refused to put myself at more risk with John. I went to the bathroom and locked myself in for the rest of the day.

CHAPTER 6

John was kept in the hospital for a week and a half. And a lot went through my mind; I could have escaped but was too afraid to do so. He did a good job putting emotional shackles on my mind. I stayed, and with each passing day I hoped he would stay longer at the hospital. At the same time, I was afraid that John would come home and catch me doing something he didn't like. I was anxious and couldn't really enjoy my ephemeral freedom. I watched television but kept my ears out for the sound of a car or John's footsteps.

Margaret, the neighbor, came back a couple of times, but I refused to answer. I wanted to, with all my heart, but my fear paralyzed me.

By the end of the fifth day, my anxiety was driving me crazy to the point that I was wishing for John's return. At least life would go back to what I knew. The anxiety made me tired and sick. I cooked and cleaned every day waiting for him. My head was hurting, my feet were tired, and my mind was torturing me. I felt John's presence in the dark, and in the morning, I heard his voice yelling at me. My mind played cruel tricks on me, and I couldn't take it anymore, John had to come back.

He finally did, and he had lost a lot of weight. He was frail and had bandages on both his arms. I had never seen him like that, it scared me. I helped him to the bedroom and helped him put on his pajamas. He wasn't saying a word, probably because I knew that it was hard for him to be weaker than me. I saw the bitterness in his eyes, but I didn't say anything. I hated seeing anybody suffer, so I helped him the best I could. He fell asleep right away. I slept in the living room, but a couple of times during the night, he called me to help him in the bathroom, or give him water. I waited in the bedroom until he fell asleep and went back to the living room. I couldn't sleep and was very uncomfortable knowing that a weak man was sleeping in the very next room.

John didn't get better at all through the night. He stayed in his bed where I served him breakfast and gave him his medication. I was playing the role of nurse and he was the ungrateful patient. In my heart I was hoping that the illness, whatever it was, would soften John a little bit. I tried to see it in his eyes, but all I saw was bitterness.

Sometimes when I helped him to get to the bathroom, I heard him curse under his breath. He hated the fact that I was helping him in even the smallest things such as: adjusting the pillow, bringing him an extra cover, helping him unzip his trousers to take a pee and helping him eat.

For all the things that I was doing for him he never said thank you, not even once. That didn't surprise me much, but I guess somewhere inside of me, I was hoping that John was a normal human being with normal feelings. But my hopes deceived me once more. I didn't know what John had contracted but he suffered a lot. He cried sometimes in his sleep, and I was there to witness it. It was hard for the both of us: John because of his illness and me because of the uncertainty. Everything was pending; negative and scary questions came to my mind.

I kept thinking, *What if John dies? What if his disease is contagious? What am I going to do? Who am I going to call?* I hated being in that situation. I cooked but couldn't eat. I just helped John eat and put the rest of the food in the fridge. John sensed my fears, I don't know how but he did. For the first time since he came back from the hospital, he talked to me.

"I am not going to die, just so you know. I will be fine," he said, looking straight into my eyes.

At that moment I knew that John was the same, if not even worse. I went into the kitchen and cried; I was doomed for life.

John was still sick. We ran out of food, and he needed to refill his pills. The first day that I told him that we didn't have food, he just ignored me. But on the third day, after I fed him cereal without milk, he decided to send me to both the market and the drug store.

"Look, do not even think about doing something stupid," he said. "I told you about what Immigration does to people like you. You are illegal until I marry you. If they catch you, not only will they throw you in jail, but torture also and put you in a small cage with rats. Trust me, I will let you rot in there."

I was naïve enough to believe him. I was still a child who had been sheltered by my parents. I believed him and so, stepped outside cautiously. John, unaware that my English was good enough to carry a conversation, gave me a list of things to say in case I got lost. In my native language, he gave me directions to the store and the drugstore. When I left the house, I read the list and laughed at him. If only he knew. Margaret saw me leaving the house, and not even five minutes later, she was behind me. She called my name a couple of times, but I ignored her. She ran to catch up with me, but I jumped on to the first bus I saw.

I didn't know where the bus was going or how much it was going to cost me. When the driver asked me for the fare, I gave him part of the grocery money. My heart was beating at an alarming rate. Not only because I didn't know the destination, but also because I had just spent part of the grocery money. John was too sick to do anything to me, but he was good at holding grudges. I stayed on the bus until I couldn't see Margaret anymore.

I got off and started to ask people for directions to the drugstore. The first person did not answer and just kept walking. The second one was sleeping on the floor with dirty clothes and asked me for money in exchange for directions. The third one, a teenage boy, gave me complicated directions that I couldn't really understand. I asked him to repeat, which he did, but I still didn't understand. I asked him to repeat for the third time, and he refused. The fourth person was an older lady, she was nice and tried to explain the best she could, but she didn't understand my accent, and I couldn't understand hers.

I took a chance by myself and started walking. Only to realize I was lost about thirty minutes later. All I could see was houses and what looked like a school. I panicked a little bit, and I wanted to scream for help. It took all my willpower not to just give up and go to the police. But the idea of being in jail scared me enough to make me keep walking. I didn't want to start asking too many questions and attract attention. When I left the house, it was almost noon, and according to John's plan I was supposed to get back by no later than 2pm. I looked at the watch that he gave me, and it was 2:15. My body was shaking and slick with sweat. I sat on a bench to regroup.a

I had two options: the first one was to ask for help, attract the police and go to jail. And the second one was to call Margaret. I thought about it for a few minutes and decided to go to a phone booth to call Margaret. Until then, I had never used a phone in

America. John didn't have a phone in his house; he only ever used his cellular phone. I knew that I needed coins to use the phone, but I didn't have any. I went to a liquor store and asked for change, but the cashier refused.

"You have to buy something to get change," he said coldly.

I couldn't spend another cent of John's money, but I also needed to make that phone call. I looked around the store and picked up a pack of chewing gum. The clock was ticking, it was already half past two. By now, John had probably gathered all his strength to get up from the bed, just to come get me. I knew his rage was powerful enough to make him do the impossible. My knees were shaking; the pressure was so high that I couldn't contain myself any longer. I sat down again, and this time on the sidewalk, in front of the store.

A couple of people stopped and gave me free money, some coins and some one-dollar bills. I smiled; maybe God was looking after me, after all. But the smile did not last very long. I saw a car cruising around the bus stop, it looked like John's car, but surely that was impossible. Then the car drove toward me, and stopped.

"Get in the car now!" That was John's voice.

I just couldn't believe it, this man was in no condition to drive, but the thought of me running away had clearly given him strength. To me, John had superpowers, just when I thought that he ran out of ways to surprise me. I stared at the car for what seemed like forever. Thinking of my sentence, and all the bad things that John was going to do to me. I finally got in the car and imagined the color of my coffin. I hoped that after he killed me, he would at least have the decency to give me a proper burial.

John didn't look nor speak to me until we got home. He parked the car and asked me to go inside. He stayed in the car to regain his strength. He struggled out of the car, and in the two steps, to finally get inside the house. The fact that I was watching him through all that only intensified his anger. He sat on the couch and looked at me.

"I am thinking of what I should do with you now," he started. "You don't deserve to stay here with me. But I am too tired to deal with Immigration, so just hide yourself in the pantry while I go buy the groceries."

I got up and went into the pantry. I sat in the dark, hearing my heart beats. He waited at least fifteen minutes, and then left for the store. I waited for his return until sunset, but John didn't come back that night. Coming out of the pantry to look at the time, I saw it was 1:15 am. I didn't know what to do, so I kept waiting. I fell asleep and woke up the next morning at ten, but there still was no sign of John. He had messed me up so much that I started to mix my emotions. I was scared that something bad happened to him, and also excited about the possibility of not ever seeing him again. That emotional combination made me laugh at myself. I decided to wait. But a couple of days went by, and I didn't hear anything. I came up with a plan: I was going to call Margaret and ask her to drive me to the police. Then I would explain to them what John was doing to me, and they would deport me without putting me in jail. I gave myself a deadline.

"If by tomorrow morning, John isn't here, I'll turn myself in."

I went back to the pantry and fell asleep. And during my sleep, I dreamed of being back in Lusa, with the rest of my family. I dreamed of my mother.

When the morning came, I woke up looking forward to a busy day at the police station. I went to the bathroom, took a shower, and brushed my teeth. But my daydreaming came to a brutal halt when I went into the bedroom. John was sleeping on the bed. Wearing bandages like he had the first time he came out of hospital. I assumed that he probably checked himself in. I stood there looking at him, and right then I realized that I was famished. My hopes were naïve, and my life was in John's hands. This life was cruel. I went into the kitchen and realized that my excitement blinded me from seeing the groceries that John had brought in. He had bought eggs, milk, bread, meat, rice, potatoes, and fruits - so much of everything that we were set for at least three weeks. I was making breakfast when John called me to the room. He looked much better than the last time I saw him.

"Make me some eggs and coffee. I need to eat something," he ordered.

I went into the kitchen and made him his usual omelet with toast. He came into the living room to watch television and eat. I served him and isolated myself in the kitchen pretending to clean. Having him in the house very ill was one thing, but having him not so ill was another story. I felt his presence with each one of my senses and organs. He was very present, and I was very uncomfortable. He was like a beast in the forest and I was a human being who had been bitten more than once. I was nervous and anxious, to the point that I threw up the food that I tried to eat.

John needed to either get back to being very sick or go back to work. His presence was suffocating me. He was home for three days, and I didn't go completely insane. But every time he called my name, I felt a lump in my stomach. He wanted water, the VCR remote control, his cellular phone, his socks, his pillows, more water, a snack, and so much more. And every morning, he made sure that I took my pill. I so carefully catered to his every need because my punishment was still pending. I was hoping to make him forget, but I was a fool for hoping.

On the fourth day, he woke up, got his breakfast, took his pills, gave me mine and headed to work. I felt like a weight had been lifted off my shoulders. I took a deep breath followed by a glass of water. I went on to do the things that I usually did. I cleaned the house and cooked. Then I sat in the living room, and for the first time in a long time I did not think of escaping. I resigned to the fact that I was going to grow old in John's house and no one was going to know my story.

My family, if still alive, would never know the type of life I lived in America. I didn't know how big Bakersfield was, or how many people were living around me, but my world felt small and lonely. I needed to adjust my thoughts and get used to living with John. All my dreams were never going to come true. I thought instead about the dreams I used to have, those big dreams.

When I was seven, my dad's niece got married to a handsome young man and every other girl in town was jealous of her. My father and her father first planned for her to marry an old rich man from another town. They planned everything, and all my cousin had to do was to show up and obey. But she cried the entire time that her father was telling her about his plan and did not dare tell him that she had a boyfriend who she adored. She wasn't supposed to have a boyfriend, as a matter of fact no girl in Lusa was allowed to have a boyfriend.

Parents arranged marriages; it was the rule and girls had to abide by it. My sister and I knew that she had someone in her life, and she did not want to marry the old man. She cried for days before the marriage was supposed to take place. Two days before the wedding day, she ran away. The town was frantic, her mother thought that someone kidnapped her, but I knew that she was safe in the next town. My mother saw how calm my sister and I were, and she concluded we knew something. She came to our room the night before the wedding and started her inquisition. We tried to deny the best we could, but it was impossible to lie to my mother, she knew us too well.

"I know you both know something, just tell me and I promise I will cover you," she said.

We stayed quiet for a while, and then she convinced us to spill it out. We told her about the boyfriend and everything else. she didn't look surprised. That night at dinner, she told part of the truth to my dad. "Today when I was going to the market, I heard a rumor about your niece." She went on and told him everything that she apparently heard from the market gossip.

The next day, my father and a group of young men went looking for my cousin. They found her and brought her back. The wedding to the old man was canceled and her father agreed to marry her to the man of her choice. My cousin made history in Lusa; it was the first time that someone had the courage to confront the norm.

She was a hero for girls like me, and from that point on, I promised myself that I would choose my own husband. I created him in my mind. He was tall, dark, and young. He was tender, giving, humble but with a strong personality. I dreamed of how much love and attention he would give me and eventually to our children. I even imagined the sound of his voice. He was perfect, as perfect as a man can be in a little girl's imagination.

CHAPTER 7

John never punished me for what I did, but he became more aggressive toward me. He insulted me for every move I made. I started to think that even my living bothered him. The food I cooked was too salty or not salty enough. The house wasn't clean enough and the fridge wasn't organized the way he wanted it. I did what he wanted me to do. I took the time to clean the house and I measured five times before I put the salt in the food. My efforts didn't make a difference.

In bed, I stopped resisting John, I gave myself willingly. I watched the tapes with him and did everything he wanted me to. I numbed myself to the point that I couldn't keep track of time. I lived for John. No more watching television and I ignored the desire to draw. In the morning, I woke up before the alarm went off and started my daily chores. I took a bath, ironed John's clothes, and made him breakfast. I took the pill from him and swallowed without making a face. Handed him his briefcase and waved him goodbye. I stayed home and kept working on making the house perfect. I refused to stop and think about the person I had become.

For two months, John went in and out of the hospital, and

never revealed to me the nature of his illness. Margaret didn't come knocking at the door, but she watched from the window. She couldn't see much, but she wanted to know what I was up to. She was like an angel watching over me. When I looked over my shoulder, I knew that she was there ready to help, and I appreciated it. In those two months, I also turned seventeen. My birthday was July eighth and I didn't realize it until the tenth. While I was cleaning John's bedroom, I looked at the calendar he kept on his nightstand and realized I had missed my birthday.

John had lost a lot of weight, but he still went to work most of the time. I hated not knowing what bothered him, but I accepted his discretion. His sex drive declined, and we only had sex once a week, sometimes even once every two weeks. I dreaded sex, and was grateful for the time off. However, it seemed like the nicer I was to John the less he could stand me. He loved it when I looked frightened all the time. John loved to dominate and scare me. But I wasn't scared anymore. I knew all his tricks and learned to deal with each and every single one of them. I cooked three casseroles of the same dish. So when he complained about one, I gave him one of the other two. When the house wasn't clean enough, I cleaned many times in his presence, and when I couldn't perform a position in bed, I tried until I got it right.

John hated the new me, and I enjoyed watching him clench his teeth at the mere sight of me. He eventually got tired of complaining about the small things. He started to complain about my physique. Some days I was too thin and others too thick. Some days the soap's aroma was too strong and others not strong enough. There was never a dull moment. But in spite of all of his capricious complaints, I stayed in character.

I spent my weekends in the bedroom, out of John's sight and only coming out to serve him food and use the restroom. I was the maid and the sex object, nothing else. He had mood swings and took it out on me. And every time he called; I was prepared for something new.

"When was the last time you washed your hair?"

I would just look at him, then he would gesture to dismiss me. I would go back to the room and wait for the next time he'd call. And he would yell, 'Come here', and I'd go running to him. But one day, he finally decided to give me a different name.

"From now on, I am going to start calling you Jen," he said.

I was like a pet he bought a long time ago and finally settled on a name. Jen was my new name, and I had to get used to it.

The first time he called me Jen, I didn't answer. Even though I was the only one in the house with me, I did not answer. Maybe I wanted to be a bit rebellious, or just hated the fact that he wanted to erase that part of me too.

Grace Munia was my grandmother's name. My father took a lot of pride in knowing that he would carry his mother's name through me. I had been called that name my whole life and nothing was going to change that. I cherished my name, and it was the one thing that still connected me to my family. John had crossed the line and I was not going to give in without a fight. I knew that fighting John was like fighting a big fire with a small bucket of water. But I took a chance.

"Didn't I tell you that your name was Jen?" he asked quietly but with an angry tone.

"Yes," I said.

"So why didn't you answer when I called?"

All the things that I had played in my mind that I would tell him, completely dissolved. I just stood by the kitchen table, helpless and defenseless, waiting for my punishment. It amazed me how much power John had over me. I felt small in front of him. I couldn't stand up to him, even when I gathered all my strength and willpower.

I was powerless in front of him and I knew it. I looked at him for what seemed like forever, and before I knew it, he came closer and slapped me. He was still weak, but not so weak that he couldn't give me a good beating. He grabbed me by my hair, took off his belt and made me regret that I ever tried to stand up to him.

"You are not worth living here, you are not worth anything. You are like the ugliest thing I have seen in my life. I saved you and this is how you want to thank me?" He went on and on.

I took the beating silently. He beat me until his strength abandoned him. To him, that was a good work out, and to me a nightmare. He hadn't touched me like that for such a long time that my body was in complete shock. It's ironic that he beat me the hardest when he was so weak. I guess he just put a lot into it. I was bruised and bleeding from more than one place. I sat on the floor until he went to the bathroom.

My flesh was hurting badly, but it was my soul that cried that night. *What did I possibly do to the world to deserve to be treated like that?* That question burned within me, I wondered and hoped that somehow, someone would answer it. But I sat on the floor for half an hour and then went to the bathroom to clean my wounds and put on some bandages. I couldn't even look at the mirror.

To add insult to injury, John called me into the bedroom to have sex. He called out my new name, and I stood up. The name that got me in so much trouble. I walked into the bedroom, where John was laying naked on the bed. I stood in front of him to make sure that he saw the bandages and the bruises. But of course, he couldn't care less; I approached the bed and got down on my knees.

Within fifteen minutes, he was tired and asked me to leave the room. He fell asleep before I finished putting on my clothes. Sat in the living room, I couldn't cry nor fall asleep. John was going to beat me to death one day, and no one would ever know. After hours of tossing and turning, I looked at the clock and it was five in the morning, I was still awake and exhausted. I was tired from thinking too much, not for the lack of sleep. I was tired of still being alive and having to go through another day with John. I found the strength to get up, take a cold shower and get started on the day.

No matter how hard I tried not to hope for something special to happen that day, I still did. I realized that as a human being, I couldn't help but hope. Hope is what keeps us alive even in adversity and atrocity. I looked out the window and I saw Margaret making herself tea. She looked at me and I felt a little better.

When John woke up everything was ready, his breakfast, his clothes, his medication, and my pills. I had to take it in front of him. Because once I took it before he entered the kitchen. He counted them every day, so he knew when one was missing. He asked and I told him that I took it already. He nearly strangled me. He choked me so hard, and then made me take another one in front of him. I thought that I was doing a good thing by anticipating his orders. I took the pill without being asked to. But John was a man that I couldn't please. And from that moment on, I learned to do things by the book, especially when it came to that pill he gave me every morning. He came to the kitchen, ate his breakfast, took his medication, gave me my pill and left.

I changed my bandages and looked at all the scars I had accumulated since I had been with John. I had at least fifteen scars of all sizes and shapes. I thought that if there ever was a scars contest, I'd probably be the champion. The thought made me smile, a little. I sat on the sofa and started to reflect on my life, where I came from and where I was going. Nothing could have ever prepared me for what I was going through with John. I thought that the worst that could have happened to me was to fall in public or turn into an old maid. But never once in my life did I imagine that I'd end up with a sex addict in a foreign country.

I was always so dramatic over small things when I was younger. When I was thirteen, there was a pair of shoes that all the girls at my school had. I begged my mother to buy me them in navy blue. The first time I asked her, she said no. The second time, she said "I'll think about it". And the third time, she asked me, "Why do you want them so badly?". The first thing that came out of my mouth was "Because everyone has them". My mother looked at me with rage and said, "I am not going to buy you those shoes because you are trying to copy everyone." I ran to my room and cried. I didn't talk to my mother for a week. She couldn't stand people who lacked a sense of individuality. She insisted that we needed to find our true selves without copying anybody else.

That lesson was embedded in my mind not because it made sense to me, but because I trusted my mother's judgment. What she said to me and my siblings did not have to make sense right away. I usually slept on it, and gave it time to sink in. Sometimes I saw more clearly in the morning and understood her. Sometimes, it took a couple of days, or months, and some other times it didn't make sense. But I trusted her enough to know that she was talking out of love and experience.

Now that I was a bit older and so far away from her, the things that she used to say made more sense to me. She told me I was much stronger than I thought. She was right; what John had been doing and saying to me didn't kill me. My heart ached and my soul was corrupted, but I was strong enough to take it. I missed my mother, and I missed home.

I looked outside the window and saw a woman going into Margaret's house. A curvy and beautiful black woman who kept looking at my window, it was as if she knew about me. Margaret joined her on the porch, and they stood there talking for half an hour. I knew that their conversation had something to do with me. And I was right because the lady came knocking at my door. I went into the bathroom and stayed there until she stopped knocking and walked away. Once again, I wanted to open that door, but I was afraid of what John could do to me, or to them. I fought the urge to open the door. I cried myself to sleep, until John came home. I was still lying on the floor when I felt a kick on my back.

"Get up!" John said.

I looked at him and wanted to spit on him. I got up and remembered that I was done cooking when I locked myself in the bathroom. I had just turned the stove off, but the food wasn't ready.

"Are you going to finish what you started?" John asked nonchalantly.

I nodded and went into the kitchen. John wasn't mad that the food wasn't ready, nor was he surprised that I was sleeping on the bathroom floor. I finished making dinner and served him. I went into the living room and pretended to iron John's clothes. His presence made me uncomfortable, and I caught myself posing, trying to look good or trying to look busy. I prayed that he wouldn't call me about the food, or to rub his back, or something even crazier.

CHAPTER 8

When I found ways to overcome the pain that John inflicted on me, he came up with new ways to hurt me. He hated that I was getting so strong, and he decided to torture me with emotional ups and downs. He would be passive with me for a week, then suddenly turn crazy and aggressive for a couple of days.

I didn't know what triggered his anger toward me, and I am not sure that I had anything to do with it. He just liked torturing me. John had now a cabinet full of medicines. He took them in the morning before leaving for work and at night after dinner. Whatever disease he had, I was just afraid that it was contagious, and every time that we were intimate, I felt like I was dying a little. My mind was so busy thinking about the disease that John had, and if I was going to die of it, that I started to have serious problems with my memory. During the day I accidentally let the food burn, or left John's clothes in the washing machine for hours. I would also forget to take a shower or brush my teeth.

I was reaching a point of insanity. I needed to talk to someone or do something about it. Every time I burnt the food, I had to clean up and make sure that John didn't find out about it. But one day, I burnt the food only for John to come home earlier than usual. As soon as he entered the house and smelt the smoke, he called my name with such fury that my heart stopped. I lost my senses. I took a deep breath and went to him. John gave me an indescribable look. He made me feel small, stupid, dirty, and shameful. I couldn't look at him, but he insisted that I did. He wanted to enjoy the look of fear and humiliation that covered my face and my posture.

"Look at me and tell me what you did this time? He asked.

I was trembling and wished to disappear. I wished that the ground would just open up and swallow me. But I was in John's control and there was no limit to what he could do to me. I was fighting the tears, but they filled up my eyes. John was having a blast; not only was he able to scare me, but he also made me cry. He was enjoying every second of it.

He grabbed me in the kitchen and made me rub the food on my skin. "You are not only going to rub it all over yourself, but you're also going to eat it. That will teach you a lesson."

He repeated this to me at least four times. I obeyed. I ate the food in front of him and rubbed it on my skin until he got bored of watching me and left the house. I sat at the kitchen table wondering why I was so afraid of him. He was just another human being, but I feared him more than I have ever feared anything in my life. The only things that I feared in my life were ghosts and cats, but only because I heard so many stories of what they were capable of.

When I was about nine, my mother's younger cousin was pregnant, and her pregnancy lasted twelve months. She was an only child and rumored to have killed her mother and twin sister at childbirth. She weighed fourteen pounds at birth but lost most of it before she was one year old. Her father never remarried and died of sadness when she was only two years old. She was raised by her grandmother on her father's side. Her entire life people told her that her parents' and sister's ghosts will never leave her alone. She had bad luck. When her grandmother took her in, strange things happened around the house. First the dogs died, then the chickens, and her grandmother had an accident after taking her to school and her leg had to be amputated. All the other relatives who lived at the grandmother's house moved out. The grandfather died shortly after, and then it was just her and the grandmother. A series of bad events happened to both of them until the grandmother died on her thirteenth birthday. From that point on, she raised herself and very few people in the family still talked to her. My mother, who was related to her on her mother's side, tried to stay nice to her. Every time she came around the house, we all stayed in our room and prayed that she didn't leave her demons behind. The moment she left, my mother called us into the living room to pray together.

"It's not that I am afraid of her, but better be safe than sorry," my mother would say.

When she was sixteen and pregnant, no one knew who had gotten her pregnant. She carried that big belly for almost a year, and finally one day she had the baby at the open market early in the morning in front of some merchants. Those who witnessed it said she gave birth to a cat who ran out as soon as it came out of her womb. We never found out the truth of that and never saw a baby. She told my mother that the baby was a still born. From that point on, I was afraid of cats. And my entire life I was afraid to run into her baby-cat who carried all the ghosts in her family.

But here I was, afraid of John, another human being that I could fight with my hands. He wasn't a spirit, nor did he have supernatural powers, but my whole being feared him. I cleaned myself up and found refuge in the pantry. I wanted to fall asleep but couldn't. My mind was scattered, and I wanted to come up with a way to confront John. My life couldn't go on like that, I wanted to be able to tell John what I felt. But no matter how hard I tried to convince myself, I knew that the fear inside had got the best of me. John controlled me and took away my ability to stand up for myself.

John came later that night and for the first time in a very long time, he made me watch porn with him and within fifteen minutes, he was all over me. I was stiff and felt so dirty and ashamed of myself. He went to the bedroom and fell asleep. I went to the bathroom and took a shower, letting the water do all the work. I couldn't look nor touch myself. I was disgusted. I stayed in the shower for at least an hour and got hungry. I wore my pajamas and went into the kitchen to eat bread and milk. This is how I am going to spend the rest of my life, I thought to myself. I was an object and I belonged to John. The past was all I had, every time I wanted to make myself feel good, I thought about my family. But at the same time, I tried to look back and remember anything that I may have done or said to deserve the punishment that I was enduring. The suffering was senseless.

I knew that John was sound asleep, so I dared open the window to see if Margaret was still awake. She was sitting in her living room with the black lady. When I first moved into the neighborhood, Margaret never opened her shades nor her windows. But when she realized that I looked for her through the window from time to time, she left all her windows and shades open, as if she wanted to make herself available to me. She only closed them right before she went to sleep late at night. I was grateful that she did that; it made me feel good to see life and freedom whenever I was sad and felt trapped forever.

She saw me and waved at me. She said something to the other lady and they both looked in my direction. I felt uncomfortable and shut the window. I didn't like the look on their faces, the compassion in their eyes spoke straight to me, and I resented it. That was *my* life, *my* fate, and I didn't want to involve anyone else. I wondered what life was like outside, and what my family was doing, if they missed me or if they were all okay. I wondered and wondered some more. I felt like drawing again, so I went into John's office and got paper and pencil to draw. My sketches were a mixture of everything. I drew people, animals, and everything in between. Once I started, I couldn't stop myself. By the time I looked up, it was three in the morning. I took all the drawings and hid them deep in the pantry where I knew John would never find them. I went to sleep in the living room.

CHAPTER 9

The next morning, I woke just on time to make breakfast for John, but he didn't come out of his room. I waited a couple of hours and went to check on him, he was breathing heavily but couldn't even get one word out of his mouth. I didn't know what to do, but he pointed me to the phone, I gave it to him, and he dialed 911. Within twenty minutes, the paramedics were there and carrying John out. They tried to ask me a couple of questions, but I was too afraid to say anything, so I kept saying 'no', and 'I don't know' until they stopped asking me questions. They took John and left me in the house alone.

Margaret saw everything, and as soon as the ambulance left, she came over. "Do you want to come over?" she asked directly.

I hesitated for a second.

"He won't be back anytime soon, I promise," she said, so I followed her to her house.

Margaret's house was warm and very welcoming. I felt good as soon as I walked in there. I felt at ease, the space was open, clean, and warm. I stood by the door for a few minutes to take it in. She asked me to follow her into the kitchen where she was making breakfast and it smelled delicious.

"Sit down, make yourself at home."

She gave me a plate of pancakes and eggs with a fruit salad, and she sat to eat with me. I was comfortable, until she started to ask me questions. She asked if I liked the food and I said yes; she asked if I wanted more, and I said yes. But then she asked me for my age and I stopped eating. Why did she want to know my age? Did she work for the immigration? I got up and left in a hurry. She tried to follow me, but I was too fast for her.

I went back to John's house and locked the door. My heart was beating so fast. *What was I thinking? What if she caused me more trouble?* I started to hyperventilate. I couldn't breathe right for a couple of minutes, so I sat on the floor to regroup. So many things went through my mind. I pictured John beating me to death or me going to jail for being an illegal immigrant. I knew that nobody would take my word over John's. He was a noted teacher, a quiet neighbor and no one would ever believe he was a molester. I took a deep breath and smiled. Maybe I was just overreacting.

John didn't come home for a week, and I tried to enjoy his absence. I was tempted to go out and go back to see Margaret, but I resisted that temptation. Although, just the thought of the feeling that I felt when I was over at her house made me feel good. The smell, the comfort, the look on Margaret's face, the light coming through the windows from outside, the pictures on the walls, and most importantly the freedom of being out of the house. I wanted to hold on to that feeling for as long as I could. I looked through the window and saw Margaret and her friend. She knew that I was looking at her, and a few times she looked at me too. Her look invited me back to her place and her expression was asking me to trust her. Margaret didn't know my story, but I could tell she wanted to help me. She caught a glimpse of my pain and offered a helping hand, but I was too afraid to take it.

The day John came home brought me back to my reality. He

74

walked in a few pounds skinnier and looking paler. He looked very tired, but angrier than ever. He limped a little bit, but I didn't dare offer my help. I went to the kitchen to start cooking something just in case. He sat on the sofa, and of course called me. As soon as I walked into the living room, I knew he was in a bad mood, and I was going to suffer.

"When was the last time you dusted this table?" he asked.

I just stood there looking at him.

"And what is this smell?" he continued.

I wanted to say it was the smell of a clean house, just air not tainted by your presence. But I remained quiet. He was holding a plastic bag that he threw at me.

"Those are my dirty clothes. Put them in the washing machine and come back to clean up this table. And make me some rice and steak." He ordered this coldly, without please or thank you.

And I obeyed like a dog who knew nothing else but how to obey her master. I finished all my chores and served John his steak and rice in the living room. I was shaking inside because I knew how miserable he would make me for the rest of the day. John was physically sick, but he was making me mentally sick. I was beside myself.

While I was serving him, I dropped a grain of rice, and he yelled. The water was too cold, the steak wasn't well seasoned, the rice was overcooked, and my being made him nauseous. He kept complaining, and I kept taking it. The saddest thing is that I let him get to me like that. *Why did I believe him? How come every good thing that I heard about me before I became John's prisoner was so irrelevant?* My parents taught me to be a strong woman. They also used to tell me how smart and pretty I was, but all of those things seemed to have taken a back seat or even worse disappeared completely from my mind. I believed what John was telling me. The negative had so much more power than the positive and I wondered why. John called me ugly, and I stopped looking at myself in the mirror. He said that I was worthless, and I accepted the kind of treatment that he inflicted on me. I lived in constant fear.

John attempted to eat but couldn't. He fell asleep after trying so hard to make me miserable like him. I went into the kitchen and fell asleep on the floor until the next morning. It must have been 5am or maybe earlier, but it was still very dark when I woke up. Every muscle in my body was aching and sore, and I had to get up slowly. I got up and walked to the bathroom.

Standing in front of the shower, I realized that I felt nothing inside. My mind felt unusually empty, and my heart wasn't talking to me the way it was used to. I stood still trying to find that voice inside of me that cried all the time, or that reminded me what a miserable life I was living. I tried to hear the voice in my head that entertained me, but it was silent. I had never felt like that before and got scared. The world around me seemed so pale and empty. I was used to waking up to my own sad thoughts. Every morning I woke, dreading another day in John's house. Each new day with a pinch in my stomach caused by the depth of my sadness. But that morning, I was not sad, nor depressed. Just empty, which felt strange.

I showered then started work on breakfast. When the sun came up, John called me into the bedroom to help him get up to use the bathroom. I did, and for the first time, I did not fear or hate him, I just didn't feel anything toward him. I helped him to the bathroom and back in the bedroom. Brought him to the telephone to call his job, and then I served him breakfast in bed. While I was doing all that he kept complaining about different things, of course. The eggs were too white, his tea not hot enough, I was too slow - the list went on. Instead of feeling that pinch in my stomach, I just nodded and went on with my chores. Nothing he said that day really affected me. I was aware that he was being spiteful, but I was completely detached from it all. I didn't feel sorry when he threw up blood, nor was I disgusted when I cleaned it up for him.

I know that I should say that I preferred being in that state, but I hated it. I needed to have feelings to know that I was still alive and still human. And that emptiness that suddenly invaded my being made me uncomfortable. I wanted to feel it. I wanted to be able to be mad at John. I wanted to be able to long for human compassion and warmth. I wanted to be mad at John and hate myself for letting him treat me like an animal. But that day, nothing went through me. I was impassive to everything. When John was taking a nap, I went into the kitchen and tried to think about all the things I missed so much: my parents, my country, my childhood, my school, but nothing moved me. I couldn't reach *me*. I was emotionally unavailable that day, and it was petrifying. My spirit was broken to the point of total emptiness.

I sat in the pantry for a couple of hours waiting for John to wake up and start yelling at me again. I almost looked forward to it. *Maybe this time I would feel something*, I thought to myself. But I tried to dig deeper inside of myself. Trying to find something that moved me, but nothing seemed to be working. I started to laugh all alone in the pantry. My misery made me laugh. I wonder how many people were going through the same pain. Or maybe I was the only one on Earth in this crazy situation.

Am I paying for a sin that I committed? There was no answer. What if God was just mad at me for something I did? The questions went through my mind. And still, I couldn't find that compassion or sadness inside of me. So, I started to recite Psalm 23. I told myself that if I died that day, at least I would go to heaven reciting a verse in the Bible. I repeated the psalm at least ten times, and each time I sought the joy I used to feel when I was younger every time we prayed with my mother.

My mother recited Psalm 23 with us when we were scared or

going through some hard times. Whether it was just bad grades or sickness, she told us that God was bigger than any problem we could face in this world. I believed her, and I believed in God. I went to bed in peace when I read the chapter and felt invincible. I found comfort in knowing that the God who created the Universe was on my side. And sure enough, I always saw the light at the end of the tunnel. By working hard, my grade improved. By responding well to a situation, and hoping for the best, things always got better in my family and my neighborhood. Life was simple, and the answers to simple problems were always within our reach. I believed in miracles, even though I never dared ask for one. I was content just believing as a child.

After reciting the psalm with my mother, I went to bed, afraid that if I stayed up someone would steal the joy from me. Once under my cover, I imagined great things. I imagined what it would be like when we were adults and my parents were older, and that we were all successful and married. My mind traveled the world, I dreamed of visiting all the continents, I dreamed of taking my parents to foreign lands. And I felt overjoyed, the possibilities seemed endless. Believing that my life would be perfect for the rest of my years. The joy that I felt the night before carried on throughout the day, I would do all my siblings' chores for them and do well at school. Because I believed, and my faith, up until then, hadn't been tried.

That night in the pantry, I kept reciting the psalm looking for that same feeling, that same joy, but it wasn't there. I stopped believing, and I didn't want to think about it. I came out of the pantry to run away from myself. I started doing things in the kitchen. I made tomato soup for John and cleaned up after myself. I opened one of the drawers and I saw the pill that John used to make me swallow every morning. He hadn't given them to me for a couple of weeks, his sickness distracted him. I tried to read the words on the packet with the little English I knew, but the words didn't make much sense to me then. I was tempted to just throw them away but was too afraid that John would find out and give me the lesson of a lifetime. I put it back with the hope to never take them again. But here is how ironic my life was, he came out of the room that night dressed in fresh clothes.

"I am going out to take some fresh air, but make sure dinner is ready when I am back," he said coldly. Then he came straight to the drawer in the kitchen, took the pills out and gave me one. He waited for me to swallow and finish the glass of water, and then he walked out of the house.

I set the dining table for John and waited for him to come back. I ate some rice and beans and waited some more. It was almost midnight and John was still not back yet. But a little after midnight, he walked in with a woman. John asked me to go into the kitchen, the woman was distracted and so drunk that I don't even think she noticed me. They went into the bedroom and spent the night.

I heard them almost all night long, mostly her. I was left in the kitchen to listen to the soundtrack of John's sexual activities. Where I come from, men didn't need to go to prostitutes. Polygamy was legal, it was frowned upon but largely accepted. Most women wished they could fulfill all their men's needs, but most of the time men ended up with at least three wives and a few concubines.

From both my grandfathers to my father and every man in our neighborhood, having more than one woman was a sign of wealth and power. I remember one of my mother's friends who waited longer than most women in our community to get married. Her name was Maya. She told people that she was waiting for the perfect man, and once she had him, she wouldn't have to worry about second wives or concubines. She made fun of all the women who had to go through being dethroned. She even made fun of my mother when she found out that my father

79

was cheating. But she finally got married and bragged about how perfect her husband was, said she had married him for love and not out of convenience.

Women in the community were waiting for the day her husband would cheat on her. Mothers sent their daughters to go tempt him. Older sisters sent their single younger sisters to go and try their luck with the so-called perfect man.

One day, Maya made an announcement, "I know that all the desperate single women in this town are trying to get with my man, but let me tell you I am all the woman that he wants, and no one, I say no one can take him from me. So you better stop trying."

As soon as she was done making the very public announcement, one of the least attractive women in town raised her hand; she stood up and walked toward Maya. The woman was at least five months pregnant, and no one had ever noticed because she was so unattractive.

"My name is Toka and I am carrying your husband's first child," the woman said out loud in front of everyone.

Maya laughed at her, and said, "If my husband cheated on me with a woman like you, I'd kill myself".

"Well get ready to do that because your husband, as we speak, he is taking a nap in my bed."

A few people, including myself and my siblings, walked with Maya to the woman's house to find her husband taking a good nap in his underwear. Maya didn't kill herself, nor did she divorce her husband. But that day taught her a lesson about men and women in our town, and she became humbler than ever.

John let the prostitute out at the back door early in the morning. He went to take a shower and asked me to go change the sheet. I wondered if he at least treated the women with respect. After cleaning, I went into the kitchen and made some breakfast for him. When he came into the kitchen, he looked much better than the day before and I hated it. He ate part of his breakfast, gave me my pill and left for the day. I was just glad that John went to a prostitute to satisfy his hunger for sex, and not me. I hoped he kept it that way. Better being the maid without the sex part.

I finished my chores and then watched television. I understood a lot of words and the programs were now making more sense to me. I watched television for the rest of the afternoon. Until John walked in on me; he came in quietly and I didn't hear him. I just felt someone grab me by my neck and I was thrown against the wall. Before I even looked up, he slapped me so hard I heard ringing in my ears.

"This is what you have been doing instead of doing your chores?" he yelled, standing over me.

"How did I not hear him?" The thought quickly crossed my mind.

I wished that I could rewind time just fifteen minutes earlier and turn off the television set. But it was too late, I was going to pay for my action. John was yelling all sorts of profanities, he threatened to take me to the police, or just let me wander the street until I got caught. He said so many things that at one point, I shut down. I wanted him to be done with it. He yelled and kicked me with his foot and yelled some more. I just took it in, without tears, and without any feeling at all.

After John finished beating me up, he told me to make his dinner. I served him then went to the bathroom to clean myself up. I sat on the floor with a warm towel, pressed it against my aching skin. I laughed at myself for forgetting that John usually came home at 5:30pm.

"Jen, get through here," he called, using that name I hated.

He wanted something sweet, and I gave him the ice cream that had been sitting in the fridge for ages. He only tried a spoonful but on realizing it was bad, he threw it at me. I wiped myself, cleaned the floor, and went into kitchen to wait for my next punishment. But John went into the bedroom and fell asleep.

I went into the pantry and stayed awake for the rest of the night. At some point in the middle of the night, I crept out to peek through the kitchen window looking to see Margaret. All her lights were turned off, and the windows shut. I knew that she was asleep, but somehow, I hoped that maybe that night was an exception. I sat in the kitchen until the sun came up.

CHAPTER 10

I had lost track of the exact time, but I knew that it was over a year since John kidnapped me. I came to the US sometime around Christmas, and it was the beginning of another holiday season. John was in and out of the hospital and still was losing a tremendous amount of weight. He never talked about his illness, and I never dared ask questions. I liked the time he was weak and needed me. My maternal instincts kicked in, and I caught myself liking to take care of him.

John's health was unstable like his mood. When he was sick, I took a break from all the beating and the verbal abuse. John knew how to use me when he was weak. He was more docile when he needed me to take him to the bathroom or help him take his medicine. But from time to time even at his weakest, the beast in him would awaken and yell at me. I remember one day he was sick, and he asked me to make him some green tea that he just bought a week ago. I couldn't find it anywhere in the kitchen.

"What do you mean you can't find it?" he said angrily when I told him.

"I don't know where it is, but I can assure you that you didn't put it in the kitchen," I said, trying to sound as polite as possible.

"Are you calling me a liar? I am telling you I bought that tea last week and set it on the kitchen table. Now you go find it!"

I left the room without saying anything, I could feel in the tone of his voice that he was getting angry with me. I was scared. I didn't know what to do, so I made regular black tea hoping that he would just drink it and forget about the green tea.

I brought the tea into his room, set the pot on his nightstand, poured the tea into the cup, and I helped him sit up straight. After taking the first sip, he threw the hot tea at me. "Didn't I tell you that I wanted to drink the green tea?" he yelled.

"But John, I couldn't find it!" I said in my dialect, trying to make myself as small as possible.

He threw everything on the floor as I instinctively stepped back. The tea barely touched my skin but it left a small burn on my right hand. I carefully picked up everything from the floor and went to the kitchen. Unable to control myself, my body shook uncontrollably. I felt a lump in my throat, a knot in my stomach. All I wanted to do was be there for him when he was sick, but John was unable to treat me like a human being. No matter what I did, or how much I did he managed to insult and belittle me. I wanted to cry, but I held the tears in.

I sat in the kitchen waiting for him to calm down and fall asleep. In my own reverie, it took a while to notice that Margaret had been watching me from her kitchen. I got up and closed the curtains in the kitchen. I went to check on John and he had fallen asleep so I snuck in to clean the tea he had spilled on the carpet. When I kneeled, I noticed the box of tea under the bed. I wondered if he had put it there on purpose just to give me a hard time, or if he honestly forgot to bring it to the kitchen. Either way, I left it there. I cleaned the carpet without making any noise, picked up his clothes from the floor, and left the room when I realized I was still shaking all over.

My emotions were overwhelming. I couldn't get myself to

stand up to John, nor could I get myself to just take the chance to leave him. Immigration would understand that it wasn't by my own choice that I was in the US. He had brought me in by force, and all I wanted was to go back to the Congo. I was between John and a hard place. Somehow, I believed everything John told me about going to jail, so much that I told myself I had to get used to living with him. But every day I felt like my heart was going to explode, or that my body was going to break into pieces. My emotions were up and down, and I was living in constant fear. My heart wasn't strong enough for what he was putting me through. I was convinced that I was going to die of a heart attack.

Before I met John and before the rebels invaded our town, nobody had ever treated me badly or even come close to breaking my heart. I was too young, and life hadn't put me through enough trials to feel real pain. The closest I came to a heartbreak was when I was about thirteen.

I had a crush on this boy in my class. His name was Kito. He was taller than most boys our age. His parents traveled a lot before settling down in Lusa for their coffee business. They took him around the world with them and had lived in Greece for a few years. He spoke Greek, German and Italian by the time he turned thirteen.

I loved everything about him. I prayed to God that he would ask me to marry him. When I saw him in class, I called out his name in silence, hoping he would notice me. But like every other boy in the class, he was after Irma. Irma was the most beautiful girl in my school. She had long hair, a beautiful figure with mahogany skin, and she wore the most beautiful clothes. She was aware of her power and used it to get better grades, because even the teachers were smitten by her. Irma used her beauty to get her way, and all the girls alienated her, including me.

I never paid attention to her until I felt like she was the

reason Kito hadn't noticed me. I wished she would get sick and stay home for the rest of the school year. Not only did she attract Kito's attention, but she also got the attention of all the other boys at the school. Tall, short, rich, poor, good looking, bad looking, it didn't matter. They all wanted to be with her or at least get her attention. Even though she was pretty, she lacked brains. She was bad at every subject at school. While I wasn't good in math, I was good at Latin, literature, history and all the other subjects that had nothing to do with math. Kito noticed that I often answered the questions in class and because he was too busy trying to court Irma, he didn't have time to study.

He asked to sit next to me every time we had a test. And that was the only time that he talked to me; when he needed to get the answers from me. I knew he was just using me to get good grades, but I didn't care as long as he paid a little attention to me. Those moments that he spent cheating from my paper were our moments together. And I felt special knowing that I was doing something for him. I let him cheat from my work, and even offered to do his homework sometimes.

Slowly we became friends, or somewhat friends. But I noticed that he never called me by my name, even though for at least two months I helped him go from being a C student to a straight-A student. He called me a 'smart girl'. At first, I thought it was like a cute name that he had for me, but with time I realized Kito just didn't know my name.

One day, I gave him back his homework and I put my name on the corner for him to see. But he tore off that part of the page and tossed it.

The next day, I wrote him a note:

Kito,
I just wanted to let you know that I enjoy being your friend
And if you ever need anything just let me know.

I am here for you, and that's what friends are for.
Truly yours,
G. Munia

The next day, I gave it to him with his homework. By the end of the day. Irma came to me with the note.

"Here, I think you forgot this in my boyfriend's book," she said, looking me straight in my eyes.

I was furious. Kito had neglected the letter that I wrote him, and to humiliate me further he gave it to Irma to give back to me. I went home and cried all night. I decided to never talk to him again. I woke up the next morning, got ready to go to school and on my way there, I kept telling myself that I would not talk to Kito, not even look at him.

As soon as I got to school, he came to greet me, and handed me his homework. "You forgot to ask me for my homework yesterday. You know that I can't do without your help!"

Kito told me that he couldn't do it without me. I took his homework and did it better than I did my own. While I was finishing his work, I kept replaying what he had told me. *Kito couldn't do this without me.* He needed me and I was there for him. I offered my help with all my heart, with the hope that he was going to declare his love to me one day. He went on like that for another month. I kept dreaming and fantasizing about him night and day, and he kept going after Irma. But for some reason, I nurtured the fact that someday he was going to realize that I loved him more than she did. I was patient.

One day the school organized a contest, where everybody had to choose a partner. I didn't want to choose a partner and refused anyone who wanted to partner with me. I waited for Kito. Irma had chosen another boy, who was better looking than Kito and richer. Kito went to her and begged her to take him instead, she said no. At the end, everyone had their partners except Kito and me. We both wanted people who didn't want us back. He wanted Irma, but she wanted someone she thought was better. I wanted Kito, but he wanted someone he thought was better than me. The teacher publicly asked Kito to become my partner, and he answered.

"I don't want her. I want Irma or nobody else."

My heart was shattered in pieces. He broke my heart. I understood then why people say that a heart could bleed. I felt an imaginary internal hemorrhage, my heart was in unbearable pain. I knew that Kito liked Irma better, but somehow, I had hoped that he was going to change his mind. I held my tears inside and pretended that I didn't care about what he said.

"I don't need a partner. I can do this by myself," I said with the little courage I managed to collect in that moment.

That day at school felt like the longest day of my life. I felt like everyone was looking at me with pity, even though I am sure that no one cared. My legs felt heavier with every step that I took. I was embarrassed and felt sick in my own skin. Kito broke my heart in pieces and stomped all over the pieces with no mercy. At the end of the day when I went home, I skipped lunch with my family under the excuse that I had cramps. I went into my room and cried my eyes out. I promised myself not to let anyone ever humiliate me like that in private or in public.

The next day at school, I ignored Kito. When he came to give me his homework, I declined politely. I didn't even want to give him the pleasure to see how much he hurt me.

"From now on, I want to concentrate on my own homework. I suggest you do the same."

"But I thought you liked helping me?" he said shamelessly.

I just walked away, and that was the last time I talked to or even looked at him. I caught myself still thinking about him from time to time but used all my willpower to try erasing him from my mind.

I deserve better, I kept telling myself.

For at least a month, my heart ached every time I thought about that day he rejected me. But thinking about it only made me stronger. I was a wiser teenager, or at least I wanted to believe that. And that was my first and only heartbreak.

What I was going through at John's house wasn't even heartbreak. My heart ached only when I thought about my family. I walked around with this pain in my chest because I missed the only people I had in this world. I wondered what had happened to them, and every day they were in my dreams. Every time the thought of possibly never seeing them again came to me, I chased it away. I wanted to believe they were somewhere out there and that they were all right.

CHAPTER 11

The longer I dealt with John, the more resilient I became. I learned to ignore him, or whenever he did or said hurtful things to me, I rebounded. I found ways to distract myself from him. I started to recite poems that I had learned when I was younger or sing songs that reminded me of my childhood. But still, I couldn't turn to God. I questioned his existence, but I didn't want to face my own doubts. The one thing that my mother taught me was the most important thing in my life. It became the very one thing that I resented: my faith.

I was grateful for the family God gave me. I was happy for the small town I was born into. I thanked him for having all the clothes that most girls my age didn't have. I went to a good school, and every summer my parents found ways to give us a good time. I had good friends and good neighbors. Both my parents were around, and they were the best parents anyone could ever ask for. I was grateful for being able to play soccer with the kids in the neighborhood. I had no reason to doubt God's existence. My life was near perfect.

Although I remember when I was about fifteen, one of my mother's cousins passed away. She was only thirty-nine years old, married without children. Her name was Shala. She was one of those Christians who spent all their lives preparing for life in heaven. She did everything according to the Bible. She believed in God with all that she had. She prayed for a husband, and she got one. Her husband was a divorced man who already had three children. But because my aunt met him at church, she believed that God sent him to her. He courted her and four months after they met, they were married. She was a virgin, and he was a man who had been with more women than one can count. But because he was a born again Christian, she married him.

His name was Maki, and his ex-wife detested him. She told people that the nine years that she was married to him were the most miserable years of her life. But she stayed married to him in the hope that he would change. He never did. Until the day he decided to divorce her and marry my aunt. And when they divorced, he took the kids with him. The law sided with her husband, and she had no one to turn to. She only saw her kids occasionally. She told people how difficult Maki was, but the people at church didn't believe her. Maki was an exemplary Christian. Always came to church on time and gave his offerings regularly. He was always willing to help the people in need, and even gave advice about relationships. It was hard to believe that such a good man could abuse his wife at home.

One day she showed up at church with a black eye and a broken leg, and still people didn't believe her. The women at the church accused her of being a woman of ill morals. They said that she wanted out of her marriage to live the life of a city girl. So, she stopped coming to church right before he announced their divorce. She returned one last time and then left town and stopped fighting to get her kids back. Maki played the victim to everyone and before we knew it, my aunt was in his arms and planning to marry him. My aunt was in her late twenties then and considered an old maid. She was ready for marriage and

Maki took advantage of her vulnerability. He was forty-four and she was twenty-nine. They married and the family was happy that the old maid of the family had finally gotten married.

Usually, the older women in the family start to look out for a pregnancy by the third month of the marriage. They waited for my aunt's pregnancy. A year went by and still nothing, my aunt started to show signs of depression. She wanted to give Maki a child, but she went on for a second year and still had no pregnancy. She went around town looking for pastors, doctors and priests, and still nothing. She fasted and spent most of her time at church praying for a pregnancy for five years, while she should have been at home with her husband making love.

People at church encouraged her to keep praying and fasting, and she did. By the sixth year, she was so thin that her husband resented her. He was the difficult man his ex-wife warned people about. He yelled at her in front of the children. He was a picky eater, and nothing she did for him was ever good enough. She hoped that somehow with all her prayers her husband would change. But after almost ten years of marriage, she looked very depressed and unattractive. She kept her spirits up, and still believed she would get pregnant and that her husband would change his ways.

But one day, she got very sick. She developed an ulcer in her stomach. Maki took her back to her parents.

"She has been nothing but trouble to me. Since I married her, she brought all her demons into my house. Even my children have noticed."

That's what Maki told my mother. My aunt suffered for a few months and died without obtaining what she prayed for. She died without the husband God had given her. She died without the children she fasted and prayed for so ardently. Her life was over, and just like that her faith was in vain.

I wondered why she died so young, and why her life had

turned out that way. I had so many questions going through my head.

But my mother scolded me when I voiced my opinions about faith and God. "Never question God, you hear me? He works in mysterious ways and we as his children, we have to wait for his time and accept his will."

The day of her funeral, Maki showed up with the kids. He was weeping and people were consoling him. He was also taking monetary donations. It was my first time seeing a dead person. Her coffin was open, and at first, I hesitated to go look, but when I saw my younger sister look, I went too. I stood there in front of the open coffin and stared for at least five minutes. I felt a lump in my throat.

My aunt who I remembered when I was much younger to be full of life was lying there lifeless. I had seen her slowly disappear and die. I was trying to read the expression on her face. She looked more peaceful than I had seen her in a long time. I couldn't help but think that it was unfair that she had to die so young. I felt like there was still life in her. She could have stayed single and accomplished so much in her lifetime. But she was gone. I wondered if she could still hear us cry and call her name. My mother came and grabbed me away from the coffin.

After my aunt's funeral, I had many questions for God. I felt that God was unfair for what he did to my aunt. I could think of a dozen other aunts that deserved to die but not her.

One day after school, I asked my mother again, "Do you really believe in God?"

She looked at me, petrified. "Yes, I do. Why do you always ask such questions?" she said.

"I don't know. I think that life is so unfair. Good people suffer and die, while all the bad people prosper." I answered my mother.

She had tears in her eyes. My mother believed in God with

all her heart, and she wanted us to believe just as much. "Everything that happens to a child of God, happens for a reason."

I looked at her like I wanted her to explain herself.

She continued. "Like I told you before, never doubt God's existence. He gives you everything you have, and he has the power to take it all away. When good people die, God takes them away from this corrupted world to be in heaven with him."

I looked at my mother trying to answer my question, and I could see that she, herself, didn't quite understand God's will. She didn't get upset this time and tried to make me understand. I pretended to be satisfied with her answer. Those questions remained unanswered, but after a few weeks they were soon forgotten. I was too busy being a teenager.

My life went back to normal, and God was my friend again. Until what happened in Lusa and John kidnapped me to turn me into his slave; all the questions I had asked at my aunt's funerals came surging back with such intensity. I had doubts about just everything in this life. I lost my faith in mankind and lost my faith in the creator of mankind. To me life was what I was living in John's house, and it was too dark. If there was a God, then he had given up on me and my family. Too much evil surrounded me, and I prepared for the worst. Although somewhere deep down, the little girl in me still hoped for a better day and that hope woke me up every day.

CHAPTER 12

John felt better after a few weeks and went back to work. I wonder how they let him take so much time off. He had spent most of the winter in his bed. And now it was spring, he felt better, and my life went back to being hell on earth.

John went back to his normal self, even though he still looked frail. By that point, he had lost so much weight that he looked like a different person. I was used to his cruelty and the darkness became a way of life. John and I were intimate at least once a week. He would come home from work, have dinner, and take me to bed. After about fifteen minutes of sex, he would fall asleep. Sometimes even on top of me.

The first time he fell asleep on top of me, he had come home in a very bad mood. He barely touched his dinner and went to sit down in the living room while I was cleaning up. After cleaning up, he called me to sit on the floor by his side and watch porn with him. I noticed that he was breathing harder than he usually did when he was sexually aroused. I just thought that he was getting sick again. I felt sad, but at the same time I was hoping that he would get sick so that I wouldn't have to sleep with him, but he took me to bed anyway.

He struggled to take off his pants, the belt wouldn't unbuckle. Then he took forever to unbutton his shirt. And finally, he took off his underwear, and took a short break. He usually grabbed me closer to him and forced me to have sex with him. But that night he just looked at me with anger and ordered me to get in bed naked. I kept my blouse on, and with fury he ripped it off me. I enjoyed watching him struggle. He tried very hard to be strong and aggressive, but within five minutes, he collapsed right there on top of me. I panicked. I didn't move and I was praying that he was still alive. Then I called, "John!" and nothing. I called him louder this time, "John!" Still nothing. I tried to push him away from me, and he opened his eyes, looked at me and said, "Get out of my room!". I think his body was giving up on him. He had pushed himself for a whole week, it was Friday, and his body gave up right there in the middle of having sex.

I got up, picked up my clothes and left the room. I looked at the blouse that he ripped and felt a pinch in my stomach. That blouse was one of the three blouses I owned. Since I had moved into John's house, he gave me three blouses, two skirts and two dresses. And they weren't even new when he gave them to me. It seems as if he got them from a yard sale. The clothes were bigger than me. I was a size two and they were between size eight and twelve. I looked like a bum in them, even though I managed to always keep them clean. Now John had ripped the one blouse that kind of fit me. I had altered it a few times; I sewed it on both sides so that it could fit me better. For the rest of that night, I tried to fix the sleeve that John ripped. And while I was at it, I also altered one of the dresses.

John was sound asleep in the bedroom, and I knew that he wouldn't wake up. I wanted to get some fresh air, so I opened the kitchen window and sat on the counter. I saw Margaret come out of her house and walk toward me. Margaret was like my constant guardian. She waited for me to give her an opportunity to talk.

When I saw her, I wanted to shut the window, afraid that John would catch me. But another part of me wanted to talk to someone other than John and myself. I left the window open as she got closer.

"Hi neighbor!" She started.

I just nodded. My heart was beating fast, and I was happy to see her. "I like it when you open the window. It reminds me that I have a beautiful young neighbor," she said.

I said, "Thank you!"

"You should come and knock at my door sometimes. I would love to have you come over again," she said in a very soft tone. She continued, talking about the grass in our yard, how she noticed that we let it grow very long. She asked me questions about John, but I kept saying, "I don't know." So after a while she changed the subject and went back to talking about the grass and the neighborhood.

I had tears in my eyes. I realized how much I longed for that human warmth. The fact that she was addressing me so personally with so much kindness made my eyes teary. There was still a little kindness left in this world and it was standing right there in front of me. My life was surrounded by negative things and my mind was filled with negative thoughts. To make myself feel better, I had to recall my childhood memories and that was it. The present was like a bad dream, and sometimes I caught myself thinking about my own death. I wondered whether I'd be better off dead than living in the house with John. I wanted to fight the tears that were about to fall down my cheeks.

Margaret noticed and asked me "Are you okay?". I told her I was fine and that I had to go to bed. She said goodnight and I shut the window.

My life didn't make sense. I felt like I had just lost something important. I missed talking to someone that I cared about and who cared about me too. I missed being loved and loving in return. I missed being taken care of. I missed my mother. I wanted a familiar face, or voice. I knew that down deep inside of me, I was capable of so much love. But with John there was neither giving nor receiving. The living room felt like an endless sea of sorrows, and I was drowning in it.

My days were easier when I didn't hope for a better day. I felt better when I resigned myself to the fact that one day, John was going to beat me to death and no one in the world would notice or look for me. But that night after talking to Margaret for barely ten minutes, I realized that I wanted to live. I wanted to be happy again. I wanted to run free, laugh at the top of my lungs and be me once more. I realized that I didn't want to die alone in John's house. I wanted to live.

I wanted to be able to grow older and see the world. I wanted to travel the world with someone I love. I wanted to meet someone who would love me with passion. I wanted to be able to put my skills to use. I knew that I had a lot to offer, but John kept me in a cage like a tamed animal. He sucked all hope, joy, and passion out of me. I was John's slave.

I wondered where my siblings were at that very moment. I hoped that they were somewhere safe. I realized that the worst day of my childhood felt like heaven compared to any day I had in John's house. Even the quiet days when John wasn't around still felt dark and gloomy. I was afraid of him even in his absence. The thought of him filled me with a sadness that I couldn't quite explain. I wondered every time I heard a car on the street whether that was him coming back. I waited for him, and sometimes even hoped that it would be him so that the waiting could stop. I wanted to keep the house clean and always organized.

John was constantly on my mind tormenting me. His presence horrified me, and his absence tortured me. I lived my life in constant fear.

After talking to Margaret, I slept better than I had before. Was it because I was reminded that there was someone next door watching over me? Was it because I had gotten some fresh air? I don't know exactly why, but that night I had a very good dream.

My mother came to me in my dreams. I was used to dreaming about her, but most of the time she was quiet in my dreams. That night, she was crossing a bridge with me. I was scared and she kept reassuring me. She kept saying "You're going to be just fine." Once we both got on the other side of the bridge, I realized that my mother wasn't there anymore, but I was holding Margaret's hand.

Then I heard John's voice, "Bring me a glass of water." I thought he was in my dreams, but then he yelled, "What the hell are you doing? Bring me the goddamn water!" I woke up. It wasn't in my dream; it was five in the morning and John wanted me to bring him a glass of water. I don't know for how long he had been screaming, but I knew long enough to get him furious. I got up and ran to the kitchen to fetch him some water. I was literally shaking all over my body. John woke me out of a very good dream. I heard my mother's voice. It was in my dream, but it was so vivid that her voice was still resonating in my head. She said I was going to be fine. I whispered to myself, "Mother, if you know how I am going to get out of this, please let me know. Show me the way because I don't know. I just don't know."

I took the water to John, and he was breathing with difficulty. He asked me to give him the sleeping pills from the nightstand, and I did. He took one and calmed down. OF course, he asked me to leave the room. I wanted to stay and watch him fall asleep. I caught myself feeling sorry for him. He seemed to be in a lot of pain.

"Leave now. And next time, do not make me call you more than once before you answer, stupid."

I smiled at myself. How could I possibly feel sorry for

someone like him? He was sick and yet he still found ways to belittle me. I needed to figure out a way to be as evil as him.

CHAPTER 13

It had been four days since I had last seen John. He had left the house sick. I watched him leave the house and knew that he was probably going to the hospital. I expected him back that first night, but he didn't show up. I went to sleep in the living room. I thought maybe he would show up late with one of his prostitutes, but he didn't. Part of me was expecting John, and the other part was hoping he wouldn't come back.

He didn't come back the second night and I was certain that he was going to be out for at least a week. For the first time, I relaxed in his absence. I took my clothes off and went into the shower and let the water run over me. Standing in the shower and having all the water run over every part of my body had a healing power to it. And whenever I was on my period, I enjoyed taking a long shower and I could only do that when John wasn't around. He never bought me sanitary pads and I used toilet paper.

I love the effect of water. Water has this pure quality to it and since my childhood I have loved being in the water. My mother used to tell me the story about when I was about a year old and got sick. The doctors couldn't figure out what I had so they sent me and my mother home and told her to let time heal me. I had a strong fever that night and my father was out with one of his concubines. My mother filled water in the bathtub late at night and just put me in it. As soon as I was in the water, I smiled for the first time in a long time. She kept me in the bathtub for an hour and when I came out, I was healed. The next day I was better and every time I was sick, or was in a bad mood, my mother would just put me in the bathtub for an hour. That's why for a long time she called me mwuna mayi, which means child of the water in Lingala. That night, I took a peaceful shower.

After my shower, I went to get something to eat. I felt lonely. As lonely as ever, my life wasn't getting any better. I was living without a future, hope or love. Emptiness was all around me in every way possible. On good days, I hoped that the next day something miraculous was going to happen. John was going to come out of the hospital and tell me that I was free from him. And that he would help me get a passport and go home. Or better yet, that someone would come and rescue me. I was able to walk out of the front door, but the unknown scarred me. I was afraid of John.

I looked outside the window to see if maybe Margaret was still awake, but all her lights were turned off and she was nowhere in sight. Every time I heard a sound I looked out the window to see if maybe it was her. But I sat in the kitchen for hours and she never came out. I wanted to go knock on her door, but I was afraid that she would turn me away. Even though she already told me that I was welcome anytime I needed a friend. I was too cautious. John had turned me into this very insecure person. I was afraid that she wanted something from me. I was afraid that she was just trying to lure me in her house and use me like John did.

But that night I wanted someone to see me. I wanted someone to look at me and notice how deeply I needed human contact. I needed to feel someone's warmth around me. I felt lonely and sad. The house felt big and empty, and I could hear myself cry for love and attention. I had never felt lonely like that before and that night it felt heavy on me. It was the worst feeling ever. Worse than any physical pain that John had ever inflicted on me. No pain came close to that feeling of loneliness and fear. I just needed someone near me, someone who cared for me. Someone I could trust. Someone I could lean on and confide in. But no one was there and I fell asleep.

In the morning I was still sitting at the kitchen table lost in my thoughts. I felt exhausted, more so mentally than physically. My mind had been racing for hours and my neck hurt. I was sick inside, and my mind was heavy. I got up and started to walk around the house looking for something to do. I just walked around for an hour and finally turned on the television and sat down to relax.

I was once again lost in my thoughts. *Who makes the decisions about who gets to be rich and pretty, and who gets to be poor and miserable?* I thought about all the children around the world who didn't have food or medication. I thought about all the boys and girls of the Congo who had lost their loved ones. I thought about all those men and women who were separated from their families and lost everything they worked for their entire lives. Then I thought about all those people I see on tv, who are so lucky and yet do not take advantage of it. I thought about people like John that I consider criminals, and how they get away with it. *Who makes the decision on who gets to be happy or unhappy?* The emptiness in my life gave me time to mull over those questions.

CHAPTER 14

By the fifth day, I already had a routine. I went to bed late and still woke up early in the morning by force of habit. I still cleaned the house and made breakfast. I sat by the window to wait for Margaret, but she wasn't around. And I missed her. The one time that I told myself that I would dare go there again, she wasn't around. Maybe she went out of town, or she moved out but whatever it was I was hoping to see her again.

I know that life was cruel to me, but I prayed silently for Margaret's return. I didn't know when or if I was ever going to run to her and tell her all about John, but I liked knowing that the option was there. I liked the idea that she was there just in case, and for those five days that I hadn't seen her I worried. *What if she was gone for good? What if she was dead? What if John killed her?* I asked myself those questions and prepared myself for the worst. I got into the habit of expecting bad things; that way when they actually happen I wouldn't be too surprised.

I spent that fifth day watching television and looking for something meaningful to watch, but all the programs seemed to be about how rich people were getting richer and nobody talked about the rest of the world. I wondered what happened to the rest of the world. Is the rest of the world so insignificant to Americans that all they found interesting was the lifestyle of the rich and famous?

Television in America had a way of making me feel even more depressed. It was a constant reminder that somebody else's life was a million times better than mine. But for some reason, I couldn't turn it off. I liked watching how much life could be better out there. Maybe I liked that those programs on TV gave me some new materials for my dreams when I felt like dreaming.

I remembered television programs back home on the one channel, we had a variety of things to turn to. We had some programs meant to educate us about the rest of the world, some to teach about nature and other inspiration. Television was meant to make people good, or at least to teach something. But I realized that priorities were different in the USA. People liked being deluded, so the media gave them what they asked for. Here is what you can never have, but go ahead; dream about it and detach yourself completely from reality.

Before I went to sleep I went by the window hoping to see Margaret. Her doors were locked and all the lights were turned off, just like they had been for the past few days. I waited for about an hour, then went to sleep on the couch. That night again, I had the dream about crossing a bridge holding my mother's hand. When I got to the end of the bridge, I realized it was Margaret's hand that I was holding.

I wanted to know what that dream meant, because when I woke that morning on the sixth day of John's absence, I missed Margaret even more. I wanted her to come knock at my door. Was my mother out there thinking about me? Or was it just her spirit looking after me? I couldn't understand the meaning of my dream, and before I started thinking too much of it, I heard a taxi cab drop off John outside.

He came walking through that door looking weaker than the

last time I saw him. I didn't know what to do. I wanted to go and help him in, but I was scared that he wouldn't like it. So, I just stood there watching him struggle.

"What are you doing standing there, stupid?" John managed to say.

I just went into the kitchen once I realized he was in a bad mood. It was going to be another day in hell. I sat in the kitchen waiting for him to call me and treat me like trash.

Later, I heard him go into the bathroom. He took a bath, and then came out into the kitchen. I stood up before he could say anything.

"Aren't you gonna make me breakfast?" he asked. He sounded mad, but not as mad as I was used to. I just took some milk out of the fridge and put it on the table for him while I was making a quick omelet for him. He sat down quietly and drank his milk, staring at nothing. I was uncomfortable and couldn't decide whether I was happy that the wait was over, or disappointed that he was home already. I made his eggs and served him with toast. He ate without a word and went to the bedroom to take a nap.

As soon as he woke up at noon, he yelled out my name. I ran to the room to see what was going on.

"Come here and massage my back for me," he said.

I approached the bed with caution. I started massaging his back as gently as possible. But he asked me to do it harder, so I went faster and harder. Then it was too hard, so I went back to being gentle. Within ten minutes, he got upset that I wasn't following his orders. He kicked me with his foot.

"You are a useless piece of shit, get out."

That tone was familiar. I went back to the kitchen happy to be out of his sight. At least I didn't have to endure his presence.

I sat in the kitchen still facing out the window waiting for Margaret to turn out, and nothing. I started to cook some roast chicken for John, in case he got hungry. He finally emerged that afternoon in his robe. He asked me to serve him lunch in the living room. He turned on the television, and somehow noticed that I had been watching it too.

"Have you been watching television in my absence?" he asked quietly.

I tried my best to remain as calm as possible. I answered, "No."

He just looked at his food and started eating. I wanted to make myself as invisible as possible so as not to attract his attention. He asked for water, so I ran to get some. And when he complained that the water was too warm, I ran to get ice cubes for him. But he only ate a little bit and fell asleep on the couch.

I cleaned the table and went back to my favorite place in the house, the kitchen. While I was doing the dishes, I saw Margaret getting out of a cab with a suitcase. She had a tan, and her figure was fuller. I realized that she had gone on a trip and I just hadn't see her leave. I felt a sigh of relief. She wasn't gone for good, the world wasn't so cruel after all. And what felt even better is that she glanced over to look if was there. Our eyes met and I looked away. I am sure she saw the relief in my eyes, even from afar. I was glad she was back.

CHAPTER 15

John left again for a couple of days, but I was used to expecting him anytime and to deal with his temper tantrums. I was burning with the need to talk to someone. I felt restless and cleaned the house more than once. My loneliness was so palpable that it physically hurt. I forgot to breathe sometimes because of my intense thoughts and the need to stop them. I felt the pain in my stomach and was unsure whether it was hunger or stress. The unhappiness inside me provided no solutions on how to get out of that hole.

I resented looking at myself in the mirror because I felt ugly and unworthy of being alive. Even my dreams and fantasies were affected by my unhappiness. My dreams were mostly tragedies, and I woke up every morning trying to analyze them. I missed those days dreaming of my mother or crossing a bridge to get to Margaret. And the days when I fantasized that I was a celebrity with fancy clothes and jewelry. When I was a teenager and knew that I would get married one day, dreaming of what kind of man I would marry. I dreamed about him all the time, and I had faith that one day he would come to me.

I remembered the first day that I got my period, waking up

and finding my underwear had a bloodstain. I knew that day would come because one of my older cousins warned me on my twelfth birthday. I had also seen them clean their cloths, since back home in my town most women did not use pads or tampons.

"You have to get ready to become a real woman. First come the breasts and then painful periods."

That morning my mother was in her room with my father, and I had to gather the courage to break the news to her. I didn't want to clean myself first because I wanted her to see for herself. I knocked at their door and waited for an answer. It took a while before my mother ordered me to come in. They were both giggly, but I needed them to get serious before I told them. I had to tell them that I went to bed as a girl and woke up as a woman this morning.

My father was standing next to their closet in his pants without a shirt, and my mother sat on the bed in her African robe.

"What is it, Grace?" my mother finally asked.

"I got my period this morning," I said looking down with embarrassment.

My father saw that I was embarrassed and wanted to lighten the mood with a bad joke. "You are a woman now; I have to hurry and find you a good husband."

I just ran out of the room crying, and I could hear them laughing behind me.

My mother joined me in my room as I was taking off my pajamas to go jump in the shower. She stood next to me and that look on her face that she usually had whenever me or my sibling did something that pleased her. She looked proud and happy. She took my hand and sat me down on my bed. My sister Mwinda was half asleep on her bed, pretending to not listen to the conversation.

My mother spoke. "Today is a great day and you should rejoice. Your father was only joking and he is as happy as I am."

"I know," I said, still looking down.

My mother held my face and said, "Your period marks the beginning of womanhood. You have to realize, now you are very capable of getting pregnant if you let a man fool around with you."

I did not want to have the sex conversation with my mother.

But she went on. "Bad boys out there would try to take your virginity away from you, but you must not let that happen. You are a princess and the man who would give your father the dowry would take you in his bed, you understand?"

I nodded yes, wanting her to stop. But my mother was very good at talking about serious issues in a very light manner. She spent that morning teaching me about hygiene and how to change and clean my cloth pad. She taught me how to deal with cramps and how to carry myself around town now that I was no longer a little girl.

"You are no longer allowed to climb trees and run around like a toddler. Men have to see a woman in you, and one day desire to marry you."

"I hope I'll end up with a better man than the ones I see in this town," I said to my mother with decisiveness in my voice.

She smiled, and by the look in her eyes I knew that she wished the same thing for her daughters. So she said, "Every night when you go to bed, close your eyes and imagine your prince charming. Imagine him the way you want him to be. What he would look like, how he would dress, how he would talk to you and how he will treat you". She paused and took a deep breath. "If you imagine him, he will come to you and be everything you wished him to be. Just be patient and be a genuine good girl."

When my mother left the room, my sister turned my way and

110

said with mockery, "I dream of a money tree that would afford me anything I want in this life".

I looked at her, and without missing a beat, she continued. "At least you know you are not alone with the far-fetched dream."

My sister was going to be one of the women in Lusa who had the courage to defy norms and useless sexist thinking. She didn't believe that girls should stop climbing trees or save themselves for a man. She was a feminist - we just didn't realize it and I loved it.

———————

I was sad and wanted to end it all. I looked in John's medicine cabinet to see what would kill me without pain, but most of the medications were foreign to me and I couldn't pick one out of the many bottles staring me in the face. Then I went into the kitchen, trying to see if there was anything that I could use to kill myself. Maybe the vinegar or the salt, or maybe if I drank the entire bottle of chili sauce, I wasn't sure. *How do I know for sure that I would be dead?* Because the last thing I needed was to end up in the hospital with John and having to deal with the consequences of a failed suicide attempt.

After a couple of hours of thinking about ending my life, I felt tired mentally, spiritually, and physically. I went to take a shower and for the rest of the evening I watched TV. I didn't care about John walking in on me, because after all, I had a death wish.

I woke up the next morning with the weight of my sadness weighing me down. My head and the rest of my body felt heavy and achy. The sun was shining bright outside, but the cloud hanging over my head was so gloomy that all I wanted to do was go back to sleep. I felt dizzy when I got up and my body was aching all over. I walked slowly to the bathroom and had a hard time pushing the door open. I finally sat down to pee and realized that I had been holding my breath. The idea of another day seemed too daunting, and I sat there for a few minutes thinking about where and how I was going to find the strength to go on.

I got up to wash my face and opened the medicine cabinet. I wanted to end my misery; I could not go on another day in this life. I looked at the medicines and picked up a box that had a couple of tablets. I took one tablet and put all the pills in the sink. There were about nine of them, and I stared at them for a while. I looked in the mirror and I couldn't see myself. The girl staring back at me was ugly and somber. I finally took all nine of the pills and hoped they were enough to help me die.

I slowly walked to the living room and lied down on the couch. Awaiting my death, I wondered if any of my family members were dead, would I see them in the afterlife? My head was spinning. I thought about my parents, about the dreams that would never come through, about the wonderful husband that I was never going to meet. My heart was beating really fast, my eyes dilated, and I felt really thirsty. I panicked; maybe I didn't want to die after all. Maybe there was still hope for me, or maybe John was never going to come back. I knew at that moment I did not want to die. My body was trembling, and I felt nauseous. I did not want to die.

I got up from the couch and ran to the kitchen. I was stumbling all over the place and managed to get a cup of water. I poured the water from the faucet and drank it fast. I was crying and trying to gag myself at the same time. I was out of my mind, feeling really scared.

The doorbell rang, and I heard it the first time. It rang again and again, but I did not have the strength to go see who it was. Then it stopped and I saw Margaret outside the window, really close to me. "Open the door, please! I want to help you!"

I stared at her and then ran to the door. I wanted her to save my life. As soon as I saw her, I started to explain to her that I took nine pills and was afraid to die.

She looked at me with compassion. "Okay, calm down sweetheart, show me what the pills look like." Margaret helped me to the bathroom, and I showed her the box of medicine that I took. She looked relieved and explained. "It's only allergy medicine. Thank God! How many did you take?"

I looked at her, embarrassed and said, "Nine." In English, I remembered my numbers.

CHAPTER 16

I woke up in a beautiful room, with the most soothing wallpaper I had ever seen. It was printed with flowers and horses all over, and the colors were blue and yellow with a little bit of brown.

The room was very simple, it had a dresser, the small bed I was on, and a vanity. The window was shut and the curtains were down. There was still enough light coming into the room for me to take a good look at it. It took me a few minutes before I remembered what had happened to me. I figured that I was inside Margaret's house.

She must have heard me sneeze, because she walked through the doorway with a cup of tea and toast. "Good morning sweetheart!"

She called me sweetheart and I liked it. I knew what it meant because I looked it up once when I heard it on TV. I liked the sound of it, and what it stood for. I looked at her walking toward me with half a smile. Margaret came closer and sat down next to me.

She smiled and said, "I brought you breakfast and some herbal tea".

I was hungry, so without hesitation I took some of the bread and started to eat. Margaret was my guardian angel, and for the first time in a very long time I felt warmth coming from another human being and I liked it. It's like one part of me was wondering about John, but the other part of me that was hungry for love, made me sit there and enjoy being cared for. I took a small sip of the tea and swallowed it hurriedly.

"I am sorry." I wanted to say more but I felt my English wasn't good enough.

She paused for a second, almost like she wanted to analyze what I had just said. Was I lying to her? Her eyes were inquisitive, but I couldn't tell her the truth. "Don't worry about it. I am a nurse, so I am more than qualified to take care of you. You took allergy medicine but not enough to overdose."

I learned English by being around John and watching TV. At least I was learning something in the midst of my ordeal with him. "I need to go home," I said to Margaret, after she watched me eat the bread like a stray dog who had just been rescued.

"If you are worried about your husband, he is not home."

I looked old enough to be John's wife, certainly, but Margaret knew that I wasn't. She wanted me to react and tell her the truth.

She continued, "I went there earlier, no one was home".

"I am sorry for the trouble, but I have to go now." I stood up and realized that I was wearing pink pajamas. Margaret got up and opened the dresser to hand me my clothes.

"I took the liberty of washing your clothes." She handed them to me.

I looked at her, before I started to undress.

"I'll be in the living room," she said and left the room.

I found Margaret sitting on the couch waiting for me to emerge out of her bedroom. Her living room was filled with lights. I was not used to that, because John usually kept the shades closed. The only light I enjoyed came from the kitchen window, and that wasn't enough. I scanned the room quickly and realized how pretty her house was compared to John's. The couch was white, and she had porcelain figurines all over the living room. It felt peaceful as I took it all in.

"I am glad you are okay," she said to make me snap out of my reverie. "You have to promise that you will be more careful next time." Her tone was very motherly and loving.

"I will be careful," I said.

She stood up to help me out the door. And as soon as I was out, she said, "Remember my name is Margaret and I am here for you. You can come back whenever, and I would love to get to know you more".

I nodded and gave her a hug. A long hug which felt really good. As I was walking toward John's house, I could feel the bitterness in my soul. I was going from light to darkness.

As soon as I walked into his house, I felt a knot in my stomach. The lighting, the smell, the furniture, the plain white walls, and John's energy in the air - it was stifling. I walked into the kitchen and began tidying up the mess I'd made trying to get pills out of my system. The night before came back to my mind, and I felt guilty for wanting to end my life. I felt bad for that moment, but at the same time it was a reminder that I had hit rock bottom.

While taking a shower, I reflected on what I'd come so close to doing. What if I had died? I knew that John would feel no remorse, so killing myself would not be a punishment for his actions. There were many people, children, and adults in the Congo fighting for their lives. And who would have given anything not to die in the hands of the rebels. I witnessed my friends and their families being mutilated in front of me. I spent countless nights lying next to cadavers and breathing the air polluted by their decomposing bodies and saw my own family fight for their lives.

"Why did I survive?" I asked myself as the water flowed

down my face. I was sad, lost and in a dark place mentally. I escaped the war back home to end up here in captivity. I didn't know where to find the strength to go on, but I decided to try.

I spent the rest of the evening cleaning the house, and then made myself a sandwich and watched TV. Still no sign of John, and I knew that something must have gone terribly wrong but there was nothing I could do about it. Wandering around the house, into the bedroom, I looked around the room and opened John's closet. I wanted to know more about him and had been eyeing the boxes sitting in the corner of his closet.

My heart was beating fast, I felt as if I was opening a tomb and was afraid to uncover some deep dark secrets. I sat down on the floor and pulled out the first box, it was yellow and heart shaped. The box wasn't locked, which surprised me but amused me at the same time. John was not as smart as I thought and believed that I would never have the courage to snoop around. I opened the box and saw pictures, lots of them.

The first that stuck out to me was a picture of a younger John in a military uniform. He was standing in front of a US flag and looking straight to the camera. He looked serious and handsome. Having never looked at him that way, the picture caught me off guard. John used to be in the military, I had to let that sink in for a while. There were more pictures of him in uniform. In some of them he was standing with other soldiers in what looked like a camp of some sort, and in others he was standing alone. He looked young and happy. So far removed from the John I knew. He was a lot heavier now and wore a permanent frown on his face.

I kept looking at the pictures and saw a picture of John kissing a girl. They looked like they were in love and on vacation somewhere tropical. She had red hair and was wearing a white bathing suit. John looked smitten by her. There were more pictures of them together in different settings and in one of the pictures; a heart was drawn in the back with the caption, 'Love of my life'.

I wondered if he wrote it or she did. My eyes were getting bigger with each picture, I was able to humanize John. For the first time, I thought of him as a human being with a past and memories. Did something turn him into the monster who kidnapped me? Or, was he born a sociopath?

I was so taken by the pictures and lost in my thoughts that I didn't hear a car outside. I only heard a key turning in the living room door. I closed the box fast and pushed the closet door. I pretended to be making the bed, just in time for John to walk in on me. My heart was about to come out of my chest as I tried to control my breathing. I was scared out of my mind and didn't dare make eye contact with John.

He asked me while clenching his fists, "What are you doing?"

I didn't respond. I finally just looked at him, and he waved his hand to dismiss me. I left the room without once looking at him.

It was late and he smelt like chemicals. I knew he was coming from the hospital and wondered why they had let him out so late. Moving into the kitchen, I waited for him to yell my name and order me to do something for him. But the night went on and I did not hear him call, he fell asleep.

CHAPTER 17

John had been back for a week, and I was getting back into my daily routine. I made him breakfast in the morning before he headed to work. I spent my days drawing or watching TV, until about half four when I made a start on dinner. John was looking better and seemed to be regaining his strength. We hadn't had sex since his return and I was hoping that somehow he had lost his sex drive.

That day he requested a steak and potatoes, and I spent all day debating how I would cook them for him, and how early I should start with the steak. I seasoned it well in the morning and let it sit in the fridge until the afternoon. I was in a better mood since I saw Margaret briefly and she blew a kiss at me. She was like a family member or a friend I didn't really know, and her existence was the best thing about my life.

When John got back, he was in a good mood himself, and his face didn't look as pale as the weeks before. I served him dinner and went to the kitchen, sat by the door to watch him enjoy my masterpiece. The steak was good so I knew that he would enjoy it. I watched him eat it like an angry bear in the wild, and I got a weird sense of satisfaction. The sad part is that in a million years,

I would never get a thank you or a look of appreciation for my hard work.

As soon as I cleared the table, I knew that sex was going to be his dessert. He played porn on TV and called me into the living room with him. This tape was new, and I was seeing things that really put me over the edge. Women were being penetrated from the back from men, and I was afraid that John would want to do that to me. He grabbed my hand and made me stroke his penis. I wanted to throw up. He eventually unzipped his pants and made me suck it. We usually took it in the bedroom, but that night John was in the moment and wanted to take me right there and then.

He made me bend over and proceeded to penetrate me from the back. The pain that I felt that night is indescribable. The more I tensed up, the more he pushed himself inside of me, and everything in me was screaming. I fought back tears and kept all my screams internal. I was quiet and stared at the wall in front of me. It took him a while before he broke through, but the harder it was the more excited he got and the more painful it was for me. I held my breath and waited for it to be over.

John got his way with me and fell asleep on the couch. I collected myself away from him and went into the bathroom. I sat on the floor and wept.

The next morning my back was aching, and I felt as if something had been taken away from me. John took my soul, my spirit, my humanity, and my ability to love myself. I felt disgusted by my own body and wouldn't even look in the mirror. This was a new kind of low, and I was completely depleted.

I made John breakfast and waited for him to wake up. He didn't for a while, and for a moment I was hoping that he had died overnight. But he got up from the sofa and went to take a shower. I had ironed his clothes and carefully placed them on his bed. He finally came into the kitchen and sat down to have his breakfast. I was standing in the corner pretending to organize the pantry, and I felt a headache take over me. This is what it feels like to serve and obey the man who was torturing me. I was his slave and John had no signs of remorse on his face, in fact he looked very happy.

John left once again and forgot to give me that mysterious pill he had been giving me, and I was glad he did. I cleaned after him and sat in the kitchen to collect myself. I needed love or affection at that point. The need for another human being was palpable and I couldn't stand it anymore. I didn't know that it was possible for me to feel so unattractive, unwanted, worthless, and filthy.

I opened the door and looked outside. I needed to be next to another human being. I needed to see Margaret. I had to find the courage to walk to her door and come up with an excuse. I contemplated the idea for a while and debated within myself. *What if she is busy? What if she rejects me? What if she wants to hurt me?* Even though Margaret insisted that I was more than welcome to go to her anytime, I still had doubts. John had taken away my ability to believe in other people, and instead instilled fear and a very low self-esteem. I just could not take another person demeaning or rejecting me, I was already too broken. After wrestling with my thoughts for a bit, I finally decided to do it. I knocked at the door and as if she was waiting for me, Margaret opened it right away.

She looked very happy to see me, and with a smile on her face she said, "Grace, it's so good to see you."

And those words penetrated my heart and entered every fiber of my being. They felt like a glass of water after a long, hot day. I felt a tingle through my body, and it showed on my face. I was happy to see her too. "Come on in, I was just about to make waffles. Maybe you could help me."

Her house was like an oasis of all things hopeful and loving. I remembered the smell of cleanliness, and the brightness in her living room. She went into the kitchen, and I followed her.

"Do you know how to make waffles?"

I responded, "No".

"Well, that's okay. I'll show you and I am sure you are a fast learner." Her ease and the tone of her voice made me feel very comfortable around her. She talked to me with a sense of familiarity and that reminded me of people back home. She took out all the ingredients she needed, put on an apron and handed me one as well.

Margaret began her lesson. "The secret to good waffles is eggs and butter. You can start battering them while I get the flour and sugar ready."

I was enjoying it and wanted to be a good student. She wasn't very talkative, and I knew that she wanted to keep me at ease. I observed her every move. Every time she looked my way, I looked down.

"Perfect! You are doing a great job," she said.

I smiled and kept battering the eggs and butter. I wanted her approval. We made the waffles while making small talks about cooking and baking. She hadn't asked me any personal questions, and I was glad she didn't. I was not ready to honestly answer, and I wasn't sure I would ever tell her the things that John had inflicted upon me until that point. The reason I came to her house is because I needed her. And being around Margaret filled me with an inexplicable joy. I felt the sincerity that came with every word she uttered.

It wasn't the same feeling that I had the first time I laid my eyes on John. I felt his negative energy but could not predict the atrocities that he would subject me to. In the back of my mind there was always guilt, maybe I should have tried harder to find my family, or maybe I should have tried harder to escape. I feared my fate and doubted my own strengths. The unknown was intimidating to me and all the conflicting emotions within me paralyzed me.

We finished the waffles and they smelled delicious. "We can sit in the living room and have some tea with the waffles," Margaret said. I just nodded. "I will save some for my son, Sebastian. He lives in San Diego, and I am driving there tomorrow to see him."

She had a son, and I could help but think about how lucky he was to have a mother like her. We walked into the living room and Margaret served us tea. I was quiet for the most part and observed her.

"Okay, are you comfortable?" I nodded, yes. "You know, you don't have to be so shy around me. I am glad you are here, at least I get to have someone to chat with."

I wasn't sure whether I was intimidated by her presence, or I just didn't know how to interact with people anymore. I was also afraid that she would discover that I was not an interesting person; therefore, not worth all the attention she was giving me.

We watched TV in silence, and I was enjoying the waffles, but was too afraid to grab another one. "You can have as many as you want. I made enough for you, myself and my son." She must have read my mind.

So I grabbed another one, and then a third one. Then I looked at the clock and it was almost 4pm, I panicked.

"I have to go, it's getting late," I said and got up with haste.

She sensed the fear in me and held my hand when she stood up. "It's okay. You are okay. I understand."

"Thank you for the waffles and tea." I took off without even hearing what she was saying. *What if John was home already? What if I didn't have enough time to make dinner?* My heart was pounding as I walked back to the house. I didn't see John's car and felt a little better. I entered the house and exhaled.

CHAPTER 18

It had been a couple of days since that afternoon that I spent at Margaret's, and John hadn't suspected anything. I felt mischievous and prided myself to have gotten away with it. Our lives were back to normal, and John was feeling better. We went back to our usual routine, and the sex got dirtier with each passing day. The only difference is that John was running out of breath faster than before, and I was just glad that our dirty rides were lasting less than ten minutes. And for the most part, he made me play with his penis and only was inside of me for about three minutes. I counted down until he got out of me, to take a deep breath. I hated his scent mixed with the smell of medication that he was taking.

Margaret had been gone for a week, and I missed her tremendously. I longed for her motherly looks and presence. And found myself hoping that she would return sooner rather than later. One night I had that dream again where I was crossing a bridge with my mother and Margaret waiting on the other side. I hadn't had it for a while and was still perplexed by its meaning. In my culture, dreams have a serious meaning. I remembered my mother telling me that they were usually an announcement for things to come, good or bad. Before the rebels invaded our town, my mother had dreamt about it. She woke up one day very sad, and while we were having breakfast my father asked her why.

She said, "I have been having this dream where we were burning in a fire".

My father looked terrified because like my mother, he was very superstitious. "And what happens after the fire?" he asked her.

"I am not sure. I can't see our faces clearly, and I usually wake up before we escape the fire."

My father said to all of us, "We have to pray about it tonight. Maybe the dream means that we are going to face an obstacle, but I am sure we will be fine".

My siblings and I were very quiet on our way to school. We were afraid of the dream, and I said a prayer internally. "God please protect my family from any harm." We were fine for a week, until the rebels finally broke into our town. Then we all understood what my mother's dream meant.

On second thought, an actual fire would have been easier and less painful. I forced myself every day not to relive those atrocious days. The rapes, the mutilations, and forced incest. We watched them take away everything we had, and I am not thinking about the material stuff. I am talking about respect, dignity, and peace. They stole our souls and I never once saw guilt in their eyes. The days that we spent hiding in the church were just as bad as when they finally found us. We somehow knew that the moment would come when they'd find us, and the anticipation was like poison in our veins.

My mother and a few of the women from our neighborhood were holding hands in prayer for hours. And I remember thinking, *God, please answer their prayers and I will never ask anything else of you.* Some men were getting upset about the prayer circle and would complain that it was a waste of time. According to them

God had skipped our town, and our fate was already sealed. I sat there with fear in my heart and tears in my eyes. I wasn't sure what was going to happen to us, but deep down inside of me I knew that life as we knew it was over.

Those days were the beginning of the end for me, and I look back and wonder what it is that we did to deserve such a fate. I wonder if our lives were already planned and that there was nothing that we could have done to prevent it. On other hand, I couldn't ignore God's existence and magnificence. I observed pregnant women and witnessed the miracle of birth. A child lives in his mother's womb for nine months and comes out to breathe air for the first time, without training or a crash course on life. A child knows how to suck his mother's nipples to acquire food and create a bond between them. I look at flowers and trees outside and realize that they have their own pulse and purpose in life. I marvel at different animals and their anatomy; they don't exist by chance. There must be a creator, the source of all majesty and energy. There must be a higher power.

The conviction of God's existence and the mystery of his will have always been in conflict in my heart. What does he expect from us? How do we get his favor and Grace? Does he live within us? And after all that had happened to me and my family, his will is even more confusing to me. I could not dare take the time to pray to him. I felt far away from his presence and was too afraid to cry out to him.

When I was about eight years old, my paternal grandmother came to live with us because she was ill and needed to get medical care. Up until then she lived in a village that I hadn't visited. My family and I live in a small town, where the lifestyle wasn't as developed as Kinshasa, the capital of the Congo, but we still had school, a couple of catholic churches, a hospital, and a city hall and a mayor. However, my grandmother came from the village and the lifestyle there was simpler. My father described it to us with so much pride. He was born in this small village called Mayi, and they didn't have electricity and water. The nearest school was miles and miles away, that's why my grandfather sent my father to live in Lusa with the catholic missionary to get an education.

My grandfather died before I was born, but I had seen a picture of him that my father kept in the living room. In Mayi, people didn't know of God. They believed in their ancestors and worshipped them. Once a month they killed an animal as a sacrifice to them, to show appreciation and ask for blessings. So, when my grandmother moved in with us I noticed that she still practiced her rituals to her ancestors and asked my dad to participate. At this point, my father had spent so much time at church, that he deemed the rituals unnecessary and an abomination to God. This created a conflict between him and his mother.

She told him, "You have forgotten about the ancestors who have brought you this far, and started to worship the white's man God".

My father would reply, "He is not the white man's God. He is God, your God. He created the world and all things in it, including you".

My grandmother would lift her hands in the air and start chanting. I didn't understand what she was saying but it was rather intense.

I asked my mother, "Do you think our grandparents and all the inhabitants in the village who have never heard of God will all go to hell? She looked at me surprised and shocked.

"They won't go to hell because we all worship the same God, but they have a different name for him."

I was too afraid to go on with that conversation, so I just went on with my day. But after a year of living with us, my grandmother passed away and my father organized a mass at the church for her. During the mass, the priest was praying for her salvation and entry to heaven. I wanted to stop the priest and inform him that my grandmother didn't believe in God, and that praying for her salvation was rather futile.

From that point, I was convinced that we, as humans, have this vain pursuit of defining God and what he represents. We give him different names and give him attribution that would humanize him. We long to be able to relate to him and make him similar to us. We create rules and regulations to impose on other people in the name of God and use them to judge others. Growing up, I knew that God existed and accepted the fact that his existence was a mystery that I would never be able to solve.

Now I was sitting in John's kitchen, the struggle that I was going through did not bring me closer to God. It made me take a step back, I felt empty and was afraid of what the future had in store for me. I was beyond the point of confusion, and I wanted to be numb. But at the same time, I was carrying a shred of hope within me that helped me wake up every morning and look outside the window and think *maybe*.

CHAPTER 19

"I don't want an omelet today. Boil the egg instead and make me some tea." John barked at me after I had spent time making him an omelet and coffee. I cleared the table while he was reading the paper and started over.

He had been up and down with his health in the past couple of weeks and I noticed the weight loss also. His skin was changing colors, and he vomited most of his meals. He was always tired and took different types of medications. He ate less and we had sex less often. After his breakfast, I watched him struggle to get up from the chair and leave the house. Once again, he forgot to give me the pill.

I made him rice, broccoli, and fish that day then for the rest of the day I drew pictures of flowers and landscapes. Every time I heard a car, I was hoping that Margaret was returning from San Diego. I missed her and hoped that I would get to spend more time with her.

That night John came home earlier than usual, and he seemed tired. His skin was turning yellow, and his eyes were red. I figured that he had gotten sick at work and left early. He sat on the sofa right away, and for a second there I thought that he was going to start watching porn and ask me to join him. But instead, he was very quiet and breathing heavily, almost like a person who had just finished a race. I sat in the kitchen waiting to hear from him.

When I had first met John, he was a heavy drinker. He got drunk almost every night and kept a variety of alcoholic drinks in the fridge. But since he got sick, John drank less and didn't bring alcohol around. For me, it meant that I didn't have to breathe the smell of it the few times that we were intimate. But that night, he asked me to serve him a beer. It was strange to me that a sick man would want to drink alcohol, but that was his poison of choice and I had to obey his order.

I served him beer and his dinner. He ate less than half of it but managed to drink more than a few beers. He fell asleep, and I cleared the table. I wondered what John's disease was and if he was ever going to recover. *What if he dies and I am the only one in the house with him? What if the police think I killed him? What if he never recovers? What if it's contagious?* I had so many questions and no answers.

I have witnessed so many people's lives deteriorate because of an illness, and it's always so devastating to watch no matter who it is. I remember one of my cousins, Fani, who had contracted HIV when I was eleven years old. She was a vibrant young lady and beautiful. The only problem is that she was sexually insatiable and spent most of her time chasing after men. Her parents were embarrassed of her, but since she was their only daughter, they had to keep her in their house and pray that she would change her ways eventually. She was tall, with a perfect complexion and curves to kill.

By the age of twenty-one, most men married or single had slept with her and women were aware of her power to seduce. She would come over to our house to visit, and I remember watching her every move. She was unlike anybody in town. She looked like one of those women we saw on TV. Dressed nicely, and her fingers were always painted in red. I was young then, but I was very aware of her beauty.

One day, rumors started swirling around town that she had AIDS, and my sister was the first one to break it to me. "She used to sleep with one of my teachers, and he died of the disease a few months ago. I am pretty sure the rumors are true," she said.

I let the shock settle in first, then said, "It would be such a loss for her family. She is so pretty and nice. I hope it's just a rumor."

My sister looked at me with mockery in her eyes. "A disease like that doesn't care whether you are pretty or not. She slept with every man in this town; let just hope that most of them were before she got sick. Can you imagine? If they all got it, they probably gave it to their wives and that means that fifty percent of this town will be dead in the next few years."

My sister and I stayed silent in our room that night, the idea of what that disease could do was scary. Back then, we didn't know much about the disease, and it was an epidemic in the Congo. False information was running rampant. People really believe they could get contaminated by being around an infected person. Men and women were dying of it, and no one knew how to prevent it.

My cousin Fani got sicker as time went on, and most people in town avoided getting close to her and her family. We were afraid of catching it and made her an outcast. She still went for walks in the neighborhood, and every time I saw her my eyes filled with tears. She looked fragile and very skinny. She didn't deserve to be treated so poorly.

My sister and I would sometimes go talk to her or help her carry her groceries back to their house. My mother told us over dinner to be careful because her disease was highly contagious.

"I am proud that you two are still nice to her, unlike most people in this town who used to praise and follow her because of her beauty. However, I want you to be careful and not touch anything that could get you contaminated." My mother had a good heart and could not stand the idea of another person suffering. She welcomed everybody in our house and even let cousin Fani come in from time to time.

Cousin Fani was a good person. She was sexually insatiable and should have protected herself better. Lusa just didn't know how to deal with a sexually liberated person like her. She brought my siblings and I gifts and would spend some afternoons with us before she got sick. But after the town learned of her disease, people started to avoid her and whisper behind her back. Her parents had no choice but to move her out of town. They sent her to live with her paternal grandparents until she died. My parents went to the funeral, but most people in town didn't.

After her death, people began to get tested and a few of the men and women had contracted AIDS also. I was young, but her story became a cautionary tale for men in our town and condoms became somewhat popular for about six months. Then we went back to our old ways. Some men started using them, but for the rest of them the pleasure of sex without condoms was too enjoyable to stop.

I overheard my uncle Richard speaking with his friends over drinks. "If it's meant for you to die, you'll die. Whether you choose to have sex with condoms or without, I personally hate the rubber and will continue doing it without it."

He believed in the health benefits of an active sex life and to him, a condom was going to slow him down. A group of volunteers in Lusa continued to educate people about safe sex, but they were met with indifference from most people.

The irony of it is that, until the day that rebels invaded our town, my uncle was one of the healthiest men in Lusa. He had a lot of concubines and mistresses and never contracted anything.

I was just hoping that John's disease wasn't contagious. I got paranoid sometimes whenever I noticed a zit on my face, or whenever I felt something unusual in my body. I wondered if John had contaminated me with his disease. But I usually snapped out of it quickly, there was nothing I could do about it. I was heartbroken that intimacy became such a source of stress and disgust to me. Sex was supposed to be a beautiful experience for two people, not what I was living with John. Even watching porn, I knew at that time that there were healthy ways to watch it, but John introduced it to me in such a vile and violent way.

CHAPTER 20

Margaret came back and I was waiting for the right time before I could go to see her. She waved at me through the kitchen window a couple of times, and I knew it was her way of sending an invitation.

John had been home for a few days, and I couldn't wait for him to either get better or go to the hospital. I wanted to talk to Margaret. He was feverish and had lost his appetite completely. He bought some canned soups and that's what he had for lunch and dinner. I made him boiled eggs and tea for breakfast.

"Next time, let the eggs boil for another ten minutes at least!" he said angrily. I nodded and left the room. Then he called and asked for a very cold beer. "Didn't I tell you to put them in the fridge?" I didn't respond and left the room. Those few days were a living hell for me. John asked me to move the TV into his bedroom, and I struggled pushing the TV stand to his room and listened to him give me instructions on how to plug it all in.

One night, he called me in and ordered me to stroke his penis and I did. At least he didn't ask me to suck on it. But the next night, after he drank his soup and his beer, he called me in. He was standing on the edge of his bed when I entered the room.

His pajama pants were down halfway, and his penis was erect. I felt repulsed at the mere sight of it. He gestured for me to get closer and sit on the bed next to him. I was looking in his eyes, hoping he would let me off the hook this time. But without saying a thing, I knew that he would reprimand me for refusing to pleasure him. So, I grabbed it and started to suck on it.

When we finished, he took a towel, wiped himself and fell on his bed. I watched him for a second and unglued myself from the bed and walked out the room. When I reached the bathroom, I threw up. I had never vomited after having sex with John, nor felt very nauseous and dizzy like this before. I wondered if I was also getting sick. I sat down in the bathroom, and I sobbed uncontrollably.

The next morning, I woke up with a headache and another bout of nausea. I felt very sick in my stomach and threw up a couple of times before I gathered the strength to make breakfast for John. The smell of boiled eggs sickened me, but I didn't want John to notice that I was sick. I was afraid he would get upset that I let myself get sick and punish me. I didn't want to give him reasons to be upset. I pulled myself together when he came to the kitchen to have breakfast.

That morning, he was strong enough to get out of the house but wasn't wearing his usual work clothes. He was wearing sweats and tennis shoes. I figured that he wasn't going to work and was probably coming back sooner than 5pm. I couldn't go see Margaret and risk the chance of getting caught.

He ate his breakfast and sat in the kitchen for at least half an hour. It looked as if he was gathering his strength for the day. I watched him and felt sorry for him. The John who was sitting in the kitchen looked nothing like the one that I met in the Congo. Back then, he looked healthier and stronger. I was intimidated by him and felt very small in his presence. But now, he was frail and barely had the courage to have sex with me the way he used to. I felt a wave of emotions for him, hatred, disgust, and pity, and wondered whether he would ever recover from his disease.

He finally got up from his chair and went straight to the drawer where he kept the pill that he used to give me every morning. I felt my heart sink and knew that he was going to force me to take it. I had been sick all morning, and wasn't sure if the pill would make me sicker. I didn't want to put anything in my stomach, and for a second, I closed my eyes and wished that he wouldn't give it to me.

He got the pill, walked toward me with a grin on his face and handed it to me. "It's been a while, it's a good thing we haven't had sex frequently since I have fallen ill," he said.

I took the pill from him and put it in my mouth without swallowing it. At that very moment, I understood that the pill was a contraceptive pill. I had my suspicions, but since I had never seen one before I couldn't be sure.

Back in Lusa, women didn't take contraceptive pills. We knew what the pill was, but no one made it available to women in our town. The average family had at least eight to ten kids, and most men had children with their mistresses. My father, like most other men in our town, birthed on average twenty-five children. The only reason some men started to use condoms was because of the AIDS epidemic, but we didn't believe in contraception and didn't bother to find out more about it. And priests and nuns warned us that it was a sin to go against God's will to give us children.

Workers from an international organization arranged a Women's Day and tried to educate mothers about birth control but no one listened. The women attended for the freebies and nothing else. Most of the foreigners who lived in Lusa only had one or two children but they were also Catholics, so how did they prevent pregnancies? I wondered. Did they take contraception against the church rules?

The only person I knew who took the pill was my mother's

friend, Aunt Shela, she was different from most women in Lusa. After graduating from high school, the Catholic Church in Lusa helped her get a full scholarship to go study in Paris. She spent ten years there and came back to Lusa, an accomplished accountant. The only problem is that she was too intelligent for any men in Lusa to want to marry her.

"She thinks she is a man, and I can't handle marrying someone like that."

"If she is so independent, she should marry herself then."

"How dare she buy a house on her own. No one would ever want to have her now."

"I bet you she likes women."

These were just a few of the comments I heard around town about her. Aunt Shela never got a chance to get married, but men were intrigued by her demeanor. She carried herself with a lot of confidence and poise, and always had her hair perfectly done. She became the mayor's concubine, and everyone knew about it. The only thing is that she didn't want to have children with him. I heard her telling my mother one day, "I am only thirty-eight, and I hope to find my own husband one day. For now, the mayor is more than enough".

My mother replied, "At least have babies with him so that you don't end up alone, in case you don't find a husband".

She laughed hard. "I have faith that I'll find someone. I am on the pill to make sure that I never end up with the mayor's baby. Have you seen him? He is ugly. His money and power are the only things attractive about him."

My mother sounded shocked when she said, "You are on the pill?"

Aunt Shela replied with pride and authority. "I am on the pill. I am not broadcasting it, but yes; I don't want to have children until I am married. Please don't judge me."

That night, my mother shared the story with my father. My

sister and I were pretending to wash the dishes but our ears were plugged to the living room where my parents were sitting.

"She seems very proud of the fact that she is on the pill, at her age that's madness," my mother said.

Without missing a beat, my father said, "I find women like her very unattractive. And you know what they say, 'a woman is like a flower and her husband is like the fence around it.' This woman is open to anything good and bad, and I would rather you didn't spend too much time with her."

That was it. My mother cut her ties with Aunt Shela, and never looked back.

My sister Mwinda and I researched what the pill was for and what type of women took it. We asked around at school, and asked anyone who would have some information about it. We finally understood what it was, and we both decided that if we got married, we would be on the pill, so that we don't end up having an army of children like most women in Lusa. From that point on, we admired Aunt Shela from afar.

Maybe being such a progressive woman wasn't such a good thing for her. I wasn't sure who I felt sorry for more, the married women with cheating husbands or my Aunt Shela, who had no stress of a husband but was lonely ninety-nine percent of the time. Even when the mayor visited her, he talked about his wife and children to her. Basically, she gave him a lot, but received the bare minimum from him. What kept her in the relationship? Loneliness, perhaps. Or just her physical needs, or maybe she was in love with him. They stayed together for a very long time, and by her forty-second birthday she realized the relationship was making her more miserable than happy. She broke up with him and moved to Kinshasa. Lusa was too small for her.

As soon as John left the house, I spit out the pill. I figured we weren't having sex; therefore there was no need for it. John was too weak to have intercourse with me. I looked at the pill for a couple of minutes, realizing it was the first time that I had taken a closer look at it. It was so small, yet capable of so much.

As I predicted, John came back early that day. I hadn't made dinner yet, and was sitting in the kitchen waiting for him. He had been eating soups only for lunch and dinner, and I wasn't sure if he would have asked for anything else that day. He glanced through the kitchen door to check that I was there and then went to the bedroom.

A couple of hours later, he finally called my name. "Can you make me steak and potatoes for dinner? And put a beer in the freezer while you are cooking."

I was used to getting orders from him with a mean tone, yet that night for the first time, he was very calm. It must have been the fatigue or he just finally decided to treat me like a human being, so I thought.

I made the dinner, and in some twisted way I was a little excited that John wasn't mean to me that day. I gave the steak extra diligence, and had a slight smile on my face. *What was it about my relationship with John that made me so confused? He was very cruel to me and spent most of his time torturing me one way or another. What did I care whether he was in a good mood or not? Why did I rejoice when he wasn't mean to me?*

I didn't have the answers to any of those questions, nor did I know who I was anymore.

That night John had dinner in the bedroom and fell asleep without bothering me. I slept in the living room and was satisfied that I didn't have to perform a sexual act with him.

CHAPTER 21

'However long the night, the dawn will break'; a proverb I heard my mother say many times. But she usually used it for the small problems we complained about as children. I never paid much attention to it, but then it had taken on a brand-new meaning. I wondered if the dawn would break for me, and when.

Weeks had passed and I hadn't seen nor talked to Margaret. She was home most of the time, but with John constantly there I couldn't take a chance to acknowledge her. I glanced every now and then, but for the most part tried my best to get her off my mind. I didn't know when John was going to get better, and I wanted to erase the hope that my friendship with Margaret ever stood a chance. It was easier for me to lose hope and to shield myself from more hurt. I tried my best not to think too much about her.

But one morning, John left without eating his breakfast. He was dressed in his jeans and a sweater, so I assumed he went to the hospital. I sat in the kitchen for a couple of hours deciding whether I should at least go say hi to Margaret and talk to her for a little bit. I debated within myself and was aware of the risk of getting caught.

I heard a knock at the door and knew it was her. My heart jumped with joy, and I took a deep breath of pure satisfaction before I went and opened the door. *Was it possible that Margaret could hear the cry of my heart? Could she sense that I had missed her?* But at the same time, I had been avoiding making eye contact with her from the window and even thinking about her too much. But here she was, once again with her perfect timing.

I answered the door, and the first thing she said was, "I have missed you, Grace".

I paused and just stared at her to savor those words.

"I haven't seen you in a while, and I just saw your husband leave a while ago. I figured I would come by and say hi."

I was still staring. I couldn't find words to come out of my mouth because so many things were going through my head. *What if John catches her here? What will he do to the both of us?* But at the same time, I realized that I love seeing Margaret and that her presence became my only source of joy and comfort.

"How have you been?" she asked again.

And I finally said, "I have been okay, and sorry I haven't visited in a while".

"No worries, I just wanted to see you and say hi. I am going to leave now to go to work, but will you promise that you will stop by sooner rather than later?"

How could I promise when I didn't have the freedom to plan anything? My existence depended on John and there was nothing that I did that did not involve him.

But I replied, "I will stop by soon. I promise".

"Okay. I am looking forward to it, and we can even bake something together." She held my hand briefly and walked away.

I was still standing at the door, when she waved goodbye from her car, and I shyly waved back. I rarely opened the door to look outside. John didn't lock the door whenever he left the house. And yet, I opened the door to the outside world but couldn't take a step to run away. I had ventured to Margaret's house, but never mustered the courage to take it a step further. John had put me in a prison that was bigger and more powerful than the door. I was broken as a person and lost the confidence to be a free human being.

He had told me that Immigration would arrest me and torture me. He had also told me that he would make up a story about me that would make me a criminal in the eyes of the law. But most of all, John had taken my right to be human and my ability to love myself. I felt like a human with a past, but no future. I was like an animal in a cage, and solitude was my best friend. I was lonely and John had put some psychological shackles on me.

The thing about loneliness is that it kills you from the inside. I was lonely most of the time and spent most of my time thinking about my past. I thought about my childhood, my school, my church, my friends, and my family. Thinking of my past was like a double-edged sword; at times it made me happy, and sometimes it made me sad beyond words. The sadness that I would never go back to the best part of my life and the thought that I may never see my family again, cut me to the very core of my being, and filled me with darkness.

I felt loneliness in my mind and saw it on my face. Every inch of my face told a sad story, and it became very visible as time went on. I saw it in Margaret's face when she looked at me. I could tell that she felt the sorrow coming out of me, but she never had the courage to ask me of its source. She didn't look at me with pity, but rather with compassion. I saw it, and I couldn't get myself to tell her how I felt. Maybe I was too afraid that she would judge me for letting it happen, or perhaps she wouldn't believe me. I didn't have the confidence to trust myself, nor did I think that another human being could really want my well-being.

I knew that Margaret was a good person, but still I felt as if I didn't deserve her love and compassion. The fact that she noticed me and let me come to her house was more than enough, I couldn't trouble her with my story. The negativity that John fed me every day about myself cancelled out all the good things that my parents instilled in me about self-esteem. Why is it that I was willing to believe the bad things that John told me and so quickly forget about the good ones I heard about all my life? Is darkness and negativity that much more powerful than positivity?

Loneliness was like a force that dominated me, and Margaret was the small crack that let the light in. All I had to do was to widen the crack and make it a gate to my freedom. I just didn't know how, and I didn't believe that I deserved it.

I was so deep into my thoughts that I didn't see the time pass. It was almost 6pm and John wasn't back yet. I seasoned a steak and also made the soup just in case. I waited for him, and by midnight he still wasn't back. I felt sick and threw up a couple of times, and the thought of interacting with him made me even sicker. So, I sat at the kitchen dining table, resting my head and fell asleep.

I woke up the next morning in the same position, not only nauseous but my head and neck were sore. I ran to the bathroom to throw up and wondered what was happening to me. Once again, the fear of having caught John's disease sent a chill down my spine. I got up from the bathroom floor and forced myself into the shower. I turned on the shower and let myself get lost in my thoughts. I was just overwhelmed with life, and the water coming down on me gave me a small sense of relief.

John didn't come back that day, and I spent the entire afternoon sitting in the kitchen expecting him. The anticipation of his return tortured me, and I had to find something to distract me, so I drew all day.

CHAPTER 22

It had been over a week and John still hadn't returned so I thought that maybe his condition had taken a turn for the worst. I was a bit afraid, but at the same time I was ready to face that next chapter in my life. Maybe if Margaret would testify to Immigration for me, they wouldn't throw me in jail and torture me. I started to imagine different scenarios of what would happen if John didn't come back. It scared me and excited me at the same time.

One afternoon, I decided that I was going to see Margaret and maybe make more waffles and drink some tea with her. I took a shower, wanting to make myself look decent for her. I cared about the way I presented myself to her, and I wanted to keep her liking me. What I failed to understand was that so far, she had accepted me in spite of my hesitation or what my clothes looked like. But my self-esteem was so low that I didn't think that anyone could really like me for me. I tried to think of conversation pieces that would make me sound more interesting to her. I read random books that I found in John's library, and I forced myself to learn a few new words, just to impress her.

I put on one of the dresses that I hadn't worn in a while, and

I noticed that I had gained a bit of weight by the way it clung more into my body. That surprised me because I didn't eat that much, and I had maintained the same weight since I was thirteen or so. I put on the dress, brushed my teeth and headed to Margaret's house. I knew the risk I was running, but the need to see her was so strong that day that it ached. I needed to see her, I craved love and attention. I spent the whole morning debating whether it was a good idea. And knew that there was a chance of getting caught by John. But I went anyway.

With each step, I felt better. I knocked once and she didn't respond. I got scared, what if she wasn't there. I couldn't handle the thought. I knocked a second time and waited a few minutes, she didn't respond. Her car was there, and the kitchen light was on. Of course, negative thoughts started to cross my mind.

Maybe she is tired of me, or she just doesn't want to see me, I wondered and started to walk away.

I was hurting inside, and convinced myself that it was true that I wasn't worthy of love. Even Margaret, who had been so nice to me, finally decided to reject me. It took that one time of her not answering for me to forget about the million times she came knocking at my door. She had shown me that she cared, so why was I so quick to jump to the conclusion that she had rejected me? I cried on my way back to the house. I was sad and more than ever felt very alone.

A couple of hours passed, and I was polluting my mind with a lot of negative thoughts. I was angry at Margaret for making me like her and rejecting me so abruptly. I started to think that I was just worthless and wished that John would just kill me and take me out of this cruel world. Life had completely changed me. I no longer thought highly of myself, and my self-esteem was non-existent.

As a child, I remembered that my father used to tell my mother that they never had to worry about me being bullied by anyone. I stood up for myself and spoke my mind, always. My thoughts were becoming toxic, every thought that crossed my mind was negative. I thought about death, hatred and the future seemed so obscure. I had lost all faith in people, humanity, and God. I believed in nothing and stood for nothing.

In the sixteen years that I lived in Lusa, only one person I knew had killed themselves. His name was Omba and he had a fraternal twin. Their father was the town's electrician, and he only had the two sons. His wife had died during childbirth. He raised the twins by himself. But by the time Omba reached twelve, his behavior started to change. He acted strange most of the time. Sometimes he would go days starving himself. He would also attack his father and brother with a machete in the middle of the night.

People advised his father to send him to a mental asylum, but the father refused. "I am his father and he is my responsibility. I will take care of my son until the day I am buried and six feet under."

Mental diseases were never discussed openly and oftentimes people were embarrassed to seek help for them. But Omba would terrorize the entire neighborhood, and people became afraid of him. One day while they were asleep, Omba took a machete and decapitated his twin brother. Their father found him in the morning sitting next to his brother's headless body crying.

"Look what I did, Father. I didn't do it on purpose," he cried to his father.

It was a school day and the town was in uproar. "We told you he would hurt someone. Now he killed his own brother."

Everyone had something to say and the father sat silently in front of his house for two days. Some of the men took care of buying a coffin and organized the burial. Omba didn't attend his twin's funeral, and no one wanted to force him to. The day they buried his brother, the father came home and found Omba hanging from the kitchen ceiling. He had hung himself. This man had lost two sons in a matter of three days and both very tragically. He never recovered, and his son remained the only person in Lusa to have committed suicide.

That had happened when I was nine years old, and I was surprised that it crossed my mind so suddenly. Living with John brought back memories from my childhood, good and bad. I was living in isolation, and I had nothing but my mind to entertain me. I thought about my life, all seventeen years that I had lived.

In my reverie, I heard a car and Margaret's voice. I ran to the window to check and saw that someone was dropping her off. She must have left at some point during the day and left the kitchen light on. Margaret was not home when I went knocking. She was not ignoring me and hadn't rejected me. I drove myself crazy for no reason.

I decided that I wasn't going to bother her that day and took off the dress and started to cook for myself. I wasn't sure whether or not John was going to come back, and I decided that it wasn't worth cooking for him. I made an omelet and ate it with bread. By the end of the afternoon, I sat on the sofa and fell asleep. I had the same dream, my mother was asking me to cross a bridge and on the other side was Margaret, smiling.

I was startled the next day by a dog that was barking loudly outside. I looked at the clock and it was 8am. I had slept for more than twelve hours and that was very unusual. What was happening to me? Was I getting sick? I was fatigued, was gaining weight and couldn't stand the smell of anything anymore. I was scared. I thought about asking Margaret to help me, but I was ashamed. Maybe she would discover that I caught a sexually transmitted disease and look down on me. My thoughts were so irrational and scattered that I didn't know what to do. Despair was a normal state of mind. I felt worthless, but stronger. I couldn't believe how much pain I was able to bear. I was living with pain every day and it hadn't destroyed me yet.

I took a shower and felt refreshed. I felt some of the emotional pain washed away with the water. I stood under the shower for almost an hour, and then I heard the door slam. I knew it was John, and I felt a knot in my stomach. He was back and my temporary vacation was once again interrupted. I got out of the shower and got dressed very quickly. He was standing in front of the bathroom door waiting for me. We stared at each other for a few seconds, and without a word he pushed me aside to go in. I stood there just to collect my thoughts, John had a way of making me feel completely unglued and worthless.

He left a bag full of medicine on the kitchen table. I hurried to warm up some leftovers, but he went to his bedroom and passed out. He slept for a few hours, and when he finally came to the kitchen he reached out for the pill and gave me one. He sat and ate his meal without saying a word or even making eye contact. That bothered me, for some reason. Was I craving his attention? I am not sure, but I hated it when he ignored me. Was something so broken inside of me that I wanted the attention of the man who tortured and raped me?

John seemed a bit frail, but strong enough to drive. He left and came back a couple of hours later with groceries. I noticed that he changed the nature of the things he usually bought. He bought green tea, more vegetables, organic lean meat, and more fruits. He wanted to eat healthier and drink less. He seemed so lost, and I felt sorry for him. I made him dinner that night, but as soon as he sat at the table he started to cough and blood came out. He sat there for a little while, almost like he was trying to collect himself. After half an hour, he got up, took his car key and left. I assumed he drove himself to the hospital.

It was almost 8pm. I wanted to go see Margaret. After seeing John's state, I knew he would probably spend the night at the hospital. So, I went to see Margaret. She was so happy to see me, as always, and she was just about to finish dinner. I wasn't hungry so I offered to help her clean up. I loved spending time with her, even if it meant standing by the sink cleaning the dishes. She was a flaming force in my life, and I think she knew it. We finished cleaning up and then sat in her living room to drink some tea and talk. We talked about her childhood and her marriage. She told me how much she loved being a mother and couldn't imagine life without her son. I listened to her. Margaret had this peacefulness about her, and I envied her. Her ways reminded me of my mother's, and I told her that.

"You never told me much about your family," she said. And I realized that we were about to enter dangerous territory. She saw the discomfort in my body language and changed the subject. "Listen, I understand if you are not ready to talk about your family. Do you want to watch something on TV?" But I just wanted to go home at that point, and she looked very disappointed.

The truth is that I wanted to talk about my family. I wanted someone to help me carry the heavy load that was poisoning my life. I needed to confide in someone, and Margaret was the perfect person. But I also knew that once I opened that Pandora box, I wouldn't be able to close it. And I wasn't sure that I was ready to take that chance. That night I left Margaret's house with a wave of feelings and thoughts. I began to contemplate the idea of telling Margaret or just taking the chance of running away. What if Immigration arrested me? It couldn't be worse than what I was enduring at John's house. I knew what John was capable of, and I was afraid to push him.

I got inside the house and sat on the couch until I felt weary enough to sleep. Thoughts were racing through my head, so instead I tossed and turned for hours. I was afraid of staying with John, as much as I was afraid to leave. I wasn't sure that I wanted

Margaret to get involved at all. I was afraid she would stop talking to me once she learned my life story. *What if I turned myself in? Would they even believe me? What would John do to vindicate himself? How long was I going to be able to handle living in those conditions?* I had so many questions and no answers at all. My mind turned into a labyrinth, and I didn't know my way out. I was a prisoner in my life and my own mind. The world out there seemed so foreign and far away, and I thought maybe I had to accept my life. Maybe being miserable and living with John was my destiny and I had to just accept it. I didn't know my rights.

That night I had the same dream. My mother was holding my hand while we were crossing a bridge, and on the other side Margaret was waiting for me. The moment I held Margaret's hand my mother disappeared. I woke up in the middle of the night, feeling restless and wondering once more what the dream meant. Was I going to see my mother again? Was Margaret supposed to play a role in my future? I wasn't sure and the uncertainty of it all was more than I could bear sometimes.

CHAPTER 23

"Instead of complaining about a situation, fix it." My father used to tell us that quote every time we complained about something. My parents had no tolerance for whiners. We could only complain about something a couple of times, then it wasn't allowed at all. They taught us that life wasn't fair and crying couldn't change that. One always has the strength to change uncomfortable situations.

How was I supposed to change my situation with John? I wasn't sure and the more I wondered about it, the more I was afraid and confused. I didn't know who to turn to and what to do.

John didn't come back that night, and when I woke up that morning, I was just hoping he would stay at the hospital at least for a week. I was growing weary of him and the depression taking over my life. I knew that if I didn't find the courage to get out of John's house, at least I would have to be brave enough to talk to Margaret.

I waited until late afternoon to go to Margaret's house. I heard a lot of noise before I knocked and wondered if she had company. She opened the door with a welcoming smile. "Grace!

I was just talking about you. Come on in," she said with so much enthusiasm.

She had company, and I immediately regretted my decision to stop by. I hadn't the courage to face other people, Margaret was more than I could handle. Yet, I took a deep breath and walked in. My body tensed up, she sensed it and squeezed my hand. I felt a little better.

There were three people sitting in her living room; her lady friend that I had seen before, a tall blond guy, and another short and good-looking black man.

"Grace, this is my friend Felicia. My son, Sebastian and Felicia's son, Joseph." They were all looking at me with surprise and compassion. I could tell that Margaret had told them about me. Felicia stood up and came closer to me.

"Can I give you a hug?" she asked, and I nodded.

She gave me a long hug and I felt her warmth. She smelled of cocoa butter, and I took in the aroma. It reminded me of some church ladies from back home. Sebastian and Joseph were young, not that much older than me, and it felt good to see young people again.

"So Grace, Margaret and I have been friends for twenty-five years. Her husband used to work with my late husband at the post office. The first time we met, we got into an argument over a pasta dish. We were supposed to organize a potluck to raise some money for our husband's friend. During the meeting, she wanted to make tomato sauce pasta and I wanted pesto sauce. We went back and forth for ten minutes, but at some point, we both looked at each other and started laughing. We realized how petty our fight was. The goal was to raise money and we almost tainted a good cause for a power struggle. From that day on we became inseparable, even our children are best friends." Sebastian and Joseph had an agreeing look.

"That's nice," is all I could say.

The conversation went on for an hour, and they were reminiscing about the past. Everyone was making conversation around the table. Felicia talked to me most of the time.

I sat there just listening to them and envied the fact that they had witnesses to their lives. They had the luxury of spending time with people they had known for a long time, and I could feel the love and the familiarity between them. They finished each other's stories and even remembered the bad times. I was a stranger in a strange land.

I wondered if I would ever have a chance to have my witnesses in my life. My family, my childhood friends, the neighbors, my teacher, and anybody who had been part of my life since I was a child. Was I ever going to be able to share memories with anyone? The thought that my life history could have disappeared filled me with.

"Grace, are you okay?" Margaret asked.

I felt embarrassed and got up to go to the bathroom. Margaret followed me and waited outside until I finished washing my face. I felt bad that I was bringing my darkness to a joyous moment between Margaret and her friends.

"I am sorry. I just have been very emotional lately, maybe it's just fatigue." I gathered the courage to tell her.

"Oh, don't apologize, my sweet Grace. We all have those unexplainable moments, and we should be the ones apologizing for going on and on about our lives and not including you." She always had a way to put a positive spin on things. Margaret was unable to be negative and I admired that about her. She led me into the kitchen with her. "Listen, if this is too much for you, you and I could just hang out here in the kitchen without them," she said while holding my face

I shook my head and replied, "Could I just hang out in your backyard for a moment? I just need a few minutes and I'll be fine."

I sat right outside the kitchen in the backyard. It was my first time in that part of the house, and it was beautiful. Margaret had vegetables growing in the backyard and everything looked organized and fresh. I was taking it all in until Sebastian interrupted my daydreaming.

"I used to come out here almost every day. It's peaceful, isn't it?" he asked.

I nodded. I just glanced at him once and couldn't look at him again. I was too embarrassed to make eye contact, and I just wasn't used to interacting with people anymore. We stayed silent for a while, and then he took a seat next to me.

"My parents had a tumultuous relationship. Whenever they got into an argument, I came out here instead of hiding in my room. I would just put some music on and pretend that I was in another world."

I was shocked to hear that Margaret used to argue with her husband, or with anyone for that matter. She seemed so angelic to me and the pictures that she had with her husband, they seemed so in love.

"They loved each other very much, but their personalities clashed a lot. I used to pray that they would divorce, but they never did," he said. I looked at him for a few seconds, a bit perplexed as to why he was sharing his story with me. "Well, my father died of a brain tumor when I was thirteen."

I didn't understand why Sebastian was sharing his life story with me. Why did he feel the need to tell me about the ugly side of his childhood? Back home, people worried more about keeping their dirty laundry to themselves. We were more comfortable airing other people's businesses through gossip. Couples pretended to be happy at home, children didn't talk to their friends about what was going on under their own roofs, and we all pretended that our homelives were perfect. But I noticed with Margaret and now Sebastian, that they carried their life story with them and were not afraid to share it. Does someone's childhood memory become their identity? I wasn't comfortable telling Sebastian my story, so I just listened.

"You are probably wondering why I am telling you all this, hein?" I nodded yes. "Well, I just have a feeling that you are going through a lot, and I want you to know that we all have baggage and struggles. It's okay to tell someone or seek help." He squeezed my hand, stood up and walked back into the house.

Margaret had been telling her son and friend about me. Maybe she hoped that it would be easier for me to talk to Sebastian since he was almost my age, or he took the initiative himself to want to help me. I stood up and went inside the kitchen, both Sebastian and Joseph were standing by the island looking into a laptop screen. Joseph looked up and smiled. I smiled back; he was handsome.

Before I walked out of the kitchen he said, "I hope that Sebastian didn't give you a lecture outside."

Sebastian pushed him with his elbow.

I responded shyly. "No, he didn't."

"Good. Let me know if he ever does. He is a psychology major in college, and he loves analyzing people. Don't let him."

We all laughed. They made me feel safe. Their aura was very light and positive. I walked out and could sense their eyes on my back. Or maybe it was just me being self-conscious.

I went into the living room to tell Margaret that I had to go. Both she and Felicia hugged me and made me promise to stop by again. Felicia walked me to the door. "I am taking some time off of work and will be spending more time here with Margaret, you should definitely come by and we could cook and do girly activities together, okay?"

I nodded. After I left, I walked to John's house with a smile on my face. I had cried and smiled so much in the last ninety minutes. The time that I spent at Margaret's house that night made me sad and happy at the same time. I felt a little hopeful again, and realized that although not perfect, there were still a lot of people in the world that were genuinely good. Margaret and her friends had given me the attention that I had been craving for a very long time, and I realized that she was my guardian angel.

CHAPTER 24

John spent a week at the hospital, and I returned to Margaret's house once more. I spent a few hours with her and Felicia, really enjoying my time. They didn't ask me any personal questions, and just let me be one of them. We cooked and talked. We laughed about everything and nothing. I stayed late at Margaret's house and wasn't really afraid to get caught.

The very next day, John came home in the morning. I was in the kitchen when he walked in, and I just took a quick look at him. I felt a wave of compassion take over me. I went back to making breakfast, but I felt a pinch in my stomach. John was sick and as much as I hated him, I also wanted to help him somehow. He walked past the kitchen into the bedroom and locked himself in until late afternoon. He called me several times to help him get up and use the restroom. He asked for soup and a beer. He wanted me to help him change his sweatpants. He needed help with his meds. The commands kept coming. Still, I felt sorry for him.

By the end of the day, he was too tired and fell back asleep and I was able to relax a bit. I was hungry like I had never been before and was craving mangoes.

I hadn't had mangoes since that week that we were hiding behind the church afraid of the rebels. Since living with John, the taste and smell of mangoes reminded me of a horrible time in my life. The few times that John had brought mangoes home, I couldn't even look at them. I associated them with death and hardship. But for some strange reason, that night I wanted mangoes more than anything and there was no way for me to get them. I made myself a sandwich, but the craving of mangoes would not go away. They had taken over me, literally.

It was almost 7pm, and I went into John's room to check what he was doing, and he was fast asleep. He looked dead. Thoughts started brewing in my head, and I considered leaving the house to go look for mangoes. I knew they were in season because I saw a few of them at Margaret's house, but she wasn't home that day and I had to get me some mangoes. I went into the kitchen to think about my plan. After fifteen minutes, I decided to take a chance and go to the market. I didn't know exactly where the market was, but I had heard Margaret mention that we had one not too far. I decided to take my chances. John usually left spare change all over the house or in his pants pockets. I collected almost four dollars. I put on my shoes and left the house.

As soon as I got outside, Sebastian was pulling into their driveway. I was hoping that he wouldn't see me, but he did and called my name. I ignored him at first, but he insisted and ran after me.

"Grace!" he almost shouted.

I turned around, trying to look a bit surprised.

"Are you so deep into your thoughts that you couldn't hear me?" he said, out of breath.

"Oh sorry, I wasn't paying attention."

"No problem, we all have those off days. Where are you headed to? Maybe I could give you a lift."

Not only was I running the risk of being outside the house while John was home, but here I was talking to a man. The thought of getting caught crossed my mind and sent a chill down my spine. John would literally kill me, but he was asleep, and I was craving mangoes. So, I agreed to a ride.

"My mother seems to have a lot of affection for you. She talks about you often, and now I can see why."

He was talking very slowly, and I appreciated it. Even though I had learned English, I still had a hard time when someone spoke fast. I looked at him and smiled.

"You seem very nice and relaxed; it also doesn't hurt that you are very pretty."

I felt very embarrassed when he called me pretty. I didn't consider myself pretty anymore. Over time, I looked in the mirror and I saw a sad face and I felt dirty inside. I took his compliment with a grain of salt.

Why did Sebastian feel the need to flatter me? Why was he being so nice? Did his mother put him up to it? Did he want to have sex with me too? I stayed very quiet.

He must have sensed my unease and apologized. "I am sorry. I didn't mean to make you uncomfortable. I meant what I said, but I can see why that's a bit odd. After all, I am still a stranger to you."

I didn't say anything, and we stayed quiet. When we got to the market, he went inside and got me the mangoes and paid for them. I waited in the car and tried my best to think positively. He came back in the car and handed me the mangoes. He looked at me and smiled. I didn't get that same feeling that I got when I first met John. My intuition made me feel at ease with Sebastian, so I smiled back. He told me about his goals for once he graduated college, and why he was spending more time in Bakersfield. He decided to intern for a non-profit organization that took care of victims of domestic abuse and sex slaves.

He and Joseph were trying to open a similar non-profit in San Diego, and he was learning the ropes. I asked him where the interest came from and he told me that his current girlfriend was brought to America by a sex trafficker from Thailand.

"I fell in love with her, but our relationship is a daily battle. She is very strong, but at the same time what she went through almost broke her. I know I want to marry her, and because of her I would fight to help other women in her case."

All I could say was, "She is lucky."

He responded, "No, I am the lucky one. Being with Shariya changed my life. She gave me a purpose."

I asked him to drop me off in his driveway instead of John's. I didn't want to run the risk of being found out. I walked quietly into the house and was relieved that John was still asleep. I went into the kitchen and devoured five mangoes in less than ten minutes. They were delicious and I felt so much better. I had to satisfy that craving before digesting what Sebastian had just told me in the car.

After eating the mangoes, I went out the back and got rid of the skin and any trace that there were mangoes in the house. I was afraid that John would smell or see anything.

That night, I replayed my conversation with Sebastian and realized that I was a victim of domestic abuse and sex trafficking. I wondered if Sebastian and Joseph could even help me. Did I stand a chance? Or would John tell a story and make them question me?

I felt like John was more powerful than me and I couldn't do anything about it. I couldn't involve other people in my twisted story and wasn't sure what the outcome would be. So I decided to just stay quiet and keep pretending that I was John's wife. In the past few days, I had done more than enough to jeopardize my life by going to Margaret's house and the market. I wasn't feeling like myself and didn't know what was happening.

I spent the night in the living room just reflecting on the past few days, and internally thanked Margaret for being such a positive influence in my life. I wasn't expecting anything from her, as long as she stayed there for me, as my friend.

CHAPTER 25

Five days had passed and John was still at home. He hadn't gone to work and was feeling a little better so he didn't need to go to the hospital. I endured the daily torture and stayed out of his way as much as I could. He spent a lot of his time in the bedroom and wasn't requesting me to have sex with him. Every time he called, I took a deep breath and hoped that he didn't have his pants down. I just didn't have the stomach to get close to him.

I cooked and cleaned while he was barking out orders. I was his slave and lived to obey him. Whether it was early in the morning or in the middle of the night, I had to be sure to be attentive to him. I was always prepared to obey his orders, and usually they were the same things: green tea, a beer, steak and fries, steak and rice or hard-boiled eggs. John was a simple man and yet very complex. I had been with him for a year and half and had never met his friends and family. The only visitors he had over were prostitutes and the gardeners stopped by once a month to mow the lawn.

His existence was very limited, and I felt sorry for him. *How could a man reach his fifties without a family? Why didn't he have friends? And where did his family go? He must have been born into a family, why wasn't he close to them?* My family meant the world to me, and I always knew that I wanted to get married one day and have children. The bond that I had with my siblings wasn't perfect, but it was the best thing about my life. We had a deep and inexplicable connection. I felt blessed to have been born into the family that I had. They created a world full of challenges, but the love was overwhelming. If given the choice, I would pick the same family and the longing that I had for them was like a dark cloud that followed me everywhere. I felt as if someone had dug a hole within me, and I had no way of filling it up.

I dreamt about my brothers and sisters often. I wondered if they were still alive, and hoped that I would see them again one day. My life felt empty without them, and the thought that I could spend the rest of my life without ever seeing them again, petrified me.

John slept for longer hours without bothering me. His sleep seemed deeper too. He would wake up in the morning to have breakfast and sleep until late afternoon for soup. Then he would go back to the bedroom and stay there until the next day. He didn't bother me as much, and his health seemed to be deteriorating every day. I spent my days in the kitchen wondering if he was going to die.

One late afternoon after I had served John his soup, I made sure that he was sound asleep and went over to Margaret's house. She was sitting there alone and was so happy to see me. As soon as I entered her house, she took me to the kitchen, and I could smell fresh mangoes.

"Sebastian told me that you are a big fan of mangoes," she said with a big smile on her face.

"Yes, I have been craving them a lot lately. Not sure why, maybe I miss home, or I am just going through a phase."

She had a basket full of them on her island and I felt good just looking at them. "Well, perfect I bought all those for you and was hoping you'd come over to take them. From now on, I'll remember to get you some when I go grocery shopping."

Margaret reminded me of my mother. She was just thoughtful with me, and I didn't know how I could ever repay her. I appreciated her love and affection for me. She gave me hope when I felt the most hopeless, and I thanked my lucky stars for her.

I spent an hour with Margaret and we watched TV together. I ate some mangoes and couldn't wait to get home and eat some more. I was too embarrassed to eat more than three in front of Margaret. I could sense that she wanted to ask me something, but maybe she was too afraid to make me uncomfortable. She glanced at me a few times and I could feel her inquisitive eyes on my side. Maybe she was just concerned about me, but I decided to leave before she asked me anything too personal about my situation with John.

"It was very nice spending some time with you, Grace. I am having dinner with the gang tomorrow, stop by if you can. Okay?" I nodded and walked out of her house without looking back. *What was it that Margaret wanted to ask me? Did Sebastian tell her that I was a victim of sexual abuse? Did he sense it?* I wasn't sure, but I felt a bit apprehensive about it. I didn't want to open that door. I didn't know what John was fully capable of and how much he could hurt all of us.

I got inside the house quietly, and all the lights were off. John was still asleep, and I was safe. The fact that I had the courage to walk out of the house while John was in the bedroom showed me that I had the courage to escape if I wanted to.

I thought about it, but my fear of the consequences scared me and paralyzed me. I didn't want to take a chance. I figured that if it was in the cards for me to escape John's house, it would happen somehow. I didn't think that I deserved to end up in John's house and be taken away from my home and family. The course of my life made me realize that sometimes life just happens.

Growing up, my siblings and I used to discuss predestination a lot. We believed in God and wondered if he had a plan for us already mapped out, that nothing we could have done would change that fact. I saw good things happen to bad people and bad things happen to good people.

Here I was sitting in John's kitchen wondering if my life was already planned for me. *What if I didn't really have a purpose? What if my life was supposed to end in John's house?* My thoughts overwhelmed me and made me feel very sad. I guess deep down, I wanted more. I wanted my life to mean more than just John's sex slave. He had taken so much from me, and there wasn't anything I could have done at that moment. My body and soul were both sick that night, and for the first time in a very long time, I wept.

CHAPTER 26

The next morning John woke up very early, I heard him knocking and kicking things around in the bedroom. I stayed in the kitchen after I made him his breakfast. I was feeling a bit sick in my stomach that day and drank some warm water to make myself feel better. I really was starting to worry about my health. Something wasn't right and I was afraid that I caught whatever John had.

He finally came into the kitchen, and I had never seen him look worse. He had dark bags under his eyes and was very pale. He looked like a ghost, and I could tell that he was not in a very good mood. He sat at the table and drank his green tea, clearly struggling with every movement. It took him a lot of strength to lift his cup to his mouth and his breathing was heavy. I stood in the corner and observed him from the corner of my eyes.

After struggling to drink his tea and have a half a cup of yogurt, he finally gathered the strength to stand up. I looked at him then turned around, too afraid to make eye contact. I didn't want him to give me the pill and was afraid that he would make a mean comment. He didn't, instead he took an overnight bag and left.

I felt relieved that he finally left the house after so many days in bed. I had hidden the mangoes that Margaret gave me and couldn't wait to eat them. I took them out of the pantry and slowly ate them one by one. I felt better with each bite. Mangoes were becoming a source of comfort for me, and I had to come up with a better strategy to get them and hide them from John.

After eating the mangoes, I went into the bedroom to look at what I would wear to go have dinner at Margaret's house. I felt unattractive and most of my clothes were tighter. I was gaining weight and the few pieces that I had were discolored from washing them so often. I wanted to feel pretty again, and I knew that as long as I lived with John, that wasn't an option. I wasn't vain but the sight of myself in the mirror depressed me. I wasn't sure what depressed me more, my spirit or my physical appearance. Or both at the same time.

My parents were very strict when it came to our appearance. Our uniforms were always clean and ironed for school. Our shoes were kept polished and shiny. They were always well-dressed from head to toe and took pride in the fact that their children represented them very well. My mother used to say, 'Being well dressed is not only good for the soul, but it's also important to present yourself well to get respect'. I understood what she said. People, unfortunately, judge you by what they see before they get to know the content of your character. The world is superficial and appearances matter.

I had nothing to work with. I didn't have much to fix my hair with, my worn-out clothes didn't fit right, and my face was covered with painful zits. I felt miserable inside and it showed on the outside. I wanted to see Margaret, but I didn't feel good about hanging out with them, especially Joseph, who I found so attractive. I was too afraid of their judgment, so I decided to stay home instead of having dinner at Margaret's.

I saw Joseph and Sebastian pull up in the afternoon, and a

few minutes later Felicia showed up. Margaret came out to meet them at the door, and they all looked very happy. I envied their freedom and their joy. I felt my sadness even more that day. I was spiraling downwards, and I couldn't save myself. Margaret glanced toward my window a few times, but I was hiding behind the shades. I didn't want her to see me.

I looked out the windows a few times to see if I could catch one of them in the kitchen. I heard their voices laughing and having a good time. I couldn't stand it, my heart wanted so badly to join them, but my emotions wouldn't allow me. I couldn't find the confidence nor enough self-love to be around them. I knew that if I felt that badly about myself, I could not expect them to look at me with love or at least respect. I hit rock bottom and for the second day in a row, I cried.

John didn't come home that night so I just made myself some soup and drank warm water. I had one mango left and devoured it in a few minutes. Like an animal, I paced back and forth in the living room. I was afraid to think too much and hurt myself. My thoughts were drowning me, and I needed to be able to control them. I sang, paced, jumped around and finally, I was too tired to do anything. On the sofa, I fell asleep. That night I had the same dream. My mother and I were crossing a bridge and Margaret was waiting for me on the other side. My mother was very quiet during our walk, and I was holding tight to her hand. When we got to the end of the bridge Margaret took my other hand and I let go of my mother without a struggle.

The urge to throw up woke me up in the middle of the night. I ran into the bathroom and everything I had eaten earlier came out. I felt dizzy and wanted to get out of my body. I felt disgusted by my own body, so I took a shower. John didn't come back at all, and I took my time in the shower. I let the water wash over me, and Joseph crossed my mind. He was so handsome and calm; I was developing a crush on him. The thought of him made me smile. I knew deep down that I didn't have a chance, but I needed the fantasy to survive. So, I let the thought linger and relax me.

When John was home, he took sleeping pills with a beer and slept for hours on end. I felt a sense of freedom and felt more comfortable sneaking out to go to Margaret. I didn't have to be afraid of getting caught.

I spent more time with Margaret and Felicia, and they taught me how to knit and cook. We talked about life, love, the world, and family. I listened to them for the most part and for every question they asked, I had short and sweet answers. I felt a little better and connected to the world. I felt a pulse coming back to me, because I had more contact with the outside world. Sebastian and Joseph spent more time at Margaret's house, and I envied their intelligence and drive. Although they weren't that much older than me, they seemed so sure of what they wanted out of life. My biggest aspiration at the time was to get out of John's house. My misery was my biggest concern. I was like an animal stuck in the cage and couldn't afford the luxury of dreams and aspirations.

My crush on Joseph was getting deeper. I just admired him, he was very intelligent and a gentleman. He had a gentle way of interacting with his mother and that made him even more attractive. He had a passion about life and devoted a lot of time researching and helping victims of domestic abuse. I listened to him talk about it to his mother and Margaret and watched him and Sebastian come up with their plan to expand their non-profit organization. I wanted to be part of it, but I was too shy to ask them. I didn't think that anything I had to say mattered and I questioned my ability to contribute to society. Even though I was feeling a little better for spending more time with Margaret, I still felt very dirty and ashamed of my life. John took away all sense of humanity and dignity. When I looked in the mirror, I saw ugliness and nothing else.

I fantasized about Joseph, and secretly hoped that he noticed me too. I wanted to look decent every time I went to Margaret's house, just in case he showed up. The irony is that I was gaining weight, my skin was breaking out and I just didn't feel good overall. So whenever we sat in the living room together, I sat quietly in the corner, and just listened to their amazing conversations. I was too afraid to open my mouth for fear of being perceived as stupid. First my English wasn't so good, and second, I didn't know much about the non-profit world. I sat quietly, hoping that no one would ask my opinion for anything. I was the one who offered to refill the teacups, wanting to be invisible.

"Grace, you don't have to clean up after us. I'll do it before I go to bed," Margaret said.

She felt bad that I helped her in the kitchen. She insisted that I just relax and act like a guest. What she didn't understand was that I took pleasure in helping her. I loved feeling like I was contributing to something and being part of her clan. Cleaning and cooking with her was a treat for me. It reminded me of home when my mother let me help her in the kitchen. I used to delight in those moments, and they made me feel like an adult. Those moments also brought me closer to my mother and allowed me to talk to her one on one. They were the only times that I had her undivided attention and I cherished them. I think the moment Margaret understood that I enjoyed helping, she let me and made them our moments as well.

John's health was still deteriorating, and he spent less time at the hospital. His schedule was practically the same every day. He woke up very early in the morning to take his medication and have breakfast in bed. And then fell back asleep until early afternoon, when he asked for something to eat and a beer. As soon as he ate, he took a sleeping pill and watched TV until he passed out for the rest of the day. He didn't have the energy to have sex with me, nor to get out of his room and give me the contraceptive pill.

At least twice a week, I would sneak out and go spend a few hours with Margaret. Right after he took his pill and fell asleep, I left. I knew the risk that I was taking, and for almost two months I had gotten away with it. Until one day, as I was walking back from Margaret's house, I heard him coughing in the bathroom. That meant that he had woken up. I closed the main door behind me and walked into the kitchen. My heart rate went up, I felt sick in my stomach as I sat down at the kitchen table. I wondered if he looked for me. A million thoughts went through my head and my palms were sweaty. I felt nauseous and my head immediately started to ache. I don't know how much time passed but it felt like an eternity. I kept hearing him in the bathroom, and it sounded like he was throwing up and coughing violently.

I was afraid for my life, and for a moment I thought about running away. I wanted to go to Margaret's house and tell her everything in the hope that she will believe me and save me. I was literally holding my breath, and my mind was racing. *What would he do to me? What if he kills me? What if he calls the police and turns me in as an illegal immigrant?* My head was spinning. And then he stopped coughing and he got quiet in the bathroom. I waited and waited. I knew the moment that he came out of that door; my life could have possibly been over.

He finally came out of the bathroom and went back into the bedroom. I waited and then he called my real name with anger.

"Grace!"

I could feel my heartbeat and my ears were ringing. I gathered the courage to walk to the bedroom. I took a deep breath before I went in. I walked in and he wasn't even looking at me. I stood there for a few minutes, and then he looked my way.

"Where were you?" he asked with his usual spite.

"In the kitchen," I responded with fear in my voice. I just assumed that he knew that I was lying.

To my surprise, he looked away from me and simply said, "Bring me a beer". It took me a moment to register what had just happened. Didn't *John realize that I wasn't in the house when he woke up, or was he just torturing me with his mind tricks?* I couldn't tell. But I hurried to the kitchen and brought him his beer.

I went back into the kitchen and took a deep breath. I dodged a big bullet. That night could have turned out completely worse. I couldn't help but laugh at myself for blowing things out of proportion in my head. I really imagined the worst and nothing happened. But just to be safe, I didn't go to Margaret for a week.

After she didn't see me for a week, Margaret came knocking at the door. She knew I was in because she saw me through the kitchen window. She knocked very gently, almost like she was avoiding getting me in trouble. She waited a few minutes after the knock and went back to her house. John was sound asleep, but I was still afraid that the knock woke him up. After a few minutes, I went into his bedroom just to check that he didn't hear anything. I heard him snoring through the door.

I missed going to Margaret's house and hanging out with my friends. I missed Joseph especially. I wondered what he was up to, and how far he had gone with his project. I missed his face, his voice, and his scent. I just longed for him, and he lived permanently in my thoughts. I thought about him randomly during the day, and he brought a smile to my face. I wondered if he knew. If he had noticed the impression he had on me. *Did he sense that I was attracted to him?* I hoped he did, but at the same time I felt like I didn't deserve him at all.

After two weeks, I went back to Margaret's house, and she was cooking by herself. She was so happy to finally see me and held me in her arms for a moment when I walked into her house. It felt good, I had missed her too. But I was also a bit disappointed that Felicia wasn't there because it meant that Joseph wouldn't most likely show up. Margaret and I went into the kitchen where she was making roasted chicken.

"It's a lot of food. Sebastian is bringing his girlfriend Shariya tonight for dinner, and Joseph might also show up with this girl that he is seeing," Margaret said that so innocently, but my heart sank.

Joseph was seeing someone, and I was going to meet her. My fragile self-esteem couldn't handle it. I kept helping Margaret peel the potatoes, but my mind was elsewhere. I actually got teary-eyed but pretended that it was nothing.

"Grace," I finally heard Margaret call my name from the other side of the kitchen. I looked up, and she looked worried. "You seem a bit off today. Is everything alright?"

I nodded. She came closer to me and stood right in front of me. "I have been meaning to ask you, but you are not looking very good physically, something is different. Are you sure you are fine?"

I nodded again and went back to peeling the potatoes. I wanted her to stop asking. I had noticed that my appearance was changing, and I wasn't ready to find out what it was. There was a chance that I had caught whatever John had, and I was too afraid to face it. She just stroked my hair and walked away.

Of course, I went home early that night. Margaret gave me some mangoes that Sebastian had bought for me. My craving for them had diminished, but I still was happy that she gave them to me. I didn't want to see the girl that Joseph was dating, and I was also preoccupied by what Margaret had said about my appearance. I was feeling sick almost every day, and barely could eat anything. I was afraid to tell Margaret that I had possibly contracted an STD through John.

I got home that night and sat in the kitchen for hours just staring at the walls. I was very afraid and hurt. It's not like I thought that I stood a chance with Joseph, but I just felt hurt. It was just another disappointment in my life. My life was becoming a series of unfortunate events, and each blow made me feel smaller and smaller. Was I ever going to feel normal again? Was my family alive? I wondered about God, life and my future. What was the purpose of all the pain I was feeling? I wept all night.

John's cough woke me up early in the morning. He was coughing violently. After fifteen minutes, he called my name, and I ran to his room. I wanted to help him. His face was abnormally red, and he looked very frail. And the stench in the room was unbearable. He smelt like sweat, vile body odor, alcohol, medication, and humidity. I felt nauseous, and I held my breath.

"Bring me some tea, right away," he commanded.

I just left the room as fast as I could to breathe. Before I went into the kitchen I ran to the bathroom to vomit.

I made him his tea and an omelet just in case he wanted to eat. I brought them to him in the room, and when I put the omelet by his nightstand, he took it and threw it at me.

"Who asked you for an omelet!" he screamed at me with such anger that I felt it in my core.

John hated me, and I wasn't sure why. I had more reasons to hate him and yet I felt a pinch of compassion for him. He was suffering. I quietly picked up the omelet and the plate from the floor and left the room.

I was hungry, it felt like I had a pit in my stomach, but I couldn't bear the smell of food so I ate a few mangoes and took a nap. I was tired all the time and could not explain the tornado within me. I was angry, emotional and sad, depressed and helpless. I was in a very dark place and lost all hope. My future was so somber and I thought to myself that if death came knocking at my door, I wouldn't mind. There was no point in my being alive. I was just carrying so much pain and darkness with me.

CHAPTER 27

"Without challenges and obstacles, we wouldn't need God and turn to him," my mother would say. "You are a warrior in this life, and I don't know an interesting person in this world who hasn't gone through some serious tribulations. Pain is what makes you grow and get out of your comfort zone. It makes you seek answers and pushes you to make decisions. Complacency is dangerous."

My mother had a lot of faith in God and life. She believed that things always panned out the way they were supposed to. As humans, the best we could do is love hard and work hard and life would just unfold the way it is supposed to, when it is supposed to.

I wanted to believe. I longed for something bigger than me, and ached for her wisdom. But something inside of me was dead and I was too afraid to reach out to God. The line of communication between me and him was broken. Or so I thought. I had lost my faith completely, but deep down I hoped for a sign or a miracle. Somewhere within me, there was silent prayer that I didn't admit to myself. There was a tiny spark that was waiting to be ignited, but I was too afraid to have hope. I was afraid that disappointment would break me for good. I chose despair because it had become a familiar place. Pain was my home.

Two days had gone by and I hadn't returned to Margaret's house. I stayed in the house, while John spent most of his days asleep. He woke up to bark orders at me, and then went back to sleep. That morning, he woke up and took a bath.

His first one in a long time, I was afraid that he was strong enough to ask me for sex. The thought made me cringe. I heard his every move he made in the bathroom, and it sounded like he was moving in slow motion and slamming everything. He was in there forever, and it got quiet at some point. I thought he had died there. I waited in the living room just in case he called my name.

He finally opened the bathroom door and screamed my name. He startled me. I took a deep breath and braced myself as I walked to him. There was water everywhere, on the floor, the mirror, the door and there were at least three towels soaking wet. He was sitting on the toilet naked, and I stood by the door afraid of what he was going to ask me to do. His penis was erect, and I knew that my fear had come true. I was afraid that he would ask me to have sex with him.

"Come here and get down on your knees," he said.

I felt as if someone had punched me in my gut. I couldn't. I didn't want to. So many things were wrong at that moment, starting with the water and the mess in the bathroom, his physical state, the smell, the tone of his voice and the fact that I hadn't been feeling well.

I found the courage to say, "I can't?"

I saw the rage in his face. "What do you mean you can't?'

I tried to maintain my composure, and hoped that maybe the desperation in my voice would inspire him to have mercy. "I am not feeling well today. Please," I pleaded.

His breath got deeper and faster. He was enraged. John held on to the sink and got up. My heart was beating fast because I knew that he was capable of anything at that point. I thought about running, but realized that it would be in vain. Everything happened really fast. He lunged at me and grabbed me by the neck, to submit me to my knees. He stood there, under the door threshold leaning on the wall and forced himself into my mouth. He forced the stroke and with every push and pull, I felt sicker and sicker. I couldn't hold it in anymore and threw up on him. He pulled me by my hair, slapped me, pushed me outside the bathroom and slammed the door. I sat on the floor in my own vomit with tears and disgust. He was cursing behind the door and I wanted to go in there and hurt him. I wanted to disappear.

I really couldn't pick myself up from the floor. A few minutes later, John came out of the restroom, and yelled, "Clean it up, now!"

I couldn't look at him. I felt an insurmountable amount of hatred for him, and I was afraid of what I could do to him.

He went into the bedroom, and I managed to get up. I spent an hour cleaning the bathroom then heard him leave the house. I was a little relieved that he was going out. I wanted to be alone in the house and pull myself together. My thoughts and emotions were all over the place, I felt completely unglued and I needed to take a moment to calm down. After finishing up with the bathroom, I went into the living room and cried. I was broken and I desperately wanted someone to hold me. I decided to go to Margaret's house.

I knocked a few times and no one answered. As I was walking away, Joseph opened the door.

"Grace!"

His voice made me feel a little better. I looked back and he had the biggest smile on his face. I needed that. I wanted to run to him and hold him. I needed him. So I walked towards him, and I hugged him. I couldn't control myself. My spirit needed that hug. I felt like I was on the brink of falling apart and embracing him was going to put me together. He didn't resist and held me in his arms for a few minutes. We stood there quietly. He waited for me to let go, and he reluctantly let go as well.

"Are you alright? What's wrong, Grace?"

All I could say was, "I am okay."

He held my hand and we walked into the kitchen. I sat down while he went to get me some water.

"Margaret is taking a shower. We have been getting rid of the weeds in her backyard."

He was trying to make conversation to relax the tension, and I appreciated the attempt. He handed me the water and sat next to me.

"Do you want to talk about it?"

I shook my head. I didn't know where to start. I couldn't explain the pain I was feeling and I knew he wouldn't be able to understand.

"Okay. I am here. We have all the time in the world. I am not leaving you alone until you tell me what is making you so sad."

I looked down at my glass of water. I was quiet, gathering my thoughts. *What was I going to tell him? Could I tell him the truth? What would happen?* I just needed to think before I opened up. He sat there looking at me, patiently.

"I miss my mother." That's what I came up with.

"Where is she?" he asked with concern.

"She is back home in the Congo. And I have not seen her for a while. I just miss her a lot."

"When was the last time you talked to her?"

How was I going to answer that one? "Well, two months ago or so. Long-distance phone calls are expensive, but I'll call her soon."

I could tell that he wanted to hug me again, but he kept his distance. He looked at me with respect. Like he didn't want to overstep his boundaries, and I wish he did.

"I understand. I am very close to my mother and we talk every day. Sometimes even more than once, and I couldn't imagine going for two months without her."

I looked up, and for the first time I really saw his face up close. There was this gentleness about him that I found very comforting. He was also very charming and he exuded a lot of confidence. I smiled and he smiled back.

I said, "Thank you."

He just squeezed my hand. "So Grace, what do you do when you feel sad?" he asked.

"What do you mean?" I didn't really understand his question.

"What do you do when you are sad? Do you pray, meditate, kick something, talk to a priest or a therapist?"

That's a lot of options, I thought to myself. *Americans had too many options and outlets for everything. Good or bad.*

"I do nothing when I am sad. I stare at the wall, or just wait until it passes," I said.

He looked at me perplexed. "How is that working for you?" he said with a smirk, and continued. "I meditate and see a therapist," he added.

"I don't believe in meditation," I said. I waited for his reaction, but he said nothing for a while.

"I see. You must find something that works for you? What brings you joy?"

"I am not sure. Drawing and reading. I don't know."

His look was so gentle. "I can help you figure it out. Maybe recommend you to a therapist, or even a priest or pastor."

I wasn't sure how to answer. "I don't know. Life, circumstances, I am not sure about anything anymore. I am not sure they can help me."

"You don't have to figure it out now. Think about it and let me know next time I see you. Ok?"

I nodded. He was offering help without being forceful or preachy.

"You know what? I study psychology. So, if you ever want to talk, I am here," he said as Margaret walked into the kitchen.

She smelled of soap and shampoo, and her hair was wet. I was disappointed that she was interrupting my conversation with Joseph. I was enjoying the time with him, and I didn't want it to stop. Margaret noticed that we were in the middle of something.

"Grace! When did you get here?" she asked with a smile on her face.

"Not too long ago."

"Well, it's good to see you. I'll let Joseph entertain you while I go make a phone call. Joseph, why don't you make her some tea? I'll be back in a bit." She left the kitchen, and I was glad she did.

Joseph and I talked for over an hour. He told me about his passion for his organization and psychology. He talked about his parents, and a little bit of his childhood. I realized that he was very fond of Sebastian. I just listened and smiled a lot. I wanted time to suspend itself. I wanted that moment to last forever. But when I looked at the clock, it was almost 7pm and I had to run. I told Joseph that I had to go make dinner. He understood, and gave me a kiss on the chick. I liked it.

I literally sprinted home, but John's car wasn't there. I let out a big sigh. I was taking a big risk by going to Margaret's house, but I couldn't help myself.

John didn't come back for five days and I didn't dare go out of the house. It was easier for me to venture out while he was asleep in his bedroom than when he was out of the house. I stayed in, itching to go to Margaret's house and see Joseph. I also was craving mangoes. Sebastian had gotten into the habit of buying mangoes and leaving them at his mother's house. He wanted me to have them.

Everyone that surrounded Margaret was kind. She attracted peace and love. She truly reminded me of my mother. And since I had been spending more time at her place, I no longer had the dream about crossing the bridge. But my mother showed up randomly in my dreams, and most of the time she was quiet. I wasn't sure what that meant, but I am glad that at least I saw her in my dreams. I also noticed that I spent less time daydreaming and thought more about conversations that I had with Margaret, Felicia, Sebastian, or Joseph.

The day John came back, I was half asleep on the couch. He startled me when he opened the front door. I was not expecting him, and I was so tired that I didn't hear the car pull in. He didn't say anything and went straight to the bedroom. I was afraid of him. Every time I was around him, I felt vulnerable and helpless. I couldn't really understand how another human being could make me feel that way. He had total power over me, and I couldn't save myself. I truly was in a prison, a cage, a place I didn't know how to escape from.

I went into the kitchen and waited for him to call me. He didn't. He went into the bedroom and slept until the morning. I slept on the couch, and that night for the first time in a very long time, I had the dream on the bridge with my mother and Margaret. I heard John moaning in the room, but I didn't want to go in there. I learned long ago not to offer him help unless he asked. I went in to take a quick shower and waited in the kitchen until the moaning stopped. He was quiet for a while. I was just hoping that he would wake up and have a beer with his sleeping pills because I wanted to see Margaret.

John woke up in the afternoon, and he asked for a steak. I cooked as fast as I could and served him it with a beer, making sure to set his sleeping pills in his nightstand. I waited for a couple of hours, until it was quiet. I peeped into the bedroom and heard him snore. I noticed that the pill container was opened and the beer bottle was empty. I was happy to finally have a little bit of freedom to go see Margaret.

Margaret was hanging out with Felicia in her backyard. They had cookies and lemonade. I was so happy to see them and felt very welcomed.

Felicia seemed particularly happy to see me. She smiled as she hugged me so tightly.

"How have you been, pretty girl? I have not seen you in a while?"

"I am alright. How are you?" I wanted to redirect the conversation toward her.

"I am good. Thanks for asking. Margaret is telling me that you were not feeling well the other day."

"Oh, I was just tired, but I am better now." *So, they talk about me. What else did Margaret tell her?* I wondered.

"You know I have a hot comb in my purse. I always carry it with me. I could press your hair if you'd like."

Margaret interrupted. "Why do you care about what her hair looks like?"

Felicia laughed. "I do care, why not? It's just that it looks like she doesn't know what to do with it. I am good with hair, so why not?" She looked at me to get a reaction.

"Thank you, but I'd rather just keep it this way." I wanted her to stop.

"Why? Are you afraid that your husband will say something? He is your husband, right?" she pressed on the issue. She wanted to understand my situation.

I just nodded. I hated lying, but I couldn't tell them the truth. I was ashamed of my life, so I wanted to keep quiet. There was nothing about me or my life that I wanted to share with anybody. I wanted them to keep liking me, so the less they knew the better. I thought about making up an elaborate story about myself, but I knew that they wouldn't believe it. I thought about telling them that I was from a good family in the Congo, and that John took me in as an exchange student. I wanted to pretend that I was happy to be there, and spoke to my family regularly. I also thought about telling them that John was my dad's friend and he took me in for a while until I figured out what I wanted to do in college.

But the truth is that I wasn't even eighteen yet, and John was not my husband, not a host or my father's friend. He was a predator who abducted me from the Congo and used me as a sex slave. I was nameless and my story didn't matter unless John released me. My only identity was 'John's possession' and nothing else. I knew that they were not ready to hear the truth. I didn't know how to tell them because I was too afraid of the consequences.

Margaret changed the subject. "Grace, do you want to help me make dinner? The boys are stopping by tonight."

I nodded. I wanted to get up and do something.

As I followed Margaret in the kitchen, Felicia grabbed my hand and said, "I am sorry, Grace. I didn't mean to make you uncomfortable. Okay?"

"I know. Thank you for caring." I meant it.

I loved that she cared enough to want to fix my hair, but I could not change a thing with my appearance because John would notice and probably beat me to death. I didn't want him to find out that I was hanging out with anybody, let alone people who wanted to give me a makeover. My hair had to stay the same not to raise suspicion.

I sat in the kitchen with Margaret and helped her cut the onions and tomatoes. We were very much in sync when we cooked together. She got the salmon seasoned and I made the salad. I cleaned the pots we used, and she wiped them and arranged them back in her cabinets.

For the most part we didn't talk about anything in particular.

Sometimes she hummed a beautiful melody and I listened. Felicia stayed in the backyard and only came in the kitchen for a few minutes to grab ice.

By the time we finished cooking, Sebastian and his girlfriend came in. I finally got to meet her; she was very pretty and very petite. They walked hand in hand, and I could tell that they were very much in love. I watched them hug Margaret and make small talk while I was cleaning the island. I just enjoyed watching the interactions between them.

And then Sebastian came towards me.

"Grace! Hi!" He gave me a kiss on the chick.

'Hi." I smiled. I was happy to see him.

"This is my girlfriend, Shariya. I told you about her."

"Hi, Grace. It's very nice to finally meet you. I heard a lot about you as well." She had a thick accent, and her voice was very pitchy. Which surprised me from such a petite woman, and she seemed a little older than Sebastian.

"It's nice to meet you," I said.

Felicia came into the kitchen and came straight to Sebastian. They hugged and kissed. They were making small talk about all and nothing, and I was wondering where Joseph was. I also wondered if he was going to bring his friend.

Margaret took me out of my thoughts. "Honey, do you want to help me set the table?"

"Sure," I quickly responded.

Margaret always made sure to include me and involve me. Sometimes, I would act like a spectator and watch them while they were talking and interacting. She would ask me a question or say something to include me. I didn't mind, but sometimes I wished that she would just let me be.

They stayed in the kitchen and I was setting the dining table in the living room when I heard a voice behind me; "Do you need help?" It was Joseph and he was all alone. I smiled.

"Sure," I answered with the biggest grin on my face. I was so happy to see him. His presence made me feel better. I had only known him for a little bit, but I was becoming very fond of him. He made me want to stay in the present and just savor it. I wanted to hold him in my arms, but I restrained myself.

I wondered why he was alone. Was his friend sick? Were they even together? But Felicia came out of the kitchen and interrupted the precious quiet moment.

"Baby, I didn't know you got here."

"Hey Mama." He called her mama and I thought that was so cute.

She gave him a kiss and stroked his head.

"I miss you, honey. You need a haircut."

Watching him acting like a child when she was around was very endearing. I missed having a mother to dote on me and look at me the way I saw Margaret and Felicia look at their sons. I missed calling my mother Mama, and my heart ached at the thought that I may never hear her voice again. My mother's love sustained me, and although I knew that we all would die eventually, never did I ever imagine that I would lose her.

We all sat down for dinner and I was praying that John didn't wake up and look for me. I wanted to stay and spend more time with my friends, but at the same time I was preoccupied by the thought that I could get in trouble. Joseph was going on about his day, and I sat across from him in awe of his intelligence. He was barely twenty-two years old, but he carried himself with so much maturity.

"I am planning on going to New York for a few days next week," Joseph said to his mother.

"What for?" she asked, surprised.

"This man that I have been talking to is willing to write a check for the organization. So, I want to meet him face to face and talk more about our project. I also want a vacation."

"Are you bringing that Britney girl?" Margaret asked.

"Why should I bring her?"

"I thought you guys were dating."

"No, we are not. She is a friend, nothing else."

"Good. I don't see you with her anyways." Felicia chimed in.

I was relieved to find out that Joseph didn't have a girlfriend. Small victory for me, I guess the world isn't that cruel to me after all. I figured that for a while maybe I could have his attention. *But what if he met someone in New York?* I couldn't help myself.

I thought about defeat all the time. I couldn't help but see life that way. *Why did I think that I didn't deserve love? Why is it that the negativity that I was experiencing with John wiped out all the positivity and love I had growing up? Did darkness always win over light?* My own mind suffocated me sometimes. I looked at the clock and I had to go. Joseph got up to walk me outside.

He came outside with me, and I was hoping that he wouldn't walk me all the way to the front door. So I stopped at the end of Margaret's driveway.

"Thank you for walking me this far, but I got it from here." My heart ached after saying that.

"Okay. It was really nice seeing you tonight. Are you going to be at Margaret's tomorrow? She won't be here, but I promised her that I'll come in to finish her backyard?"

He wanted to see me, and spend some time with me. I felt my heart jump with joy. Joseph liked me.

"Sure, I'll try." I sounded awkward. Thoughts were racing through my head, and I couldn't think of anything else to say. I just walked away.

He stood there looking at me as I walked toward the house; I could feel his eyes following me. When I reached the door, I looked back and waved. He waved at me and smiled.

I got inside the house and breathed. I didn't realize that I was holding my breath. He literally took my breath away. I started to think to myself if I sounded stupid or if my voice cracked - maybe I should have said more? I replayed our conversation a few times for the few minutes I stood by the door. I have never felt this way before. Joseph was occupying my mind. I cared about the way I talked to him and wanted to please him. They knew I wasn't married to John and were waiting for me to tell them the truth.

The house was quiet and I could hear John snoring. I walked quietly to the kitchen and sat down. I needed to catch my breath. I didn't know what I was going to do with Joseph. I couldn't afford to let him get too close to me, and at the same time that was all my heart desired at that point. I belonged to John, and I had a secret to keep. Joseph was a very curious guy who asked a lot of questions. I needed to come up with a good lie about my situation with John. But I wanted to tell him the truth. I wanted to open up to him, and let him help me. I was drowning in my own thoughts that night.

John didn't bother me that night. I heard him go to the bathroom at some point, but he went back to the bedroom until the next morning when he screamed my name, and woke me up. I ran to his room to see what had happened, but he just wanted breakfast. He startled me with his scream, and I didn't have the time to process what was happening to my body. I was feeling particularly weak and nauseous that morning, and being in the bedroom with that stench made it worse. I just left the room and went into the kitchen.

We were running out of groceries, and John was not in a condition to get out of the house. We had two pieces of bread and stale milk, and I was too afraid to go back into that bedroom to tell him. I stood in front of the pantry trying to come up with a miracle. I reopened the fridge at least five times and wondered how I hadn't noticed that we ran out of food. I had lost my appetite and whenever I was hungry, I ate at Margaret's house or ate the mangoes that Sebastian bought me. My mind was scattered, and I was too preoccupied with all the weird symptoms in my body.

As I stood in front of that pantry, I remembered that Joseph would be waiting for me at Margaret's house. I wanted to see him and just talk or listen to him. I didn't want John to be upset about anything. I wanted him asleep in his room, and out of my way. Life couldn't even grant me the simple pleasure of spending time with Joseph.

I didn't have a choice, I had to tell John. I went into the bathroom to wash my face, and just take a moment before I endured his wrath.

I only spoke to John in short English sentences. He didn't know that I spoke English. To him, I could only manage a few words, and could only understand his orders. Besides, we never had conversations, he ordered me, and I obeyed. The last time that he heard my voice was in the bathroom when I refused to perform oral sex on him. Now, I had to figure out a simple way of telling him that we don't have food in the kitchen. So, I knocked and waited. When he didn't answer, I knocked again.

"Come in!" he yelled.

He saw me, and I could see the surprise on his face.

"Where is my breakfast? Didn't I ask you to make me breakfast?"

He was already angry, so I said without making eye contact. "We don't have food in the kitchen."

He was silent for a while, and I just waited by the door for his reaction.

"You really are stupid. Why didn't you tell me sooner? You ugly and stupid thing!" His insults still hurt. They made me feel terrible, and I could feel the tears coming up. I fought the urge. I didn't want to give him the pleasure of seeing me in tears.

"Get out of here!" he shouted.

I left without lifting my head. Back into the kitchen, waiting for my sentence. John was very good at making me feel bad and small. He took pleasure in seeing me broken. A day that was supposed to be a good day with Joseph was already starting in such a negative tone. I thought that maybe he would be too tired and fall back asleep. Or maybe he would just go out and not come back, ever, but he didn't. He didn't even come out of the bedroom. I heard him coughing and moaning, but he didn't come out for a few hours.

Time was moving so slowly; I was looking at the clock and wondering what Joseph was doing. I just hoped that I could see him that day, so I waited for John to say or do something. The anticipation was killing me, literally. Finally, late in the afternoon, John came out of his room, still in his pajamas, but with shoes on. He called me into the living room where he was standing, holding on to the couch.

"Put some shoes on, let's go," he said.

I hurried back to the kitchen and put on my shoes. Where was he taking me? I was afraid. I wondered if he was taking me somewhere to kill me or turn me in or just get rid of me somehow. I was afraid, and when I came back to the living room he saw the fear on my face. He smiled. The man was sadistic.

He drove and I was in the passenger seat. It was always so uncomfortable to be so close to him. I resented his smell, his breathing, and just his being in general. I sat next to him with my eyes looking out the window. He was quiet and I could tell that he enjoyed sensing my fear. The drive was really short, and we ended up at the market. He parked the car and handed me a piece of paper that he had in his pants' pocket. He had taken the time to make a list of groceries, and he wanted me to go inside the market without him.

He handed me some cash from the glove compartment.

"Just figure it out, and if you can't, ask a clerk. Don't do anything stupid, I am warning you," he said, in Lingala. My native tongue.

I was glad to get out of the car and breathe. I could sense his eyes following my every step, and he parked in the handicap parking right next to the store window. He was afraid that I would run away, but what he didn't know was that I didn't have the courage, nor the confidence to do anything. The chains that were holding me captive were psychological.

I wandered around the store trying to find my way. The list had cereal, tea, potatoes, rice, steak and beer. I am sure that no one was looking at me, but I felt very self-conscious. I was under the impression that people could see the shame that I carried with me. In my mind I stood out from the crowd, and people looked down on me. I felt inferior and small. I wanted to hide. A clerk came to ask if I wanted help, but I just shook my head. I didn't have the courage to look him in his eyes. It took me a while to find all the items, when I went to pay the cashier tried to make small talk, but I didn't really talk back. I just smiled at her.

John was watching me, and as soon as I exited the market, we made eye contact. He was waiting impatiently. He was unaware of the power he had over me. John didn't realize that he had instilled enough fear in me and taken so much of my confidence and self-esteem, that escaping was not an option for me. I was able to go to Margaret's house, but I would have never had the courage to tell her the truth. He didn't realize that his plan to break me had worked perfectly. I felt incapable of being a strong human being. My existence depended totally on him. I got back in the car, gave him the change and we drove back quietly.

We passed Margaret's house and I saw Joseph's car. He was there and probably waiting for me. I felt a knot in my stomach. I was so afraid that he would be so disappointed and take his affection away. We got back inside the house and I just took the groceries back into the kitchen. John sat on the couch. Of all days, he chose to hang out in the living room the day I was supposed to go to Margaret's house.

"Make me a steak and put the beer in the fridge, right away." The irony of it all.

As I was cooking, I pulled up the shades in the windows. I didn't want John to catch a glimpse of Margaret's kitchen. I was too afraid that Joseph would see me and wave. I knew that I wasn't going to see Joseph that day, and wondered what he would think of me. I wanted to scream and shout. My heart was aching. Joseph was next door waiting; just a few steps and I couldn't get to him because John had me that day.

I served John his dinner in the living room and he spent the rest of the day on the couch. He was going in and out of consciousness, because he only took half of his pill. I spent the rest of the day in the kitchen hearing him snore and moan. I realized that I hadn't eaten all day, but the stress took my appetite away. I was hungry, but food was the last thing that I wanted. I wanted to be at Margaret's house with Joseph. Nothing else mattered at that moment. My desire was simple and yet impossible to get. I was desperate and helpless.

Was it just bad luck, coincidence, karma or just life? My life and all of its vicissitudes were a mystery to me. Once again, I wondered what determined a person's life and destiny. *Were we predestined to certain things? Or was it all up to us? Did we inherit luck from our parents?* From what happened to my family back home, to this small event today, my life baffled me. I reached a point where I just wanted to give up altogether. I thought about not going to Margaret anymore and cutting all contact with her. It was just too hard. I didn't care about life or death; I was already in hell. I cleaned up after John then went into the pantry and sat on the floor. It was the only room in the house that made me feel safe and far away from him, especially when he was in the living room.

CHAPTER 28

The next day, I woke up very early and every inch of my body ached. I went to the bathroom quietly and showered. The water was soothing, and I wished I could have stayed in it longer, but I couldn't take the chance. I got out and took a good look at myself in the mirror. I was unrecognizable. My face was full of blemishes, my body looked a bit deformed and the spark in my eyes was gone. I looked joyless and lifeless. There was nothing familiar left of the girl that I once was. I couldn't recognize myself not only physically, but within me, my spirit felt different. The worst version of me. I was trapped and John had the key to the cage.

I had two dreams that night. The first one was of my mother and Margaret on the bridge, and the second one was of me and Joseph. I dreamt of the day we could have had. Sitting on the patio in Margaret's house, just talking and drinking lemonade. The dream felt real.

In the kitchen that morning, I thought about that dream over and over. It was just a dream, and it made me feel so sad he was so out of reach for me. I felt as if life would never be kind enough to let me get close to Joseph. What if I fall deeply in love with him? What if I could never get close to him and become his friend? To protect myself, I had to stop thinking about him, and cease all visits to Margaret's house. For me, getting so close to something I couldn't have felt like torture. It just added to the sadness that was already filling my heart and soul.

John was still on the couch, and he got up at some point that morning to go to the bathroom but came back to that same spot. I think he was tired of his bed and wanted a different space, or maybe the smell bothered him too.

He called me at around noon to make him something to eat and to get him a beer. I was always shocked that he still drank so heavily, considering his fragile health. He drank alcohol with all the medications at the same time. He didn't care. John had given up on life. He had no friends, no family, no job and his health was declining. His aura was so dark and heavy that I pitied him.

John didn't take his sleeping pill that day, and he called my name more than I could bear. He wanted tea, a beer, a blanket, another pillow, his socks, his laptop, water, more tea and many more things. I wished he would just fall asleep, but he was up until later that evening. He finally decided to take the pill. I was holding my breath in the kitchen and tensed up every time I heard him move. He made that day grueling for me, and I reached a state of complete despair.

I closed the shades in the kitchen windows because I didn't want Margaret to see and knock at the door. But I also knew that she had enough sense to leave me alone whenever she saw John's car in the driveway. She knew that something was wrong in my relationship with John, but she wanted me to open up to her. She never pressed for answers, and gently made me feel comfortable enough to speak to her. Margaret opened her house and arms to me, but I wasn't ready to take that leap. I went to her house, but I didn't let myself crumble in her arms. I knew that John was capable of evil and made sure that he wasn't aware of my friendship with Margaret.

I missed my family a lot that day. I thought about my childhood and the simple things I had taken for granted: my freedom to be myself, a hug, a kiss, a simple 'I love you', my mother's meals, a clean and uncluttered house, my friends, and school. I wanted to believe in a higher power, and wanted so desperately to see the light at the end of the tunnel. My situation seemed so hopeless, and the sadness was overwhelming.

Somehow, the next day I woke up in a better mood. I wasn't as sad as the night before. I am not sure why. Maybe my dreams had something to do with it. Joseph was the first thing to enter my mind that morning. Even though I had told myself to stop thinking about him, I just couldn't. The more I tried, the more I thought about him. My efforts were futile, so I let myself be transported by fantasies of the life we could have had. I heard his voice a few times from Margaret's driveway or backyard and felt a leap in my stomach.

John slept on the couch that day, and many more days after that. The cage that I was in got smaller. With him in the living room, my movements were restricted. I stayed in the kitchen, and I waited to go to the bathroom until he was asleep and snoring. I didn't want to give him the chance to insult me or yell at me, by passing by the living room when he was awake. I held it, sometimes for a couple of hours until I could go.

One day I wanted to pee so badly, but I could hear him in the living room coughing and moaning. He was awake, and I was too afraid to go to the bathroom. I held it in for a couple of hours. I used all kinds of techniques to keep it inside. I sang in my head, counted to three thousand, thought about my life back home, and paced back and forth in the kitchen to no avail. My bladder was going to explode, so I just left the kitchen to go to the bathroom. As soon as I reached the living room, our eyes met. I stopped for a second, and sure enough he gestured for me to get close to him.

I really needed to pee, but I also had to obey him. When I got closer, he unzipped his pants and gestured for me to get down on my knees. I stood there in front of him, hesitated for a few seconds. I couldn't move. One step would have made my bladder explode. His penis was half erect. I looked at it and peed myself. I couldn't hold it in.

His reaction was so visceral. He looked at me with horror and kicked me with his legs. I was embarrassed, but my bladder thanked me. He proceeded to insult me and call me every name in the book. At least I didn't have to perform oral sex on him, his half erection went down, and I was free to go to the bathroom.

I was so focused on how good my bladder felt, that I didn't feel the pain of his kick until I was in the bathroom. He had kicked my knee, and I felt the excruciating pain once all the excitement was gone. I felt too many things at the same time: pain, relief, fear, and sadness. I just sat on the floor and pulled myself together. I sat quietly and tuned out John who was still yelling in the living room. I took a shower and sat in the bathroom for a while.

The need to belong was in the fabric of my being and I couldn't deny it. I was born into a large family with a strong sense of community. Everything we did was in a group. I shared a bedroom, as well as breakfast, lunch and dinner with others. I walked to school with my siblings and shared friends with them. My life was always tied to a family member, whether it was one of my parents, a sibling, an aunt, an uncle or cousin. I realized that I had never had a chance to really think about myself as an individual.

My parents instilled moral values in me, and I just accepted them for what they were. I acted based on what they had instructed me to, and always made sure that my decisions didn't bring shame to my family. *Who was I? What were my dreams?* I had always thought that I would grow up to become a teacher, get married, have children, and accept whatever else life had in store for me.

But sitting in the bathroom, I realized that my life was like a written script up until John abducted me. I never consider my own feelings and thoughts. Did I really want to be a teacher? Did I want to get married? Did I truly want children? I felt lost. At the same time, I felt guilty for reasons that I couldn't quite grasp. I felt soiled by all the involuntary sexual acts I performed. The restlessness within me was palpable. I was quiet and still most of the time, but there was a war of feelings and thoughts inside of me.

I was sitting on the bathroom floor with my head resting on my knees. I felt heavy with sadness, but John brought me back to reality with an aggressive knock on the door. He was incapable of leaving me alone. He interrupted my peace, my moments of sadness, my hope for a little happiness and my life. He was just there, present in everything and anything. I just wrapped a towel around my chest and opened the door. He was standing in front of the door with a look of hatred on his face. I just walked past him, holding my breath.

"Please don't hit me," I whispered under my breath.

I couldn't take another hit or punch. I went to the pantry where I kept the few items of clothing that I had. I put on a dress that I hadn't worn for a few weeks, and it felt a bit tighter. I was losing weight at some point, and then I gained it all back. I knew that something was wrong with my health, but I decided to ignore it. I had no one to turn to, and if death decided to take me, I welcomed it. I had nothing to live for. I washed my skirt and underwear in the kitchen sink and hung them on a chair. I knew that John wouldn't come to the kitchen that day and would probably call me a few times to order me around.

I stared at my clothes hanging on the chair. I was seventeen years old and I had just peed myself. Nothing in my life had prepared me for the emotional and mental suffering I was enduring with John. I witnessed a lot of bad situations and circumstances back in the Congo, but misfortune seemed to be something that happened to other people, not me, not my family.

Joseph was on my mind a lot. I wondered whether I actually had a crush on him, or my mind was using him as a coping mechanism. Maybe I just needed something to help me escape my daily routine and the misery that was my life. I wondered what he was doing and if he was thinking about me too. Was it possible to fall in love with someone so quickly? What made me sad was the fact that we really didn't have a chance. I lived with John. I belonged to John and that was that.

As humans, do we always want the things that we can't have? I felt like Joseph was unattainable for me, but I couldn't snap out of fantasizing. Although my father used to tell me that if you really want something, you have to go after it and work for it. My father showed me the meaning of hard work. He was an entrepreneur who started with nothing. He started with a construction company and made a lot of money at first.

But when the economy slowed down, the business took a hit. That didn't stop him; he started a trading and messenger company between Kinshasa and our town. People were able to get goods and exchange letters with their loved ones in Kinshasa. He charged a small fee, and the business was doing so well. He never gave up, and even though we sometimes were short on money, not once did we not have food on the table. He and my mother provided for us, and gave us a very good childhood. When times were hard, we knew it, because my father became moody and argued with my mother a lot. We eavesdropped and heard them argue about money.

I would hear my mother tell him, "If you didn't have so many mistresses, maybe you wouldn't struggle so much. You spread your money all over town when your entire family relies on you as well. Do you ever think of how that makes me feel?"

She rarely complained about my father's philandering, but some days when her back was against the wall, she cracked. My father's persistence was not only good for business, but it was also good to pursue and get any woman he wanted. My parents and other adults in the family thought that they did a good job hiding things from us, but we were curious and oftentimes investigated or eavesdropped to find out what was going on. My father had taken wives from his friends and cousins.

When he wanted a woman, he went after her and got her. It didn't matter whether or not she was married. One of our neighbors, Pierre, who was a widower, had traveled to Kinshasa to have his sister help him find a wife. Because he had some money, he was convinced that any woman would follow him back to our town, as long as he promised her comfort. He was gone for a couple of months, and when he came back he brought a beautiful woman with him. He proudly introduced her to everyone who would listen to him brag about how he got her. He was so proud of himself and single women in our town hated him. They were mad that he just didn't pick one of them. And men were jealous that his wife was prettier and more refined than their wives. His wife's name was Nanga and she was the talk of the town. Her clothes and hairstyle stood out.

The first time my father saw Nanga, it was at church. My mother usually went to the early mass so that she could get home and cook lunch. So we went to the 11am service with our dad. We saw Pierre and his wife at the entry of the church and he introduced her to my dad. We all watched her in awe. She was pretty. My dad pretended to be unimpressed and rushed us to get inside the church. His reaction was very odd. She had made him uncomfortable for some reason. Once we were all seated, I noticed that my father would turn in Nanga's direction whenever the priest asked us to close our eyes to pray. He was almost salivating, and I smelled the trouble. The following Sunday, my dad was extra nice to my mother and helping us get ready for church. He usually let us get ready and only checked before we left the house. But that Sunday, he made sure that we woke up on time.

"We don't want to be late for the Lord today, children." His enthusiasm was very odd to me, and my sister felt the same way.

"We all know why he is so excited to go to church today," she said.

I knew what she meant, but we didn't dare discuss it further. We felt bad for our mother, and imagined that it was hard to have a husband like my father. He was a good husband, a good father and a good provider on one hand. On the other hand, he was a cheater and a self-centered man. He made her feel insecure with all his affairs, and yet she never had the courage to leave him. Divorce was not an option in our culture back then, and the few women who had done it had to endure the shame for the rest of their lives. So she stayed with my father, out of love and duty.

As soon as we got to church and sat down, I could see my father's eyes looking around anxiously. He was looking for Nanga, and I knew it. At some point he was shaking his legs, and that is how I knew that he was losing his patience. He got up to go outside.

"Don't move, children, I'll be right back." He went outside and came back with a smile on his face.

Nanga had just arrived with her husband. He relaxed a little bit. And whenever we closed our eyes to pray, he looked back and stared at her. My father was smitten. I had never seen him look at my mother with those eyes. He looked at my mother with respect and affection, but the look for Nanga was of passion and excitement. I wondered at that moment if marriage reduces a woman to being a 'friend who is there to raise the children'. Were men incapable of lusting after their wives at home? Did passion and excitement disappear once a man marries a woman and has children with her? I noticed the same pattern for all married men in my family. They didn't look at their wives with excitement.

Pierre still lusted after his wife because she was fresh and hadn't borne him a child. I was sure that after a couple of years and children, he wouldn't be showing her off the way he was doing then. But my father wouldn't give him the opportunity to look at Nanga as the 'mother of his children'.

After a few Sundays, my father got close to Nanga. One Sunday, Pierre wasn't feeling good and she came to church by herself. I saw my father's eyes get big and his smile grow. He never usually bought us ice cream after church, instead always rushing us back home. But that Sunday, he decided to take us to the ice cream stand right outside of church and went back to the exit of the church to wait for Nanga, who was still inside greeting the other churchgoers. Once she came out, he spoke to her and I saw her laughing really hard. My father's charm was working. They talked for a while, and then my father came to talk to us.

"Hey kids, your uncle will take you guys back home. Tell your mother that I am staying behind to tend to some church business. I shouldn't be too long. Okay?"

We just nodded. Our father saw his opportunity to have Nanga all to himself, and he took it. We walked home with one of my father's cousins. Our walk home was very quiet. I was angry with my dad, and I could see my sister holding back the tears. My brother didn't care and the twins didn't really know what was happening. Once we got home, my uncle made up some excuse for my father to my mother and I just walked into the bedroom. I couldn't look at my mother because I knew something that she didn't know, but very much involved her. My uncle was talking to her and pretending that everything was alright. Like every other person in my father's family, they loved my mother, but also were friendly with all the mistresses. They couldn't betray my father, but at the same time had affection for my mother. So, they were caught in the middle. My mother usually knew what was going on, but she had to play along. She so gracefully dealt with the life that God had given her, rarely complaining.

Nanga became my father's mistress and left her husband. Pierre cursed my father and promised that he would seek revenge.

"I will get one of your daughter's pregnant one day," he said to my father.

But my father was too busy enjoying his victory. He had seen a woman he wanted, went after her and got her. My sister would say, "It's just survival of the fittest. Some people are meant to win and some to lose. Even nature has predators and their prey. I don't even think there are consequences. I just hope that when I am older, I am more like dad. The winner and the fittest".

My father spent a lot of time with Nanga at first, and my mother cried in the bathroom about it. That's what happens whenever he had a new woman in his life. He spent a lot of time with them, and my mother had to wait until the excitement wore off. The moment one of his mistresses started to have children, he spent less time with them. He loved the children and treated them fairly, but the mother became ordinary. Nanga wasn't an exception.

After she gave my father a baby boy, he spent less time with her, and had the nanny bring the baby to our house. I saw Nanga in the market or at church and she had faded. She didn't look as happy and excited as the first time I met her. Pierre still longed for her and wanted her back despite everything that had transpired. The gossip was that he brought her gifts late at night and hoped that one day she would take him back.

Nanga wanted my father. I overheard her say one day that she thought that my father would leave my mother and marry her. She was willing to wait, and people looked at her with pity. My father always came back to my mother, and the countless mistresses he had knew better. They were happy with their situation. He offered them houses, maids and allowances. He treated the children the same way he treated us. But he spent every night at home, next to my mother. Nanga thought that she was different, but she wasn't. As time went on, she lost her self-confidence. She looked bitter and angry all the time. She started pressuring my father to spend nights with her, but he wouldn't. People around town were talking about them and their arguments. Sometimes, they fought outside of Nanga's house. My father began to avoid her altogether.

She went back to Pierre. My father made sure that my half-brother spent most of his days with us. Pierre was content having Nanga back after two long years. Life went back to normal for him. We saw them at church and I could see the look of dissatisfaction in their eyes. Pierre wanted Nanga, and she wanted my father. They both wanted something they couldn't truly have, and I felt sorry for them. My father went on with his life unbothered by the damage he had caused to my mother or anyone else for that matter. He found a new mistress and got her pregnant too. The cycle started over.

In spite of all the things that my father did to my mother, I still somehow believed in love. I liked Joseph and I had never felt like that before. I looked at John and wondered many times if he had been in love. I saw the pictures he was hiding in his closet of a woman, and wondered about her. *Were they married? Was he in love? What happened to her?* John was an unsolved mystery and the longer

I lived with him, the less I understood him. His wickedness was predictable, but his background was unknown.

At times, I caught myself feeling compassion for him. It pained me to see him suffer, only for him to throw an insult at me and remind me that he was not worthy of my compassion. John had pushed me to my limit and I wondered whether or not I would reach a breaking point. He had violated me in ways that I didn't think possible, and yet I didn't have the courage to escape. I was caught between John and a hard place. Afraid of the unknown. That his word would trump mine if we went to court, the police, or Immigration. He had the power to destroy me, so I stayed and complied.

John and I were stuck in the house for a couple of weeks. He spent most of his time on the couch in the living room. He had asked me to move the TV back to the living room, and he only got up to go to the restroom. The entire house reeked of sweat and alcohol. He left the house twice to go to the market, and brought back beer and vodka. He mixed alcohol and his sleeping pills. I didn't dare to get out of the house, because the couch was in front of the main entrance. Even though I had decided to stop visiting Margaret, everything in me longed for her. I also missed Joseph madly.

Every time John fell asleep after a meal, I hoped that he wouldn't wake up. But he did, every time, and he managed to be more evil with each passing day. I couldn't get used to it. With every insult, I felt smaller. I tried to convince myself that I was stronger, and that his view of me was irrelevant, but I couldn't. His negativity was like a poison being injected into my vein. John had reduced me to nothing. I was an object. His object.

Pain and sadness inhabited my mind and spirit permanently, but sometimes they hit me harder than usual. I had days of total darkness, when I could feel the sadness completely take over me. It overwhelmed me, and I didn't know where to turn. I needed an outlet, and that's when I realized that Margaret had been instrumental in helping me cope. I didn't have her, and I needed her positivity, her light. My sadness was too big to handle. My heart felt heavy, and all I could do was sit still. I sat in the kitchen and stared at the wall. My thoughts jumped from one place to another and back again. I saw no end to my predicament.

I just couldn't silence my mind. My body was still in one room, but I traveled through time. I wondered again and again what I had done to end up with John. *Where did I go wrong? Why was my fate tied to someone like him?* I tried to think positively but I couldn't.

My parents had called me Grace after my grandmother and because it was my mother's favorite word. She believed that when someone has grace, they go through life obtaining all their wishes.

"Grace calls for miracles," she would say, and I believed her. I believed that my life would reflect my name. I never thought that I would be extremely successful, but I strongly believed my life would be easy and happy. The plan was mapped out, and grace was supposed to carry me through everything in life. I wondered if I would ever see my family again. Those days I was convinced that I would never feel happy again. And I had to force myself to get used to being sad. But could one ever get used to abuse and sadness?

I heard Margaret and Felicia a few times coming in and out of the house. I dared to open the shades from my window twice to catch a glimpse, but she wasn't in her kitchen. She also didn't come looking for me. I wondered if they talked about me, or even thought about me.

John's cough was getting worse, and he spent a lot of time in the restroom vomiting. I cleaned after him every day. He came to the kitchen once and caught me opening the shades. My heart stopped, and the look on his face sent me a chill. I didn't expect him to wake up, but for some reason he didn't find the strength to yell my name, so he came to the kitchen barely standing on his feet. I just heard his breathing as I was staring out the window, as I turned around, he was just standing there, looking at me. I just closed the shades and stood by the sink. I knew he wanted to throw something at me or at least punch me, but he was too weak. After what seemed like an eternity, he exited the kitchen.

I heard him go out through the back door. The shed in the backyard was off limits. But that night, he unlocked it and went in for a while. I thought he went to get a machete or chainsaw to kill me. If it was my time to die, I was ready for it. I was numb and wasn't sure what to expect from John anymore.

He came back to the kitchen completely out of breath. He had four pieces of wood, and a hammer. As soon as he walked in, he dropped them on the floor. He was covered with sweat, and his face was bright red. I thought to myself that it would take more than four pieces of wood to create a coffin. He wasn't making eye contact with me, nor was he saying anything. He sat down and was breathing heavily. I didn't know what to do, so I stood at that same spot by the sink and the window. After a few minutes, he stood up, grabbed one of the pieces of wood with the hammer and came towards me. What's almost funny is before he came back in the kitchen, I thought that I would be okay if John decided to kill me. And yet, as he was approaching me with the hammer, I got afraid. My heart was beating fast, and my mind was traveling a million miles in a second.

He got next to me and pushed me out of the way. He took the piece of wood and hammered it across the window. He took the other four pieces and shut the windows with wood crossing them. He closed my window to the world, literally. He wanted to make sure that I didn't see or interact with the outside world. I watched him nail each piece with strength that I hadn't seen in him for months. John was so evil, and his anger towards me pumped adrenaline through his system. If I wanted to escape, I would use the front door when he was out. Why did his twisted mind think that I would use the back door or the window? John was my prison, not his house.

He finished hammering the nails to the window and left the kitchen. I was standing on the same spot, just astounded by what had just happened. John was very angry, and I thought he was going to kill me, or at least hit me. But he was so wrapped up in his rage that I became invisible to him, even though I was the very object of his wrath. I heard him breathing hard in the living room, and I prayed that he would just fall asleep. He didn't. He called me the first time, while I was still recovering from the shock and I didn't move. The second time, I went to him.

"If I ever see you trying to open a door or a window in the house, I'll hurt you." I stood in front of him, frozen. "Do you understand?" He was speaking in English, which means that he knew I understood him. "You are in this country illegally, and if someone catches you we could both be in trouble since I am letting you stay in my house."

Letting me? I couldn't believe him. He didn't let me stay in his house; he kept me as his prisoner. I was forced to stay with him, but in his sick mind he looked at it as a favor to me. I started to wonder if John was aware of his sickness. Was he just unaware? Or, he made the choice to pretend he didn't see the madness in his life? His entire existence didn't make sense to me. From the fact that he abducted me, and had me in his house as a slave, to the fact that he still drank a lot of alcohol in spite of his illness. Maybe his denial was a defense mechanism, or he was just completely detached from reality and normal life.

He took a long pause and looked down. "Don't just stand there; go make me something to eat."

I hurried back to the kitchen. The window was gone, and the room felt smaller and darker. The kitchen that was once my refuge, felt hostile. I wanted to crawl out my skin. I wanted to die. With my eyes filled with tears, I had to start cooking. Every move required a lot of effort from me. From getting the steak out of the fridge, to grabbing the pots and pan, I felt distressed and destitute. I had to make dinner for John. The man I hated, and who mistreated me. I didn't have a choice. That was the cross I had to carry, and it was too heavy. Life was intolerable. I didn't know how long I could endure the pain. Every time I thought that it couldn't get worse, it did.

I went through the motions, and made him a steak with potatoes. I served him with his beer and hot tea. I made sure to put his sleeping pill close to the plate. I needed him asleep, so that I could breathe. I held my breath when he was awake and in a bad mood. I knew that at any moment, he could do anything to hurt me. He was predictable for certain things, but for the ways he chose to torture me, he wasn't. We hadn't been intimate for a while, so he fed his obsession in different ways.

He ate his food very slowly, and carelessly. There were pieces of food on the table, the floor, his laptop, the couch. He spilled some of the beer too. When he called me to clean the table, I couldn't believe how messy the small area in the living room was. His hands were shaky and he seemed a bit disoriented. He was holding the remote in one hand, and the glass of beer in the other, but in his confusion he tried to put the remote in his mouth. I truly pitied him. The medication and alcohol kicked in and his system probably could no longer handle the combination.

I cleared the table and got out of his way. He didn't call me for the rest of the night, and when I peeked through the door, he was fast asleep and snoring.

I was asleep on the floor in the pantry when I heard John coughing violently in the living room. It was the middle of the night, and I was in the middle of my dream. I went into the kitchen to wait in case he called me. For a few minutes he stopped coughing, and I felt relieved. As soon as I walked back in the pantry, he started again. I sat on the floor, listening to him. I could tell he was in a lot of pain and he needed some medical attention. But John was stubborn, and I knew that he always waited until the last minute to go to the doctor.

I couldn't fall back asleep because of his cough, and I almost wished that he would let me help him. After a couple of hours, he called me and I hurried to the living room. I wanted to help him.

"Bring me some water!" he ordered.

He looked like he was on his way to hell. His eyes were glassy, his skin was red and he was sweating profusely. I went into the kitchen, and my heart was aching. I couldn't tell whether it was empathy toward John, or me. But I felt the knots in my stomach tighten. John was dying right in front of my eyes and I couldn't do anything about it. And I thought about the implications of his death in my life. There were just too many.

He drank the water and wanted another glass. After the second glass, the coughing subsided. He was still on the couch staring at the wall in front of him. John was pitiful. His life was sad. I went back to the kitchen and sat at the dining table. The sun was slowly coming up, and we hadn't slept much.

When I was in the Congo, I loved the break of dawn. I loved hearing the rooster outside, and it was quickly followed by my mother's voice. She would start calling our names from the kitchen and then come to our room. She would lean over by the bed, and gently call my name. "Wake up, honey! Today is the day that the Lord has made, you will rejoice and be glad in it." She would say. My mother was a walking Bible. She quoted it every chance she got, and made us memorize her favorite verses.

Mornings in our house were synonymous with peace and love. We created chaos because we had to share the bathroom, but my mother was a tower of strength and calm. Living with

John had made me resent mornings, and nights for that matter. The break of dawn for me meant another day to deal with John and his cruelty. It meant another day of anger, sadness, nostalgia, and depression. I had my nights at least when he would sleep in the bedroom, and leave me alone. Now that he was sleeping in the living room, my nights were unpredictable. I couldn't sleep soundly for fear that he would call me and I wouldn't hear him. I had to be half aware, and some nights I heard his voice in my dreams. I was living in constant dread of him and my morning meant just that: another day as John's slave.

I longed for my mother's voice and presence. I had never appreciated that simple gesture of her waking me up and hearing her voice. Her positive energy set the stage for my day, and carried me through my childhood. I would have given everything, including my own life, to hear her voice again, to talk to her and be in her presence. A part of me was missing and my heart was still bleeding. In my heart I knew that she was no longer alive, because I didn't feel her. I could still feel my siblings, but I didn't feel my mother. The world felt empty, and had she been alive, she would have found me. She would have looked for me, or at least my body to bury me. She was a gentle and kind woman, but my mother was relentless when it came to her children. It hurt me to admit to myself, but I knew she was gone. She came to me in my dreams to tell me something, but I couldn't understand it.

I wondered about my siblings and missed them every day. I prayed that they were all okay somewhere, and the funny thing about blood is that I felt their presence still. I felt connected to them and their souls. I just didn't know if I would ever see them again, or if I would come out of John's house alive. Every day, living with uncertainty.

John gathered the strength to shower early that morning. He took a very long time in the bedroom before he finally called me. I found him sitting on the bed, breathing heavily. He was naked.

The sight of him made me sick. The sight of his naked body made my skin crawl. I had a visceral reaction that morning, and had to pull myself together in front of him. His penis was erect and I wondered how that was possible. He coughed all night and looked ill, but somehow he still craved sex. He gestured for me to get close to him, and my body tensed up. I hesitated, but he gave me a threatening look. I knew I didn't have a choice. He owned me, and I had to do as he said. Without speaking a word, he commanded me to get down on my knees and pleasure him.

There were tears coming down my face, but John was unbothered. He moaned and made repulsive sounds. He grabbed my head and pulled it toward him. He didn't care about the tears or the expression on my face. John didn't look at me as a person. I was just an object.

Within a few minutes, he ejaculated on my face. I felt small and dirty. I sat on the floor, while he got up and got dressed. I was invisible, and could not find the strength to unglue myself from the floor. He finished getting dressed and left the room, then I heard him leave the house.

I sat on the floor with John's scent lingering in my mouth and my body. I could still feel his hands on my neck and the sound of his moans in my ears. I wanted to get up and run away, but at the same time I couldn't even gather the strength to get up from the floor. The weight of my situation was on my shoulders, and I couldn't get up. I wept for at least an hour.

When I finally decided to get up, my head and heart felt heavy; tears used to make me feel a little better. Whenever I was hurting and cried, I felt like I washed away part of that sadness. And I remembered my mother telling me to 'always allow yourself to shed tears whenever you are in pain. They will always make you feel better'. But that morning, my heart felt like it was going to burst out of my chest. I walked slowly to the bathroom, and I avoided the mirror as I got under the shower. I didn't want to look at myself. I didn't have the heart to face my emotions through my eyes. I turned on the cold water and let it wash away John's scent. The water made me feel a bit better, but I couldn't stop thoughts from racing in my mind.

I thought about my parents, my siblings, Margaret, Joseph, the Congo, and my life. I couldn't stop my mind, couldn't calm myself down. I was breaking from the inside and couldn't stop it. That morning in the shower, I knew I had to ask for help.

After a long while in the shower, I got out only because I felt hungry. I made myself a sandwich and devoured it in a couple of minutes. The kitchen was so dark and somber. I thought about Margaret and her friends. I hadn't seen her and wondered if she missed me at all. I wanted to see Joseph and explain why I didn't show up that day. But I didn't know whether or not John would come back, so I didn't dare leave the house. Even though I had decided to leave Margaret alone, I couldn't. I wanted to see her. I wanted to feel loved and looked at as a human being again. My soul ached for humanity.

We didn't have many groceries left, and I was craving mangoes again. I ate different things throughout the day to get rid of the craving, but nothing was working. I ate rice with sugar, bread, some meat with potatoes. I stuffed myself to the point of making myself sick. By the end of the day the craving wasn't gone, but I was too nauseous to want to eat anything else. I threw up half of the food I ate and went to the pantry to fall asleep. John didn't come home that day, and I felt relieved. I didn't want to see him and I needed a break from his toxic presence.

CHAPTER 29

It had been five days since John left. I assumed he checked himself into a hospital. We were running out of food again, and I had to eat white rice with sugar for breakfast, lunch, and dinner. The first two days I had the luxury of eating steak and potatoes, but that ran out too. I was learning to ignore my craving for mangoes and constant fatigue.

I watched TV sometimes, and realized that I definitely understood English better. My brain didn't hurt so much from trying to understand everything. I paced back and forth, and heard Margaret's voice from her backyard. I missed her, and it surprised me that she didn't knock at the door after all this time. She usually waited until John's car wasn't in the driveway to knock. But this time, she left me alone and I hurt a little bit. I felt a bit abandoned by her. I was tempted to go see her but every time I thought about the effort to come up with lies and excuses, I gave up. And I didn't know what to say to Joseph.

I looked for paper and started to draw again. I hadn't for a very long time, and it showed. My strokes were not as smooth as I remembered, but after a few tries it felt natural again. I drew faces with sad expressions. I tried to draw Joseph's face, but I couldn't, my mind could make up his facial features. I never really made eye contact with him for long. I was afraid that he would see in me what I was trying so hard to hide. I knew his scent from that one time he hugged me. Joseph did everything with intention and purpose. When he talked to me, I felt connected to him. He listened and always had the perfect answer. I kept trying to draw his face, but I couldn't quite get it.

I gave up and decided to clean John's bedroom and air it out. The house had windows and doors that I could freely open, but John decided to shut the kitchen door completely. His mind amazed me. I opened the bedroom window and took in some fresh air. I vacuumed and washed his clothes. When I was done, the room looked so much better and didn't smell so much like him. I didn't know how he would take it, but it gave me something to do.

I also organized the pantry and made more space for myself on the floor. Since John left I slept on the couch, and I was hoping that he would go back to sleeping in the bedroom. But just in case, I was making the pantry a bit more comfortable. I cleaned the kitchen and the living room. At the end of the day, I felt tired and my mind quieted down a little bit. After taking a shower, I got dressed, I went back to the living room, got down on my knees and prayed.

"Father, give me peace of mind. And if John contaminated me with his disease, please heal me."

I wasn't sure that my prayers were going to work, but in my loneliness God was my only friend. Back on the couch, I tried my hardest to stop the voices in my head. I wanted to feel calm for once. So, I sang to myself quietly until I fell asleep. I dreamt about my mother and Margaret on the bridge again. It woke me up in the middle of the night. I decided that if John didn't come back that next day, I would go see Margaret. I wanted to see her and just feel her affection.

I woke up very early the next morning, and it felt good to sleep on the couch as opposed to the floor in the pantry. The few days that John was out allowed me to not only sleep on the couch, but spend the night without the fear of being called and yelled at. The fact that I had decided to go see Margaret gave me something to look forward to. I planned my day based on John's return. I told myself that if he didn't come back by late afternoon, I would just go visit Margaret and spend an hour or so with her. I had to keep myself busy in order to ignore the anticipation. I took a long shower and while I was there, I said a little prayer.

"God please, keep John wherever he is. Don't let him come back today. Amen."

God was like a genie in a bottle, I really needed him to answer that prayer. Actually, I repeated that prayer internally all day. I was asking God to keep John sick for my own benefit. *What if John was praying to get better and come home?* I wondered how that worked. *Did God or the universe take turns at answering people's prayers? What happens if one person's prayer cancels out another's prayer or wish?*

It reminded me of a time when I was eleven years old, and we had a singing contest at school. The competition had many stages of elimination, and at the end it was me and one of my classmates, Marie. Two days before the final sing-off, I overheard her tell her mother to stop by church on their way home because she wanted to light a candle and ask God to make her the winner. I had thought about praying about winning, I was sure that I would be the winner. On my walk home from school that day I thought about going to church too, but I decided to go home instead and pray in my room. When I got home, I sat down with my family for lunch but looked preoccupied. I wanted to be done with lunch and go to my room to say a prayer.

My mother noticed that my mind was somewhere else, and

she asked, "What's on your mind? You seemed bothered by something."

I hesitated before answering. I was too embarrassed to admit that I was afraid of my competition. But then I decided to tell her the truth and maybe she would pray for me too, and both our prayers would cancel out Marie's prayer.

"I overheard Marie tell her mother to go to church and pray about winning the competition in two days. I am just worried that she'll win, but I really want this."

My sister Mwinda looked at me with disdain. My parents and my siblings laughed at me.

"You are acting as if the prize is a trip to America or a car or something. The prize is two books and a t-shirt. Come on!" My father continued under his breath. "Books and a t-shirt. That's a joke."

My mother gave me that look she gave me every time she wanted to teach me something new. "Honey, in life you should never worry about what the other person is doing. God has a plan for you, and if he wants for you to win the competition, you will. Besides, worrying about the competition distracts you from focusing on your own life and work."

My father looked up from his plate of fufu, and said, "I disagree with your mother, never underestimate your competition. Keep an eye on them at all times. Know what they are made of, and if they look a bit stronger than you then work harder to beat them. Although, I don't understand why you are stressing about two pitiful books. All that money that I pay for this school, and they can't even give children better prizes?"

My father had a hunger for life that my mother didn't. He wanted everything to be bigger and better. My mother saw the good in everything and as long as her children were well healthy and happy, nothing mattered to her. I was a mix of the two of them, and that day I went into my room and said the most ridiculous prayer.

"God, please help me win the competition. You could give Marie something else, but this win is mine. Amen."

The next day at school, I kept my eyes on Marie. I observed her whereabouts and her demeanor. She seemed relaxed and very sure of herself. All of a sudden, she seemed larger than life. She looked taller and smarter that day. Me on the other hand, I was stressed and anxious about the competition. I refrained from talking because I didn't want to strain my voice. I was a nervous wreck, and asked the Principal to send me home early. The knots in my stomach gave me a headache. My mother was surprised to see me home so early.

"Why are you home early? Don't you have your last rehearsal for the competition this afternoon?"

I couldn't tell her that my over-stressing made me sick, so I just said, "I am not sure, maybe the goat we ate for dinner last night made me sick. I've had diarrhea all morning."

My poor mother believed me. "I had a feeling that the goat wasn't good. My poor baby, I hope the rest of your siblings and your father don't get sick too."

I just nodded and went to my room. The walk of shame.

The next morning, I had a fully-fledged fever and broke out in hives. My prayer had backfired, or just my craziness and overthinking. Or it was just a coincidence, the goat really did make me sick. I will never know this answer. I stayed home from school that day and missed the sing-off. Marie won and that weekend she came to visit me with her mother at our house. She brought me fruits and gave me one of the books she won. I could tell that she genuinely felt concerned about me, and her mother was very nice too.

"I just felt alone without you up there. I missed your energy and your good humor," she said cheerfully.

She was not looking at me as a rival, but rather a pal during the competition. Her heart was in a good place, and although she wanted to win, she never wished me harm. She figured there was enough space on the stage for the both of us. At eleven years old, Marie understood life better than I did. Or maybe she was just born with a positive disposition.

I spent my morning pacing back and forth. Watching TV and cleaning the house at least twice. Every time I heard a car approaching, I prayed that it wasn't John. We didn't have anything to eat in the house, and I was really hungry. I made the last bit of rice and ate it with sugar. I didn't want to let my anxiety get the best of me, so I sat down to draw. Sketching pictures of what I remembered from home: the courtyard where we played soccer, my school, the church, and my childhood house. I felt very inspired and for a few hours I didn't think of anything else but what I was doing. I didn't care about the noise outside, or the passing of time. I focused on drawing and let my mind travel to my childhood. I let myself remember life before John.

When I finally looked up it was 5pm already, and there were no signs of John. I went to the bathroom to wash my face and decided to go to Margaret's house.

I put on a dress, combed my hair and put a bit of olive oil on my face. I was breaking out and it was difficult to look decent, but I tried my best. I wasn't sure what she would say or the questions she might ask. I had to think of a lie to explain why I hadn't visited her. Every time I lied to her she knew, but I didn't have a choice. I couldn't tell her the truth and she understood, but she still asked sometimes hoping that maybe one day I'll find the courage to tell her what was truly going on with me. So I decided that if she asked, that day I would tell her that it's complicated, and one day I would tell her the truth.

I walked to Margaret's house with excitement, and hoped that she was alone. I just wanted to spend time with her. I needed her maternal affection, wanting to feel a bit normal again. I knocked very shyly and within seconds she answered, as if she was expecting me.

"Grace! I was just thinking about you." She held me in her arms for a long time.

I took her in, her scent, the warmth of her body, her gentle and yet firm grip and her presence.

"Come on in, sweetheart. How have you been?" She was happy to see me.

"I have been good." She held my hand and we walked to the kitchen.

"I was warming up leftovers from yesterday to have dinner alone. Do you want to join me?"

I nodded. I hadn't had a decent meal in a while and Margaret's food was always so comforting. As she was getting the food ready, I sat by the island and listened to her catch me up on what I had missed. Sebastian and his girlfriend had a new apartment, and they organized a march to raise money for victims of rape and domestic abuse. Joseph was able to get some funding for their non-profit also, and they were thinking about getting an office in San Francisco, or maybe Oakland. Felicia was on vacation in Jacksonville, Florida, to visit her family. And Margaret had been busy just helping Sebastian and Joseph with research. I wanted her to tell me more about Joseph, but I didn't dare ask her.

"You know you should get involved with the boys and help them out with what they are doing. That would be good for you," she added.

I wanted to help, and I needed the help. I was a victim of

John and keeping a dark secret in plain sight. She made us some fresh lemonade and put some cookies in the oven. I helped her set the table outside, and we sat down. The pasta felt like the best meal I had ever eaten, enjoying every bite and going for seconds.

Margaret loved it when I ate her food. She also enjoyed the company while I was just happy to be there with her. I got the cookies out of the oven when they were ready and took them back outside to our table. She never asked me why I hadn't visited her, but she told me repeatedly that she had missed me. I had missed her too.

"It's good to see you, really. You know I am always here if you need anything. Okay?"

"Yes, I know and thank you." I felt like a human being again, and I took great comfort in that.

Although the moments I spent with Margaret were brief, they had such an impact in my life. They brought me some joy and gave me a little hope to carry on for another day. She did it so effortlessly and never expected anything in return.

I spent a couple of hours with Margaret and enjoyed the comfort of her presence. She told me more about her upbringing and her college years. She was born in Baton Rouge, Louisiana, the only child of a schoolteacher and an electrician. Her parents were still alive and were retired. She visited them twice a year, for their birthdays. She moved to Bakersfield when she got married and became friends with Felicia.

She spoke fondly of the people in her life. Her life was transparent, and her positivity radiated from her eyes. Life vicissitudes did not leave her bitter. She still had so much faith and hope in her heart that it was contagious. Margaret's presence made me feel hopeful. I listened to her and enjoyed the stories about Sebastian when he was a little boy, and his plea for a little sister.

"He begged me to give him a little sister for years, only

because his best friend when he was eight had a sister," she said with a smile on her face. "I tried, but for some reason I couldn't get pregnant a second time and I gave up.

When it was time to leave, Margaret packed some food for me and cookies. I was afraid that John would come home and find the food, but I needed the food so I took a chance. She packed enough for a couple of days, but I was planning to visit again. I helped her clean the kitchen and do dishes before I left. We found our rhythm again. Margaret and I were always in sync. With or without words, we had a strong bond and I held on to it.

"When will I see you again? she asked as I was about to leave her house.

"Soon, I hope."

She held me in her arms, and I knew that she wanted me to tell her what was on my mind. And I wanted to unburden myself, I felt the need to tell her, but I resisted. I wasn't ready. My stomach was in knots. I didn't know what would happen once I told my story. Would they even believe me? What would be the consequences? My fears paralyzed me. I just didn't have the courage to talk, yet. I promised to visit again and left.

I walked back to the empty house that represented my personal hell. The energy was different in John's house. The air was heavy, and it felt more like a graveyard. Every time I returned to John's house from Margaret's I felt the difference, but that night I got chills. Sadness, sickness, depression, anger, and death made the walls thick and the mood very somber. John's house had a very bad aura, and I was living in it. It affected me physically, mentally, and spiritually.

Once I wrapped my food in a plastic bag, I hid it at the bottom of the fridge. John rarely opened the fridge, but I still had to be very cautious with him.

I wanted the feeling of peace that I felt at Margaret's house to linger at least until the next day. I tried to control where my thoughts were going and fall asleep. I didn't want to think about my childhood, my family, John or anything else. I felt the need for stillness and calm. But I realized that my mind was a difficult thing to control.

I controlled my thoughts for a few minutes, and then they jumped all over the place. I went back and forth between stillness and a scattered mind. It became an exercise that I enjoyed. At the end of the night, the negative thoughts won. Voices in my head were telling me that I would die at John's house, or that I didn't deserve Margaret's love and affection. Joseph also crossed my mind.

The negative, once again, outweighed the positive. I wanted to feel good so badly. I wanted to feel loved and admired. The love that Margaret gave me came to my life so unexpectedly, and at a time where so many bad things had happened, that I was afraid to hold on to her sometimes. Afraid that something bad would happen again or that she would stop loving me for one reason or another. Misery and sadness took root in my being, that I was unable to see the good in life or in people. I forced myself to see the light, but it was always temporary. Darkness always took over.

The next day I woke up to a quiet house again. John didn't come and I was glad. I took my time in the shower and let the water make me feel good inside and out. After my shower, I made myself some warm milk and ate some of the cookies Margaret had given me. I savored them. They were so good. The kitchen was dark and stuffy. I wanted to take down the woods that John had nailed across the windows, but I didn't dare. I stared at the wood, and missed the days when I was able to look out the window and dream.

I watched TV until early in the afternoon. And at some point I dared open the door, and saw Joseph's car in Margaret's driveway. I wanted to see him, and talk to him. I changed into a dress, brushed my teeth and combed my hair. I gathered the courage to go to Margaret's house. I thought about John, but the need to see Joseph that day was stronger than my fear.

As soon as I knocked, he opened the door. His smile made me feel warm inside. He pulled me to him and held me. I needed it. His touch was gentle and strong at the same time. His scent was manly and soft. I abandoned myself in his arms and took him in.

"I was just thinking about you. How are you?"

He was thinking about me. I let that sink in. Joseph thought about me too. I wondered how much and how often. Because I thought about him all the time.

"I am good. How are you?" I said shyly.

"I am excellent. This is an exciting time for us and I wanted to fill you in. Margaret just left, and I came to pick up a document that she prepared for me. Do you mind going to my mother's house with me? Then to the printing place? We could run some errands and catch up?"

He was making plans with me. I felt alive and part of his life. I felt important in his eyes, and deeply touched. I couldn't find words, so I simply said okay. I watched him gather some paper from Margaret's house. He went to the fridge and grabbed two bottles of water. I was watching him with admiration. When he finished he finally looked at me.

"Are you ready?"

I nodded. He grabbed my hand and led me outside the house. He locked the door behind us. I was scared that John would see us. I was afraid that we would be out of the house for too long and John would come home. At the same time, I had Joseph next to me and the world faded away. I felt normal.

He opened the passenger door and let me in. As soon as he got in, he looked at me.

"Is everything okay?"

He must have noticed the questions in my eyes. Or maybe the

fear of getting caught, mixed with the feeling of complete exhilaration from being with him. I looked at him with a smile and said, "I am good. I am happy to spend time with you".

During our drive to Felicia's house, we talked about his work and school. I envied him, and hoped that one day I would be able to be so passionate about something.

"What do you want to do when you go to college?" he asked.

I thought that I wanted to be a teacher, but wasn't sure anymore. So I decided to be honest and told him. "I don't know."

He smiled. "Don't look so disappointed in yourself. I am sure you'll figure it out. I changed my mind so many times, and still have doubts about psychology. So trust me, life is not meant to be a clear shot."

He had wisdom beyond his years.

"What about love? I am assuming that the old guy is not your husband, right?"

I took a deep breath. I was afraid of the questions, but at that moment I wanted to have a good time with him, and make him feel that I trusted him. "No, he is not my husband. Our situation is complicated. When I feel ready, I will tell you." I didn't say much, but I felt as if that answer was the most honest that I had been. I didn't want to shut the door. Maybe Joseph could help me.

I gathered the courage to ask him. "What about you? Are you in love?"

He stopped at a red light and looked at me. He wanted to say something, but stopped himself. "I think I am. I am not sure, but I truly think I am. I hope she feels the same way."

Any other day or time, I would feel sad or depressed to hear that. Thinking that he was talking about someone else. But that day, in his car, Joseph's heart spoke to my heart. Something was happening between us and we couldn't stop it. We were quiet for a while until we got to Felicia's house.

The house looked very similar to Margaret's, at least from the outside. Once we got in, I could smell Felicia in it. It smelt of vanilla and cocoa butter. The house was decorated in all brown and beige. She had pictures on every wall. And the majority of those were of Joseph.

"Come in and make yourself comfortable," he said. "And please don't mind all the pictures of me."

He walked toward the hallway. I walked around the living room, looking at the pictures. They were of Joseph as a baby, as a toddler, as a boy playing soccer, practicing karate, riding a bike, winning a trophy and many more. As I was staring at one particular picture of him standing in a tuxedo with a girl in his arms, I felt his presence behind me.

"That's my high school prom night. Not too long ago. Three years to be exact. I hated high school and couldn't wait to graduate and go to college," he said with a nostalgic tone.

"Why?" I asked.

"I don't know. I wasn't invested in it at all. I felt as if it was holding me back. I was looking forward to graduation. Although, when I look back I wish I had taken the time to enjoy and get to know my classmates."

We talked for a few hours and he made us some sandwiches. The moments that I spent with Joseph were perfect. At some point, we sat on the couch next to each other and our legs were touching. I didn't want it to stop. Ever. He showed me more pictures of him in high school, and that same girl from his prom night was in a few of them. So, I couldn't help but ask if she was his girlfriend.

"She was. I knew her since I was twelve and had the biggest crush on her. In 9th grade, she finally agreed to be with me and I was so happy. For three years, we were inseparable. We spent every day together and shared everything. She moved to England for college and I stayed here. I was very sad at first, but with time I got used to it."

I loved the way he approached life and wished that I had as much faith in the process. Or that I trusted my fate more. I just lacked the confidence to believe in anything. Even the moments that I was spending with him felt unreal to me. I had an inside voice that kept telling me that I didn't belong there with him, or that he would find out about me and be appalled. I was incapable of just being. I looked at the time and couldn't believe that it was past 7pm. I didn't want to panic, but I gently asked him to take me home. He didn't object and we got in the car.

On our drive home, I was praying that John wasn't there. *Please, please God, let me have today,* I was hoping and wishing inside. All the scenarios played in my head. What if John came out of the house to hurt Joseph? What if he killed us both? What if he just waited for me inside and then killed me? My mind was racing and my heart was beating fast. Anything could have happened. Joseph sensed that I was tense, so he reached out for my left hand. We looked at each other for a moment. I felt a brief sense of calm and smiled at him. He could read me very well. Joseph understood me in a way that no one else did. I felt very connected to him, and being with him gave me a sense of hope. He reassured me, even if it was usually temporary.

As we approached the house, I noticed that John's car wasn't there. Joseph, without even hesitating, dropped me off at Margaret's driveway. He understood that something wasn't right in my relationship with John. He stopped the car, and gave me a kiss on my cheek.

"It was great spending the afternoon with you. Even though I didn't get to go make my copies," he said, laughing.

"I enjoyed it too. I hope you can still get some work done," I said and exited the car. Joseph had entered my heart completely.

John's house was cold and dark as usual. It seemed even darker after the afternoon that I had spent with Joseph. I went from such a high to feeling low in an instant. That house represented despair, sadness, depression, sexual oppression and reduction of my humanity. I didn't turn on the light. I went to the restroom in the dark, and then came back to lie down on the couch.

I could still smell Joseph, feel his touch on my hand, and his soft lips on my chick. He was very gentle with me, and was always so careful to not overstep his boundaries. But I still felt closer to him than I did with John who I had had sex with so many times. What I had with Joseph was intimate and pure. I felt safe with him, and wanted more of him. I had crushes on many boys before, but what I felt for Joseph was exhilarating and peaceful at the same time.

Was I too young to truly fall in love? I wondered. My mother married my father when she was only nineteen, and sometimes wondered if it was too young. I wondered if she would have had the courage to leave him had she given herself time to grow and mature before marriage. *How soon is too soon? Or, how late is too late?* I marveled at the fact that I already picture the children that I would have with Joseph. He was my fantasy. The man who showed up in my dream. He didn't tell me that he liked me directly, but I sensed it. That night, as I was laying down on the couch, I whispered to myself, "I like you, Joseph."

CHAPTER 30

I was awakened by a kick on my head. John came back and found me on the couch. He had hit me hard with a plastic bottle he was holding in one hand and groceries in the other. I jumped and he was standing right in front of me. My head was in pain and my heart was beating fast. I stood in front of him for a few seconds to collect myself. I was probably having a dream because I thought that I was still in the Congo. Even when I saw John's face, I still needed a moment to register what was really going on. I went around him and ran to the kitchen. I looked at the clock and it was almost noon. I slept too long and peacefully.

John sat on the couch and the living room smelt of medication, sweat, and heavy body odor. He called me a few times to serve him, but then he fell asleep. He didn't look good and I was hoping that he would stay asleep all day. He did. John wasn't getting any better. His health was still deteriorating, and he looked like he could die any time. Then I thought about the villains in all the books I read as a little girl - they didn't die.

I thought about one of my dad's aunts, Granny Mantana, she was the meanest person I knew. She was my father's paternal aunt and he felt the need to take care of her since all five of her children had died. None of them had lived past their twelfth birthday. Her husband divorced her and most family members abandoned her. My dad was the only one left. But life had made her bitter beyond repair. She saw the bad in everything and everyone. Her energy was heavy and every time she came to our house, we all went hiding in our bedrooms. She scared me. But the crazy thing is that she outlived so many people. Whenever we heard of a death in the family, we thought it was her, but it was always someone else. Someone nicer and more pleasant. She died about two weeks before my sixteenth birthday and her death came as a shock to all of us. Apparently, she was sleeping with her neighbor, and his wife sent someone to assault her in the middle of the night. Granny Mantana was old, maybe in her early eighties, and it was surprising that she still had a lover. Let alone someone else's husband.

Over time, as I thought about John's death, it reminded me of my dad's aunt. John was like a villain who was going to outlive most people. Sometimes I wished that I had the courage to hurt him, but I didn't, and I couldn't. I was unable to hurt or kill. Even with all the bad things he did to me, I still couldn't truly hurt him.

I slept through the night, and he didn't bother me. He woke up early and went to the bedroom. I was relieved that at least I wouldn't have to deal with him in the living room. I made him breakfast and waited for him to call me, but he didn't. By late afternoon, he asked for cereal. I brought it to him and waited until he fell asleep and snuck out to Margaret's house.

She was working on a project for Joseph and Sebastian when I got there. So I kept her company in the living room. I was watching TV and she was filling out some papers. I felt at ease in her presence even in silence. I watched TV for an hour and to my surprise Joseph showed up with Sebastian. My heart took a leap from inside my chest. I was so happy to see him. He gave

Margaret a kiss and came to sit next to me. He looked and smelt good.

"I didn't know you'd be here. I would have stopped by earlier," he said so casually.

"I got here not too long ago," I responded shyly.

From across the room, Sebastian chimed in. "You wouldn't have come earlier. I waited in your house for three hours before you woke up from your nap. And still your mother had to force you to wake up."

Joseph threw a pillow at him. Margaret looked at them with amusement and so much love. They went on to discuss work related matters and I sat there listening to them. I envied them. I wanted to be part of something meaningful. I wanted my life to matter to someone. I wanted to feel passionate about something. After an hour, Joseph asked me to go to the store with him. I hesitated and Margaret insisted that I go.

"It would do you some good."

Joseph added, "Come on. I have to find some materials to make banners for the fundraiser we are organizing on July 8th."

I was startled by the sound of that date. It was my birthday. I was going to be eighteen on July 8th. I didn't even realize that the date was approaching. "July 8th is my birthday." They all looked at me with surprise. They were astonished that I had revealed something about myself. I was more taken aback at myself. It just came out.

"How old are you going to be?" Sebastian asked.

"Eighteen. I am going to be eighteen."

Joseph came close to me and put his arm around my shoulder. He felt the discomfort in me. "Perfect. I'll make you a birthday cake."

Joseph and I left the house to go to the store, but instead of going to the store, he took me to a coffee shop. It was getting late, maybe a little past 7pm, but I didn't care. I wanted to spend some time with him. And maybe talk about my feelings. I was in a weird place emotionally. I was going to turn eighteen away from the people who meant the most to me, my family. I didn't even realize that I had been at John's house for almost two years and my life lost its meaning. I had dreamt about turning this age. When I was younger, it meant my entry into adulthood. I couldn't wait to sit at the table with grown-ups, and even be able to discuss marriage and children with my mother. I looked forward to it, and now that it was almost here, I didn't want it to come. It was supposed to be a big event in my life, but instead it was going to be a reminder that I was a prisoner. I couldn't put words to my feelings at that moment. I was beyond sad.

Joseph held my hand and led me to the coffee shop. He said something but I wasn't paying attention. I was too deep into my thoughts.

"Grace?" He finally jolted me out of my reverie. "What do you want to drink?" I looked up to the board and they had almost twenty types of drinks and didn't understand any of them.

"I don't care. Pick for me." I knew of juice, soda, water, milk, coffee, tea, and alcohol. What else were they serving? And where did they all come from? For a few minutes, I stared at the board trying to really understand the variety of drinks. They didn't make sense to me. After a guy behind the bar served us drinks, we found two chairs and sat down.

"So, it's your birthday in two weeks, hein?" Joseph was trying to break the uncomfortable silence between us.

I nodded.

"I remember my eighteenth birthday. My mother threw a big party. Even though I asked her not to. She couldn't help herself. Plus, I was graduating high school and got into college with a full scholarship. She had a lot to celebrate. That was only three years ago but I remember it as if it was yesterday."

I listened to him, and realized that even though he was very mature for his age, every now and then I saw a boy. A boy with needs and big dreams. Joseph fascinated me.

"What were your dreams for this big day?" he asked. Then waited for the answer.

"I wanted to go to school to become a teacher. I also thought that I would get married young and have children." I had the courage to reveal parts of me that I hadn't for a long time.

"Why are you talking as if you won't be able to do those things anymore?"

I didn't know what to say. Despair had taken a toll on me. I was a girl without a past, without a future, and definitely without dreams. John had taken everything from me. I had moments of hope, especially after spending time with Margaret and Joseph. But that feeling of hope was always temporary. Once I went back inside John's house, I fell back into the same despair. I felt hopeless and Joseph wanted to know why I spoke in such a manner. I couldn't say anything. So he changed the subject. Silence was my refuge. I just smiled and he understood that I couldn't talk about it.

We spent a blissful hour at the coffee shop. He told me about his misadventures with Sebastian and his high school friends. We laughed about his first girl crush when he was six years old. He told me of his father and his childhood. I shared just a little bit about the Congo. I told him about the warm weather, the mangoes, palm, and avocado trees. I told him about the strong sense of community and the never-ending need of young people to escape and go overseas.

"Did you ever dream of coming to America?" he asked.

"I did."

"Is it what you imagine it would be?"

"Not at all. Now, I dream of the Congo. I miss my country, and the simplicity of certain things there."

Joseph looked at me with intention. He listened as if he wanted to discover me. We talked more about life.

I looked at the clock and it was past 8pm. "We have to go," I said gently, but panicked inside. I had lost track of time.

Joseph just stood up, took both our empty coffee cups to the trash, then held my hand to the car. He came to the passenger side to open the door, and before I went in, he leaned in and kissed me on the lips. It was a gentle kiss. I closed my eyes and took it in. That moment was perfect. I went inside the car and watched him go around. My heart was beating fast and I felt transported into another world. Joseph just kissed me. He liked me too.

The drive was mostly quiet. We both were too afraid to say anything to ruin the moment. I didn't need any words, apparently neither did he. He held my hand and we just enjoyed each other's presence and touch. I wanted more of him. I felt my body and my mind crave him. I needed to feel him closer, but I had to fight the urge. I didn't even understand the pull. It was a strange feeling and I had never felt like that before. I didn't feel that way about John at all.

As we got closer to the house, I snapped back into reality. He pulled into Margaret's driveway and came around to let me out.

"Okay. I'll see you soon," he said. "I'll be at Margaret's house tomorrow. If you have time, stop by." I hugged him and walked away.

I couldn't make a promise because I didn't know what awaited me behind John's door. I prepared for the worse. Joseph stayed in his car watching me. I didn't turn around, and before I went inside the house, I said a prayer. I opened the door very quietly and the house was dark. I shut the door behind me and waited to hear something. I stood there for a minute and waited. John was snoring in the bedroom. I was safe. I breathed. I felt lucky. The perfect ending to a perfect day.

I went into the kitchen and sat there for a while. I wanted to take it all in, and replay my conversation with Joseph. I thought about what I said, feeling I could have said it better. *Or what if I said too much or too little?* I touched my lips a few times. I wanted to feel his lips on mine again and again. I wasn't used to that type of euphoria at all. I couldn't believe that something so good was happening to me.

I went into the living room and leaned back on the couch. Wanting to keep thinking about Joseph, I closed my eyes and replayed the day again. I also built an entire life around him. I dared dream of our wedding day, our house and children. I imagined spending time with him and growing old. After a few hours of dreaming of Joseph, I heard John's footsteps coming out of his bedroom. They brought me back to reality. My reality was those footsteps. John was my reality. I got up from the couch and laughed soundlessly at myself. I thought *why even bother dreaming of Joseph.* I was foolish to think that I had a chance with him. I was torturing myself with the fantasies of us. I knew I had to stop but thinking of Joseph became my oxygen. I needed him as an escape from my life and all the sadness that surrounded me.

John came out of the bathroom and went back into the bedroom without bothering me. I could go back on the couch and relax. I fell asleep thanking Margaret for bringing joy into my life. Maybe she was my guardian angel after all.

John left early the next day. I was still on the couch when he passed by me. He didn't ask for anything. I watched him struggle to open the door. He was weaker than the day before, and probably was going to the doctor. As soon as he shut the door behind him, I felt nauseous and ran to the bathroom to vomit. The nausea was becoming less frequent, but I still had it sometimes.

I sat on the floor in the bathroom and felt alarmed. I needed to talk to Margaret about my health at least. I didn't want to wait until I reached John's stage. I decided to go see her and talk to her. I cleaned the house and showered. I waited a few hours before I went to Margaret's house. I had to think of ways I would tell her about my disease. What if she asked me many questions? What if she wanted to talk to John? I was nervous, but I knew that I had to tell her somehow.

By early afternoon, there were still no signs of John. So I went to Margaret's house. She watched me from the window as I walked to her house. So she opened the door before I knocked. My heart was palpitating. I wasn't sure how I would tell her and when. As usual she gave me a big hug.

"Hi honey! How are you?"

"I am good. How are you?" She pulled me toward the couch.

"I am great. I feel a summer flu coming, so I took some meds and decided to rest a bit. But it's so good to see you. Although, you don't look so well yourself."

I took the opportunity to tell her. "I know. I am not feeling well. I haven't for a while. I am not sure what is wrong with me. I was nauseous and tired all the time. I lost weight, then gained it back. I am afraid that I might be dying." I said that very quickly and tears were coming down my cheeks. I was a ball of emotions.

She listened and held my hand the entire time. I felt like a little girl crying for a mother. She held me in her arms to calm me. "I think I know what you have. I have had my suspicions for a while, but I didn't know how to ask you. You might be pregnant, my dear."

I felt like someone had just punched me in my guts. I couldn't be pregnant. I couldn't be expecting the devil's child. I was supposed to have a baby with Joseph. I started sobbing and screaming. "No, no, no."

"Calm down, Grace. Calm down." She held me tighter. I couldn't handle it.

After a long time in her arms, Margaret held me up. "I even

bought a pregnancy test the first time I suspected it. We are going to take a pregnancy test, and if you are not, then I'm sure we have nothing to worry about. If you are, we'll deal with it together. I promise. Okay."

I was speechless. She went to her room and brought back a stick of some sort. She asked me to follow her in the bathroom. That was the longest walk of my life. "Okay. I am going to wait outside. Pee on the stick, then call me. Okay?"

She left and I stood there. My heart was pounding. I felt dizzy and sick. I couldn't believe that I was maybe carrying John's child inside of me.

Margaret knocked a few times to ask if I was okay, but I wasn't ready to find out. I wasn't responding to her. Margaret was used to my silence. I finally did it and opened the door. She was waiting right outside. She came in and looked at the stick.

"We have to wait a few minutes to find out. Everything will be alright. I'll give you my word."

We waited and waited and waited. My gut felt like it was going to explode. After what felt like an eternity, she picked up the stick and said, "I was right. You are pregnant". I collapsed on the floor. The little hope that I had of life outside of John's house was gone. I was his for the rest of my life. Margaret sat down on the floor with me. She just held me for a while.

"I have to go. I'll come back tomorrow, so we can talk." That's all I had the courage to say.

"I'll be here waiting for you. Before you go, wash your face."

She left the room. I looked at myself in the mirror and knew that something had to change. Either I had to accept my place in John's house or tell Margaret and run the risk of getting in trouble with the law. I washed my face, went into the living room, kissed Margaret and left her house. We didn't exchange a word. She knew I was a seventeen-year-old pregnant woman by a much older man. She wanted me to ask for help.

I walked slowly to John's house and before I opened the door I heard a sound coming from the inside. I didn't see John's car outside, so I thought it couldn't be him. I hesitated before I went in. I waited for a few seconds, and it was quiet again inside. I thought maybe it was my imagination. As soon as I opened the door, I saw that the lights were on. My heart sank; John was back, and I was caught. I wanted to just turn around and run away but before I could think it through he lunged at me. He pulled me by the hair.

"So this is what you do when I am not home? You stupid whore." He kicked me everywhere. My stomach, my legs, my back, I couldn't catch my breath. "You'll see what I will do to you, tramp." He was breathing hard, and his eyes were dark.

He pulled me outside of the house to the shed. He kicked the door and threw me in there. I fell on the floor and buried my face in the dirt. He locked the door behind him and came inside. He chained my arms and legs around a pole. He was doing it with so much anger that I felt the metal penetrating my flesh. I was bleeding, but he didn't stop. I was screaming and begging him to stop. My heart was beating so fast that I felt a substance come up my throat.

"John, please stop." I begged.

But the more I begged, the more he kicked and tightened the chains. I stopped and closed my eyes. Once he finished, he kicked me again and left the shed.

The smell in there was indescribable. It smelt of something dead and rotten. I could hear the rats moving around. My body ached so much that I couldn't even move. I was chained around a pole, and I was bleeding. The room was dark, but a little bit of light was coming through the ceiling. I was scared and in pain, but I couldn't cry. I was hurting for the child inside of me too. On one hand, I didn't care if it died. On the other hand, I already felt affection for it.

I had to calm myself. I stopped struggling with the chains and sat still. In my stillness, I could identify where each pain was coming from. My mind was in trouble because of the pregnancy. My body ached because of the beating from John. My heart hurt because of my family, my life, Joseph, and Margaret. I was falling apart, mind, body and soul.

I couldn't shed a tear. I fell asleep despite the pain. My sleep was interrupted by rats, and every time I moved, the chains sunk into my skin. I was tired. When the morning came, the light coming from the ceiling hit my face. I looked up and took it in. *What if this was my last day on Earth?* I wondered. Then I remembered that I was pregnant. I didn't really have time to process it the night before. If I died in that shed, the baby would probably die with me. If John continued to beat me, that would have also hurt the baby. I cared. I was going to be a mother and I already wanted to protect my child. Even if it was John's baby.

I was hungry and my body ached. I didn't know whether John was still inside the house. I couldn't hear anything, except cars and trucks passing. I hoped that he would bring me food, or at least water. I was drowning in my thoughts and worries. I couldn't find a way to quiet my mind. At times, I felt like hitting something to feel better. The pain was insurmountable. Fear of the unknown had taken over me. The hours passed and no signs of John. I could see from the ceiling that night was falling. My hunger had subsided, and I was getting used to the pain. I smelt of dried blood and sweat. Margaret must have waited for me. I wondered if she had told Felicia, Sebastian, and Joseph.

I tried to remove the chains and free myself, but all my efforts were in vain. John made sure that they were tight. He used the little force that he had left to punish me. I didn't see his car outside. He must have left it at the hospital and taken a cab. Had I known he was home, I would have stayed at Margaret's or run away.

The immigration prison couldn't be worse than what I was enduring in the shed. Besides, in prison I would have had the company of other illegal immigrants. I should have run when I heard a sound coming from the house. I just couldn't imagine that John was inside and would catch me. I thought about all the what-ifs, but they didn't matter. They never mattered. Life happened and I had to find a way to escape John's house. But I didn't have the strength to break away from the chains. I fell asleep despite everything. My body was swollen, and my head was hurting badly. I still found a way to sleep. I needed to rest somehow.

Hunger woke me up that second day. My stomach was eating itself. I felt an excruciating pain and my body was shaking. I heard footsteps approaching the door. It was John, and I saw his feet under the bottom of the door. Holding my breath, I was hoping that he had brought me food or water. But I also feared that he had come to torture me. He stood there for a few minutes, and then walked away. He probably just wanted to make sure that I was still inside. I was relieved and disappointed. I needed water, and I wanted to pee badly. I was inhaling and exhaling to ignore my bladder, but to no avail. Every time I tried to change position, it hurt. I didn't want to pee myself, I just didn't. The thought of it disgusted me because I knew that I would have to sit on it for a while and smell it. I decided to hold it just a bit longer. But at some point, I just let it go. As I was peeing, I cried. I had hit yet another low. I was reduced to an object.

I was sitting in my own urine, and I could smell it for hours after. I was hoping to die at that point. I implored God to just take me, but I was breathing for two. The child inside of me deserved to live. I didn't know how far along I was, but I figured that it must have been three to four months. That's how long I'd been feeling sick and missed my period. I thought I had caught

John's disease, but I was just pregnant. In all my childhood dreams, I had pictured the perfect husband, the perfect pregnancy and the perfect baby. But my life at almost eighteen was nothing close to what I had imagined. I was in hell with no hope for the future. And I cried for the innocent child inside of me.

I fell asleep for a few hours and was woken up by a few rats biting my legs. I screamed. I was horrified at the sight of them. A few of them ran away, but two vicious ones kept biting me. I was kicking and screaming until they finally gave up. I lost all my strength. I couldn't fight anymore; not for my life, not for the child inside of me or anything else. I was exhausted. My breathing was shallow, I was hungry and thirsty, and I peed myself a few times. I could tell that it was night time from the crack in the ceiling. It was the end of my second day, and John still hadn't tried to come in. No one heard my screams and no one was looking for me. I actually started to laugh. I was delirious. Laughing at my own misery. I was too tired to cry. Too tired to feel, too tired to hope and to fear death.

I felt the light from the ceiling hit my eyes. It was my third day and I grew numb. The stench, the pain, the hunger and the thirst felt normal. My body wasn't mine anymore, and for some strange reason, I felt more alive. I was in tune with all my senses and emotions. I felt my heartbeat and my mind think. I felt my flesh breathing and my insides working. I became in tune with the sounds coming from outside. Whether it was a car or a bird. I felt, heard, and smelt everything. I also became very aware of the life that I was carrying. I am not sure if I created the connection in my head, or if I could actually feel it inside of me. A few days before that, I wasn't even aware that I was expecting.

I heard John's footsteps approaching again. He couldn't help himself. He was addicted to inflicting pain, and was tempted to come inside to torture me. But he stopped right in front of the door, and walked away after a few minutes. I wondered what was going through his mind. What happened to him in his life that made him so sick in his head? Was he even aware of it? I wanted him to come inside and take me out of my misery. But that would be too easy; torturing me was much better. He needed to see me in pain to feed his sick soul. I didn't know what to expect from him. Every next second could have been the end for me, or the beginning of a new suffering. I surrendered. I couldn't think about the next moment because the one that I was in was already hard to digest.

Rats didn't get close to me anymore. Maybe they were also disgusted by me. I saw them running around me and sometimes they stopped to look, and then carried on. I could smell myself and I didn't care anymore. I was between life and death, nothing else mattered.

Right before nightfall, I heard John's footsteps approaching again. My heart started beating fast again. He stopped in front of the door and I could hear him catch his breath. After a few minutes, he opened the door slowly. As soon as our eyes met, I looked away. He didn't look good. I couldn't look at him for too long. He shut the door behind him and walked towards me. His steps were heavy and slow. I looked down. I wasn't sure what his intentions were, but I knew that they weren't good. He came near me and stopped. He kicked my legs. He was too weak to kick too hard, so it didn't hurt.

"Look at me!" he ordered. I didn't. "Look at me, I said!" I still didn't. He laughed. "You think you are tough, don't you?" He lifted my head to face him. I closed my eyes. "Open your eyes and look at me."

I still didn't. He was getting upset and I could feel it. I wanted him to kill me. At the moment between the life I was living and death, I chose death.

He kicked me again and again, but because I was chained

against the pole, my body wasn't moving much. He took the keys out of his pockets and opened the lock. The chains fell. He only left one chain attached to my right hand. He took off my clothes and pulled me towards a beat-up chair on the other side of the room and attached me to it. I was grunting and moaning the entire time but didn't say a word and kept my face down. I didn't want to give him the pleasure of eye contact.

"You smell like a dead dog," he said with disgust and hatred in his voice. "I don't even know what to do with you. You are worthless to me now. A burden."

I was chained to the chair that John was sitting on, and I was on the floor. "What do you want to do? Do you want to please me? Maybe then I'll let you come back inside."

John wanted me to perform oral sex on him in spite of the smell that was coming from me. I hadn't showered or brushed my teeth in three days. I could feel my stomach turn, but I still managed to turn him on sexually. He took his pajama pants off and pulled me towards him. I resisted. He tried to pull me harder, and I resisted again and looked the opposite way.

"What are you trying to prove? You'll do as I say, right now!" He barked and I didn't move. He stood up from the chair and kicked me. It was so painful I let out a scream. He kicked me in my naked stomach, and that's when something happened inside of me. He kicked the innocent child inside of me, and I bent over to protect it.

"You felt that one, didn't you? Do you want me to kill you? Do you?" He kept screaming at me.

He pulled me by my hair and when I opened my eyes to finally look at him, I felt enraged. I felt a strength take over me and I kicked him hard on his penis.

John was shocked that I dared kick him. He bent over and I pulled the chair with me. He caught my leg as I was trying to run away, but I kicked him as hard as I could. He didn't have enough strength left in him to restrain me, so I freed myself from his grasp and ran out of there. The chair was heavy, but I knew that I had to keep running. I went through the kitchen and out the front door. It was dark outside, and I saw Margaret's car in the driveway. I managed to pull the chair attached to my wrist all the way to her door, and I knocked.

I kept calling her name, and after what felt like an eternity, she opened the door. I collapsed in her arms.

EPILOGUE

It's been six years and seven months since that night. John was arrested but died before his trial. He had liver cirrhosis and spent less than three months in prison. The day his lawyer called to announce his death, I felt nothing.

I was still pregnant at the time and refused to let the hatred I felt towards him affect my child. My brain didn't even process the news. I was preoccupied with the fact that I was carrying a child in my womb, and one day I would have to explain to them who his or her father was. The memory of the night I escaped is still blurry to me. According to Margaret, I was incoherent when she took me to the hospital. I only remember waking up the next day and panicking about John. Margaret reassured me that I would never have to worry about him again. I fell back asleep and didn't wake up until the next day. I remember the sense of peace that took over me, and I slept peacefully.

During my pregnancy, Margaret and Felicia kept telling me how my sadness would affect the baby. So, I focused on positivity although it wasn't easy. I cried a lot and isolated myself sometimes. I wanted the baby to be born healthy to a happy mother, but the weight of my past overshadowed the positivity some days. The future scared me. I felt too young and too broken to take care of a child, but Felicia reminded me of my strength.

She kept saying to me, "All the baby needs is your love and you have plenty of it in your heart."

I believed her and held on to those words until the baby was due. The baby was born healthy, and I called her Mwimpa which means 'beautiful' in Tshiluba, a local Congolese language. Giving birth to her restored my faith in life and redirected my life more than I could have imagined. The road to recovery hasn't been easy, but worth it. Right after John's death, I had nightmares and feared he would somehow come back and hurt me. Counseling has helped me overcome my anxiety and the darkness I felt toward life.

Joseph and I are getting married in a week and I could not have been more excited. He and I moved in together a year ago. We took our time to get to know each other first before our relationship became romantic. I lived with Margaret for five years, and both she and Felicia helped me through the most difficult years of my life. They loved me through the pain of recovery as a victim of sexual abuse. They taught me how to become a mother to Mwimpa.

I went back to school and obtained a bachelor's degree in sociology. Sebastian and his girlfriend are now married and expecting their first child. Felicia became my daughter's godmother and grandmother since Joseph was in the process of adopting her.

I haven't found my family, but I will never stop searching for them. I still feel connected to them profoundly and I feel their presence in the universe. I am not sure which one of them is still out there, but I hope to find them one day. My life is not perfect, and I will never be able to fully understand why I had to go through such an ordeal. But with Joseph and Sebastian's organization, I have been able to help men and women who have been sex slaves and trafficked. Being of service to others has been another form of therapy for me.

My life became a testimony that anything is possible. Now, I understand the dream, Margaret was the person who was going to help me cross the bridge from pain to recovery. My mother sent her to me. I've accepted the fact that I do not have the answers to the mystery of life and learned to embrace uncertainty.

There is a higher power and we do not need to understand it. Maybe we will get it one day, or maybe we won't. Either way, I am learning to be grateful for the life I have.

ABOUT THE AUTHOR

Anita Yombo was born and raised in Kinshasa, the Capital of the Democratic Republic of Congo. She currently lives in Los Angeles with her son, Adam. She has always been interested in psychology and is drawn to books about human experiences. Anita spends her free time reading and taking nature walks. *Between John and a Hard Place* is her first novel.

SHARE YOUR THOUGHTS

I would love to know what you thought of
Between John and a Hard Place!
You can write a review with your thoughts at:
- Amazon
- Goodreads
- Facebook

Connect with the author:
Twitter: @Anita_Yombo
Facebook: Anita N Yombo
Email: anitayombo@gmail.com

Made in the USA
Monee, IL
23 February 2022